love falls

ESTHER FREUD

BLOOMSBURY

First published 2007
This paperback edition published 2008

Copyright © 2007 by Esther Freud

The moral right of the author has been asserted

Bloomsbury Publishing Plc, 36 Soho Square, London W1D 3QY

A CIP catalogue record for this book is available from the British Library

Paperback ISBN 978 0 7475 9319 5

10 9 8 7 6 5 4 3 2

Export paperback ISBN 978 0 7475 9498 7

10 9 8 7 6 5 4 3 2 1

All papers used by Bloomsbury Publishing are natural,
recyclable products made from wood grown in well-managed
forests. The manufacturing processes conform to the
environmental regulations of the country of origin.

Typeset by Hewer Text UK Ltd, Edinburgh
Printed by Clays Ltd, St Ives plc

www.bloomsbury.com/estherfreud

For my sister, Bella

'I DON'T KNOW IF I've ever mentioned my friend Caroline,' Lambert said as a thick white plate of kedgeree arrived at the table and was set down on the linen cloth in front of Lara, 'but I had a letter this morning, and . . .' He paused to acknowledge the arrival of his chops. 'It seems she's not at all well.'

'Oh. I mean, no. I don't think you have.' Lara stared down at the slivers of browned fish, the gold yolk of the egg, the parsley sticking to the rice. She wanted to start but it seemed rude. 'Is she very . . .?' She never knew if you were allowed to mention age to people who were old. 'Is she . . .' She said it brightly. 'Very old?'

'Well . . .' Her father took up a sharp knife and cut into the meat. 'Not terribly. A few years more than me. Sixty-ish, maybe?' He sighed. 'Quite young.'

Lara nodded as she scooped up her first mouthful, the soft grains cinnamon and clove-scented, the tiny seeds of caraway cracking between her teeth, and wondered when, if ever, she would think of sixty-ish as young.

'It made me wonder,' her father continued while the waiter poured tea, 'if I shouldn't visit. She's taken a house in Italy for the summer. She takes one every year, her late husband was Italian, and every year she invites me, but this time . . . this time I thought I actually might go.'

He looked down then, frowning, giving Lara a chance to observe him, see how this declaration was affecting him, a man who made it a point never to leave London, had not left it, as far as she knew, since before she was born. Why, she'd asked him once, do you never travel? And he'd shrugged and said why travel when you're already in the best place there is?

For a while they ate in silence and then, still chewing, he fixed Lara with a look. 'Have you ever been?'

'Where?'

'To Italy.'

Lara shook her head. She'd been to India with her mother on a bus, through Belgium, Germany, Greece and Turkey, through Iran (although they'd called it Persia to make the days pass faster) into Afghanistan and across the Khyber Pass. She'd been to Scotland too, had lived there for seven years, so maybe that didn't count, but she'd never been to Italy.

He was still looking at her. 'I thought maybe you'd like to come.'

'With you?'

He nodded.

'Really? I mean yes. I would.'

They smiled at each other – a seal on their pact, and then spirals of alarm, of dread, of delirious excitement shot through her body with such force that her appetite disappeared and finishing her breakfast seemed suddenly as arduous a task as being asked to plough a field.

Lara's father, Lambert Gold, lived in a dark and thickly padded flat halfway up a wide, carpeted stairway. There was a small kitchen, a small sitting room, a large study, and a bedroom into which she'd only ever glanced, but which had a pale-green plant of such beauty growing up against one wall that it always surprised her, it seemed so out of keeping with the dark interior of the rest of the flat. Through the half-open door the heart-shaped leaves and twining stems seemed to be actually breathing, stretching towards the light, shivering very slightly in a breeze, the leaves always in spring colour, whatever time of year. This plant was the one thing that reminded her that Lambert had ever known her mother. She also had a plant, a lemon-scented geranium on a low table beside her bed, but unlike Lambert's – for which she didn't have a name – the geranium was forever changing, ageing, growing new shoots, darkening and lightening with the time of year. The stalk was gnarled and brown, the dead leaves dropped in a little curling pile on to the plate below, but when you rubbed against it a scent so rich and airy filled the room that it made you stop whatever you were doing, and breathe in.

Ever since she'd known her father, and it bothered Lara sometimes that she couldn't remember the day they'd met, he'd been writing a history of Britain in the twentieth century. Some sections of it had already been published, a fact he railed against, because each time this happened it meant his work schedule was disrupted by requests for articles, interviews, letters to which he must reply. There was a sense about him that he was warding off interruption, must really, ideally, never be disturbed, so that it meant the few people who did see him felt themselves to be the chosen, and every second spent in his time was a gift bestowed.

Lambert's real name was Wolfgang Goldstein. As a child he'd been known as Wolf, but he'd renamed himself three months after arriving in London, seeing his new name in print for the first time the day after his eighteenth birthday when he'd written an angry letter to *The Times*. Why did you choose Lambert? Lara asked him, wondering what she would call herself if her own name – Lara Olgalissia Riley – ever became more of a burden that it was worth, and he said he chose Lambert because it was less threatening than Wolfgang but still related, a sort of private joke to himself. He'd come across it in the obituary pages of the newspaper, William Lambert 'Bertie' Percival, a colonel in the army who'd died peacefully in his sleep. What had his letter been about? She always forgot to ask him – and when she did remember the moment was never right.

Lambert was fifteen when he first came to England. He'd been sent out of Austria in the year before the war, the precious only son of his parents, and as if this was to be his fate, to be precious, he'd been taken in and fostered by the Holts. Sir Anthony and Lady Anne had four grown children, a flat in Belgravia and a house in Dorset, where for his own safety Lambert spent the first years of the war, trawling through their ancient library, shaking the dust off books that had often not been opened for years. The Holts had doted on him, considered him a genius with his perfect English, his knowledge of music, theatre and art, and would sometimes invite their friends to consult him on his understanding of the politics that had made Austria and Germany so ready to rally behind Hitler in the war.

Lara's mother Cathy had once met Lady Holt. It was a chance meeting. Cathy and Lambert were walking along Piccadilly towards Green Park, when Lady Holt, a stout woman with small piercing eyes, had swung out through the doors of Fortnum and Mason. Lambert had introduced

4

them, said Cathy was a student of English literature at the college where he lectured, but Lady Holt had screwed up her eyes until they were almost invisible and glancing at Cathy's pregnant tummy had asked if it wasn't terribly tiring, studying so close to her time. 'I'm surprised your husband allows it,' she said.

Cathy looked at Lambert, and seeing he had no intention of enlightening his adopted mother, she stuttered and mumbled and shook her head. 'No, it's not tiring at all,' she'd blushed.

'But why didn't Lady Holt think you were his girlfriend?' Lara felt affronted – on her mother's behalf, and – if you could be affronted on behalf of yourself while still in the womb – for herself too, but Cathy only laughed.

'Your father always insisted he would never marry, never have children. Said he wasn't fit. Well, at the time I didn't believe him. I was only nineteen. But Lady Holt obviously understood him better.'

'But why?' Lara didn't understand.

Cathy put an arm around her. 'It hasn't turned out so badly, has it?' and she kissed the side of her head.

Lambert and Lara were travelling to Italy by train. The train, Lambert decided, would be more civilised, more comfortable than a plane – they could dine in style in the restaurant car, but they both knew the thirty-six hours of the journey would give him more time to adjust to the idea of leaving Britain. 'We've got a very early start, so it may be easier if you stay the night at me,' he suggested. 'Then we'll be sure we don't lose each other at the station.'

'Right,' Lara agreed, as if this were all quite normal, and so, on a warm evening in July, three months after her seventeenth birthday, and one week before the Royal Wedding for which the whole of London was being swept and decorated and prepared, she heaved her bag up the steps of his Kensington block, rang the bell, and prepared to spend the first night of her life under her father's roof.

'Welcome, please, come in.' Lambert nodded formally, his accent, for some reason, unusually pronounced, and for a moment they stood self-consciously together in the hall. 'I've eaten,' he said, as if this might be a worry, had better be made clear, and, even though she assured him she'd eaten too, he backed into the kitchen where he opened the fridge. It was tall and white, much larger than the one she and her mother owned, but much emptier too. There was half a lemon, a bottle of old milk and something flat wrapped in white paper.

'I have some tongue?' he offered tentatively.

But she told him she'd had macaroni cheese. 'I ate with Mum,' and she patted her stomach as if she really had.

There was no spare room at Lambert's so instead he made up a bed for Lara on the sofa in his study with a sheet and a tartan rug he used to drape over himself when he was cold. But hard as they searched they could not find a pillow. Eventually they discovered that the leather seat of his arm-chair came away if you tugged at it hard enough and so they wrapped it in a towel and propped it up on the end of her make-shift bed.

Goodnight, they said, once Lara was in her nightie, having brushed her teeth and washed her face, and she tried not to listen as he took his turn in the bathroom. She read her book, shutting off her ears to the arc of his pissing, the clunk and roar of the flush, and then, some minutes later, the choking humorous gargle as he rinsed his mouth. She slept lightly, the ridges of the buttoned leather sofa making her dream she was at sea, shifting between one smooth wave and the next, and then too soon, but also after an endless buffeting, she heard the pull of the sitting-room curtains and felt bright sunlight stream in against her face.

'Morning,' Lambert greeted her, and seeing she was awake he moved off to the kitchen to fill the kettle.

It was wordless, their arrangement, seamless, as if they'd lived together all their lives. Lambert stayed in the kitchen while she pulled on her clothes. Then he, still in his dressing gown, shut the door into his bedroom, while Lara slipped into the bathroom, washed her face, examining it with microscopic scrutiny in the harsh morning light, grimacing at the dark round of a pimple lurking below the surface of her cheek. She brushed her hair, arranging it so that a strand fell over the spot, and then, dissatisfied, she fluffed it up so that it didn't fall so flatly on her head. Don't look, she told herself, still looking, knowing her attempts were hopeless, and despair settling like a black umbrella collapsing, she arranged her features into one of optimism, and forced herself away.

Lambert already had the tickets. How did he get them? It seemed inconceivable that he'd gone out and bought them – made his way to the station – stood patiently in a queue. Or maybe someone had done it for him? Someone practical, who knew about these things. Lara looked them over in the taxi. Two return tickets for the boat train, from Victoria Station right through to Pisa. All they had to do was find the platform, the train for Dover, their seats.

Lara followed him, sticking close as they hurried through the mass of people, straining her eyes for a clue to the right platform. It was early, but the station was crowded, backpackers sitting like flocked seagulls on the ground. Families, dressed for a day out, on their way south to Eastbourne or

Brighton, and businessmen, with matching suitcases, trousers pressed to a fine point above their shoes.

And then, with a jolt, Lara realised she'd lost him. She looked around, saw only a sea of summer heads, and as she searched more wildly, clutching the handle of her bag too tight, she was gripped by the desolation of someone who has given up all responsibility. Christ, she thought, I have no ticket, no idea where we're going, and then she caught sight of him again, taking his change, stowing a sheaf of newspapers under his arm. 'Dad!' she yelled, and it shocked her to feel how quickly she'd become a child.

There were only five minutes now before the train was due to leave. Lara felt the imagined whistle blowing right under her skin. But Lambert moved towards another kiosk, where, taking his time, he bought a box of matches and a packet of Gitanes. You can buy them at duty-free, she would have told anyone else, but she stood obedient while he chose and handed over change. Three minutes, she hissed just under her breath, and then, turning, he began to run, his bag flying, his shoulders jostling people with all the time in the world. 'Excuse me, so sorry.' His apologies floated back to Lara, running behind, and then they were at their platform, hurtling along its length, pushing the bags ahead of them, leaping aboard their train.

'It is very important,' he panted, 'how you leave your destination.' A whistle blew and the sound of doors slamming rattled every carriage.

'More important than how you arrive?' Lara sank gratefully down into a seat.

'I'll tell you tomorrow,' he smiled, and he opened up a paper and with convincing nonchalance began to read.

*　　*　　*

8

As a child Lara had seen very little of her father: the occasional summer ice cream, a trip once to a bookshop where she was told she could choose anything she liked. She'd picked out a copy of *Little Lord Fauntleroy*, with a sky-blue cover and tall brown writing. It was something she still owned, and whenever she caught sight of it amongst her books, mostly old paperbacks and battered hardbacks bought more for their beauty than their content, she felt a vague unease, as if, aged ten, she'd made too sentimental a choice. Should she have chosen one of his books? she wondered, knowing it would have been ridiculous if she'd asked for his study of Europe in the years between world wars, or the book he'd written about Great Britain, his adopted country, about how the people had changed so radically during the immediate post-war years.

After India, when she and Cathy came to live in London, they began to meet more often. They met for breakfast in hotels, the old and formal kind, Claridge's or the Dorchester, and sometimes, at the end of the day, she'd meet him at the entrance to a museum where just before it closed they'd pace fast round exhibitions.

Less often she visited him at his flat, where occasionally, forgetting she was there, he would finish a telephone conversation and then go back to his work. Lara would sit in his kitchen, leafing through old auction catalogues, ancient treasures about to be bartered for at Sotheby's or Christie's, or spend an hour reading every lurid page of the *News of the World*.

Lambert's kitchen was piled high with newspapers. Why doesn't he throw them out, she wondered, but when she inspected the dates she saw that often they were just the accumulation of a week. But why buy so many? Surely they all said the same thing. Sometimes she'd watch him, too little time to read them, flicking through each page, scanning it, as if there was something he was hoping to find out.

Eventually, on these afternoons, Lara would put her head round Lambert's door and see him, a pen in his mouth, staring into space. 'Dad . . . I'd better go now,' she'd whisper, and he'd start out of his seat when he realised she was still there.

That morning they'd barely had time for breakfast. Just an apple and a cup of pale tea. Lara had brought the remaining apples with them, thinking they'd only rot, left in their bowl. She'd packed them into her bag with an unopened bottle of Perrier that was standing in the hall. She opened the Perrier now and took a gulp that fizzed so fiercely in her throat she almost choked.

'Steady on,' Lambert said, and he reached out for a drink.

She didn't know if it was the fizz of the water or the act of sharing the unwiped bottle but she suddenly felt quite heady with excitement. They were going away. Setting off on an actual holiday! Until now, she hadn't quite believed it, and to hide her excitement she turned to the window and looked out. They'd left London behind, were already rumbling through a suburban landscape, were soon rolling out through scrub and fields. She looked over at her father, but he had closed his eyes and was gripping the bottle of water by the narrow top of its neck.

Although the train was full, with people standing in the corridors, they were alone in their first-class carriage, the dark seats, wider than standard, draped with head-protectors, like the starched white pinnies of a hotel maid. Lara knew it was wrong, felt the unfairness of it in her bones, but all the same she stretched luxuriously, ate an apple, threw the core out of the slip of window, watched it drag backwards in the wind.

She thought about her mother, as she'd left her the evening before, rinsing lettuce for a salad, and it occurred to Lara that she'd never asked her what she planned to do. Maybe Cathy would do what Lara did when she was away, have a party, upset the neighbours, eat tinned vine leaves for breakfast, take baths three times a day. Suddenly she felt supremely happy, the sun streaming in through the window, aware she was at that perfect stage of a journey, safely begun but with no danger of having to arrive.

She thought of how miserable she'd been on the last day of term, only ten days before. How cowardly she'd felt when she'd missed her chance of saying even one word to Clive – Clive, who for three terms she'd dreamed of, yearned for, fantasised about, and who still, for all she knew, didn't know she was alive. She'd sat behind him every Monday in history, too distracted by the black curls of his unbrushed hair, the wide shoulders of his donkey jacket, to take more than the most illegible notes. And then she'd made a decision. She'd talk to him at the college disco, the finale of all the Wednesday lunchtime discos, where for three terms now she hadn't danced. Lara and her best friend Sorrel swung in and out of the swing doors, hovered by the curtained windows, whispered in dark corners, and always there was the suspenseful feeling that something was about to happen.

That Wednesday she'd stood near Clive, waiting, nothing between them but a stack of chairs, and then, just when she was sure she'd plucked up enough courage, a girl from drama A level swept in, and without a moment's hesitation took Clive's hand and pulled him out on to the floor. And he'd allowed it. It was as easy as that. What kind of a spineless idiot was she to have been so afraid? Why was she so stupid? She closed her eyes against the vision of the two of them, Meg and Clive, only half an hour later, kissing hungrily behind the stage.

'My God.' Lambert sat up with a start as the train began to slow. 'Here already,' and they gathered up their bags and shouldering themselves into the scrum, they prepared to crowd off the train.

There was a bar on the boat, already beery with overflowing ashtrays, and a canteen into which Lara hungrily peered, but it was in the restaurant that Lambert had decided they should eat. By the time they found it there was only one table free and almost as soon as they'd sat down they were asked if they would share. Would they? Lara had no idea. But Lambert nodded his head courteously and a man, too sleek and well-groomed to be British, introduced himself and immediately began to open up a conversation as if this lunch had been pre-arranged.

He was a professor of medicine, from Belgium, involved in research, and soon it was clear that he had heard of Lambert, recognised him now, was thrilled to have this chance to talk to the great man. Ideas were exchanged, opinions, names and theories introduced, and to Lara's surprise, Lambert, who always protested he hated to see too many people, loathed having to discuss his work, was nodding, interrupting and admonishing the Belgian with real pleasure in their every word.

Lara sat and listened, hoping to find some way to contribute, aware she should be concentrating, hoping she might even retain something of what she knew to be great talk, but soon she realised she was listening too hard to take in anything, and so instead she excused herself and went out to find the loo.

She made a detour past the shops, the information desk, the duty-free and then, seeing a door open, she stepped out on to the deck. She was high up, the sea swirling dark-green and menacing below. She leant over the rails, pushing her feet between the painted poles, and thought how easy it would be to slip. Shouldn't they be more solid, shouldn't the temptation to slide through unnoticed be put further out of reach? Lara pulled herself back. Gulls screamed and dived around the boat and children ran squawking along the ramps.

She walked to the very front of the ship where couples huddled out of the wind, their faces bright with spray and happiness, their arms around each other, the remnants of their packed lunches scattered along the wooden bench. She scanned the shoulders of the men for signs of Clive, longing to see him in this unlikely place, wanting a chance to turn fate around, to claim him, or even say hello, but although there were a number of dark-haired, donkey-jacketed men, none of them, quite obviously, was him.

Lara suddenly remembered she was meant to be having lunch. She turned and ran, slipping through the nearest door, rattling up and down the metal stairs, losing her way, then finding it again at duty-free, back past the canteen, the information desk, and there they were, her father and the Belgian, still talking, the waiter having given up on her, clearing the plates. Lara sat down with a small nod of apology and there was a pause while it was decided no, they wouldn't need dessert.

'First class?' Lambert asked a guard on the platform at Calais. '*De première classe avec couchette?*' but the guard shook his head haughtily and said there was no first class on this train. He seized the tickets and flicked them mockingly. No couchettes either. Not for them. For a moment they both examined the tickets, disbelieving, and then, realising they were losing precious time, they boarded the train and began searching for two seats.

It seemed impossible, but there were not two seats together the whole length of the train. Anxiously they moved from carriage to carriage, peering into compartments where people, already ensconced, looked up with hostile eyes. Who were they? Lara thought. Where had they come from, how had they settled themselves so soon? She began to hate them, they looked so smug, as if they owned their seats, had inherited them, had not a thing in common with her at all. Lambert looked defeated as he let yet another heavy door slide shut, and Lara had to stop herself from reaching out to take his arm.

Maybe he shouldn't have left London, the safety of his study, the largeness of his reputation; and then just in time they came across a carriage where a buxom woman with quantities of luggage had taken up three seats.

'*Excusez-moi, pouvez-vous enlever vos baggages?*' Lambert asked in chivalrous French, and with perfectly good grace she stood up and began to stow away her bags.

Lambert sat beside the woman and Lara opposite him. They smiled at each other, relieved, and Lara opened up the Perrier and took a swig. She leant across to offer it to him.

'Thank you,' he said, as if it were champagne, and he held it as he had done before by its neck.

They nodded to each other, consolidating their ritual, and it pleased Lara just as much as if they had clinked glasses and said cheers.

Whistles blew and doors, heavy as walls, slammed shut.

14

They were moving slipping out of the station, into France, away from the sea, towards Switzerland, the Alps, towards Italy, and Pisa.

'Do you know any Italian?' Lambert asked later, when half the people in their carriage were asleep.

'No.' Lara thought for a moment, and then with some alarm. 'Will that matter?'

Lambert leant towards her. 'The rudest thing you can say to an Italian, worse than' – he flailed around – 'your mother is the mistress of a two-headed chimpanzee . . . ' He lowered his voice to a whisper and Lara looked round to check they were not about to be overheard. 'Is *Porca Madonna*.'

'*Porca Madonna*,' she whispered back, and the lady with the luggage snapped open her eyes.

It was three o'clock when they boarded the train and by seven they were starting to feel hungry.

'Shall we find the restaurant car?' Lambert suggested.

Lara imagined the evening spent sipping wine, eating delicate courses, broken up maybe by a sorbet or a bowl of soup. They would sit at a narrow table, set for two, with a ruched curtain and a lamp, the tassels hanging down in a fringe of burgundy while a waiter hovered over them in white gloves. It was a scene from a film, she knew this, or from a novel she'd once read, but she still looked forward to entering into it for a night.

Before leaving their carriage they stowed their bags carefully, nodding to the woman who had just eaten the entire contents of one basket, hoping she understood this meant she was to guard their seats with her life.

Out in the corridor, all along the train, there were people standing, leaning up against the windows, smoking, eating, talking, stretching their legs. 'Excuse me, *excusez-moi*.' They sidled past, enjoying this journey, the warmth of the evening light slanting in, the shudder of the wheels below. There was something strangely pleasant about the way the train threw you from wall to wall, gently enough to rattle you, but not enough to hurt. But after four or five carriages it occurred to Lara there was no smell of food.

'Excuse me,' Lambert asked a man coming the other way. '*Il y a un restaurant?*'

The man put his head to one side and paused to think. '*Non*,' he said, making the word hop, '*non*,' and smiling he went on his way.

At first it seemed easier to disbelieve him, so they pushed on, the thud of the rails less pleasant now, jolting up through their feet, throwing them off balance, until it became clear the man was right. There was no restaurant car. No buffet. Not even a trolley serving tea. They turned around and wove their way back towards their carriage, learning to leap when the train swerved and to use their fingers to press themselves out from the windows and the walls.

Eventually they reached their carriage and, relieved to see their seats, already as familiar as home, they sank down. Lara picked up the Perrier and took a swig. It was warm and flat. She held it out to Lambert. 'No thanks.' He shook his head. She peered into her bag. There was one apple left. She took it out and offered it. But again he shook his head. Preserving rations! she thought. Lambert had taken up his newspaper and folding it over so that she was faced by a full-page photograph of Lady Diana Spencer, with only one week left before she became wife to Prince Charles, he began to read.

Lara drew her legs up and examined the photo. It was Diana's hair, she decided, that made it so difficult to like her. Her hair, all feathery and hanging down over one eye. She was twenty. Three years older than Lara, and she wondered what Cathy, or even Lambert, would say if she was about to marry a man just entering middle age. But then again, Lambert had been forty-one when she was born, and Cathy only nineteen. But it was different. She couldn't really explain it, but Lambert was ageless with his Old-World accent and his store of knowledge, and her mother had proved just by having her that she was free and reckless and fierce.

The train slowed to a halt. It was starting to get dark, and the station, lit up, threw the dusk into relief. Doors swung open, people shouted and then along the platform Lara saw a man with a trolley.

'Look.' She pointed, her face pressed to the window, and even as they watched, a scrum of people gathered round, thrusting money, helping themselves, emerging with huge sandwiches, packets of biscuits, cans of drink. 'What do you think?'

Lambert began searching through his wallet for the foreign money he'd exchanged, but even as he did so a whistle blew, people scattered, and the train began to move.

Next time, Lara promised herself, but the next time, although she stood on the steps, waiting for her moment, clutching a large franc note, she found she was too terrified in case the moment she stepped off the train it would start up and she would have to run the length of the platform, like Omar Sharif in *Doctor Zhivago* when he was travelling to a small town in the far east of Russia, not knowing that the woman he really loved, Lara (after whom she'd been named), would be living there too. Doctor Zhivago had been pulled back on to the train by a carriageful of people, all reaching out to him from a wide-open door, whereas she'd be relying on the arms of her father, who might not even know that she'd been left behind.

Around midnight, her stomach contracting now with hunger, she plucked up enough courage to get off the train, get as far as the trolley, point to a roll, the slice of cheese, the frill of lettuce visible between the soft rounds of the bread, but just then the whistle blew, and even though it turned out to be for another train, Lara ran so fast back to the steps of their carriage she thought her lungs might burst.

'Shall I try?' Lambert suggested, but the thought of his nonchalance, his slow ruminations as he counted out change, made her so anxious it took her appetite away.

'Please don't,' she implored him. 'I mean, really, I'm not hungry,' and pressing her face into the corner of the window as if it were a pillow, she closed her eyes and pretended to sleep.

Through the black of her eyelids she conjured up the train platforms in India, crowded with men selling baskets of samosas, puri, dosas, bags of dried chickpeas and nuts. If you didn't want to get out you could thrust your arm through the window, or even order a train meal from the comfort of your carriage. The meal was delivered at the next station, served on a tray divided into sections, each one filled with rice, dhal and vegetable curry, with little pots of yoghurt and chutney on the side. The food was comfortingly familiar. It was almost identical to the food they served at Samye Ling, the Tibetan centre in Scotland, although the yoghurt on the train was thinner and the chutney when she tried it burnt her tongue.

Lara was four when she and Cathy moved to Scotland. They'd lived, until then, in a flat not far from Lambert at the top of Ladbroke Grove. They'd moved after Cathy had a letter from a friend telling her he'd found the answer, and that as soon as possible she must come to study Tibetan Buddhism with His Holiness who was living in a camp for refugees in the foothills of the Himalayas. If she could get herself there she could benefit from his teachings and all her misery would disappear.

'What misery?' Lara asked when Cathy told this story, but Cathy always looked at her as if she was missing the point.

'Anyway,' she continued, when people asked what had brought her to this valley in Scotland, so heavily planted with Christmas trees it seemed always on the verge of growing dark, 'I couldn't get myself to India – not then, anyway, and so instead we came to live here.'

They found a house to rent on the top of a hill, and a year later Lara started school. The school was in the village, just beyond the Buddhist centre, Samye Ling, and all the children regarded her with as much curiosity as if she was from Tibet herself. They'd circled her and prodded her and sniffed at her clothes. They'd stared in disgust at the food she unwrapped for her lunch – crumbling home-made brown-bread sand-wiches filled with lettuce and Marmite – and the sight of her mother, having walked the two miles from their cottage, waiting in wellington boots at the gate.

But Lara didn't really care. Her mother was happier. The long hours of meditation left her light and calm, and most holidays they had visitors, guests they could see from the upstairs windows of their cottage, toiling along the valley road beside the stream. And once a year they hitchhiked to London. They walked with their bags out of the village towards Lockerbie and then they'd get a lift at least as far as the motorway, where they'd pride themselves on reaching London before the end of the day.

*　　*　　*

When Lara woke it was morning and her father's legs were stretched across the gap between their seats. She could feel his toes as they pressed into the flesh of her thigh, see the pale skin of his legs where his trousers had ridden up, the fine black hairs, the ridge of bone along his shin. Very, very carefully she inched herself away. Lambert stirred, looked as if he was about to wake, and so seizing her chance and yawning as if it was involuntary, she shifted along the seat until she was free. But Lambert continued to sleep, his head resting against the window, his mouth a little open as he breathed. Lara glanced back at his feet. They looked so harmless now, unprotected even, falling outwards into the gap she'd left, but she didn't move back.

The train began to rattle and the outposts of a station came into view. Signs flashed by, names she couldn't catch. Bin . . . Binar . . . 'Where are we?'

Lambert was awake, stiffly taking back his legs, lowering them down into his shoes. 'Binario. I think.'

They looked at each other. They were definitely in Italy. Just a few more hours and they'd be there. In celebration Lara took out the Perrier and sipped a few drops, handing it over for Lambert to tip the last gulp into his mouth. She took out the apple and, using a trick she'd learnt at school, twisted it until it snapped in half. She ate her half slowly, the juices, sharp and sweet, stinging the inside of her mouth, and she looked admiringly at her father as he discarded his core, slinging it out of the window with at least three mouthfuls left. Lara devoured hers down to the stalk until there was nothing but the shimmery husk of the core where three pips hung exposed. Afterwards she felt hungrier even than before, her stomach twisting and contracting, remembering and regretting all the meals she'd ever left, half-eaten, on her plate.

Just then they reached another station. Bin . . . Binar . . .

Binario. They were there again. Or maybe she'd been so taken up with her apple that she hadn't noticed they'd not moved. She leaned over to look at her father's watch. It was eight o'clock now and they were due to arrive at two. She looked out on to the platform. There was no sign of a kiosk or a trolley, even if she'd had the courage to get off.

Lara got up and stretched, and then to pass the time she wandered the length of the train, peering into carriages, trying not to gaze too longingly at the people, so well prepared, unpacking their breakfasts, pouring themselves hot cups of coffee, tearing off hunks of white bread. She felt thinner already, lighter, her clothes looser on her, after just two missed meals, and she thought of the diet she had subjected herself to at the end of the autumn term, one day of nothing, three days of fruit, and as a reward, a small portion of cottage cheese, which had tasted as delicious as anything she'd ever tried. And it had worked. She'd been slinky and beautiful for the college Christmas party, if not a little pale, but what had been the point, when she'd been too freezing cold to take off her coat and still too cowardly to talk to Clive.

When Lara got back to her carriage they were at Binario again. Lambert looked at her and shrugged, and laughing, hoping suddenly that they'd never arrive, they shared out the pages of the newspaper and settled down to wait.

They were met at Pisa station by Ginny, Caroline's cook. She had been watching out for them on the platform (or *binario* – as they'd finally understood it to be called), and when she saw them she swooped down and took hold of their bags. Ginny was an English woman who had driven out from her village in the Cotswolds, and was very kindly stopping en route to pick them up. She was a large woman, the colour of hay, with gold flecks in her hair, and freckles on her arms and face that ran together in lion-coloured dots. Her clothes, which were abundantly flowered, made her look even larger, but her voice when she introduced herself was small and high.

'What fun!' she squeaked. 'A summer in Italy!' and it occurred to Lara it would be just the four of them – Caroline, Lambert, Ginny and her. 'Shall we head straight off?' Ginny said cheerily. 'The car's not too far away, but parked rather precariously,' and Lara shot a quick look at Lambert to see what he would say.

'Yes,' he agreed, not mentioning they were ravenous. 'Of course.' And obediently they followed Ginny out of the station.

The car was a 2CV, bright-yellow, and heady with trapped heat. Lara climbed into the back with both their bags and, as they sped out of Pisa, Ginny began to tell them in great detail how dangerous the roads in Italy were. Crashes, pile-ups, accidents by the day. She chattered happily, but Lara found it was hard to adjust to the idea of being squashed flat by a lorry when her main concern was that she was about to die from lack of food. Would it be . . . could we? And then by the side of the road she saw a stall piled high with fruit.

'STOP!' She was unable to contain herself, and although Ginny became flustered, forced to veer over on to the wrong side of the road, she did manage to stop.

Lambert got out and Lara scrambled after him. Together they stared at the sweet hard oranges, the grapes and outsized apples, the trays of figs, deciding eventually on a kilo of peaches, felted and sweet-smelling.

'Food,' Lara sighed as she bit into the first one, leaning over to let the juice splash on to the ground, and Lambert took one himself and devoured it in three quick mouthfuls.

'Come on then,' and he held the door for Lara.

She sat in the back of the car with the brown paper bag of

peaches on her lap and ate another, then another.

Lambert glanced round. 'I wouldn't eat too many more,' he warned, and from his look she assumed it could be dangerous.

'All right.' She folded the bag, turning the soft paper over and over, thinking how strange it was that this was the first piece of advice her father had given her, and although she knew she was being overly dramatic, she couldn't get out of her mind the story of the woman who, on being liberated from Auschwitz, was given a sausage by a well-meaning soldier, and on devouring it had rolled over and died.

Everywhere Lara looked they were surrounded by hills. There were large blue hills in the distance, and others, smaller and more barren, sloping away on each side of the road. The hills, however steep, were divided into fields, some planted with lines of olives and all without exception home to a house or a cluster of houses at their very top, as if every available opportunity must be taken to reach for cooler air. The houses were beautiful, the colour of the earth, terracotta, ochre, the dust-pink of cement. They were decorated with vines and jade-green shutters, each one more beautiful than the last. Lara gasped and pointed to the first six or seven, and then seeing she might go on for ever gave up and simply noted them, letting them pass.

Ginny had a map spread out on her knees and occasionally she paused at a crossroads and glanced down, but she seemed quite amazingly efficient, confident of the way, and so Lara closed her eyes and listened to her telling Lambert how she'd done a cookery course in this region and more often than she could remember had come to cook for English families summering out here.

'One family, can you imagine, just a married couple and their friends, brought a masseur out with them.' Lambert must have nodded because she carried on. 'I was allowed to take advantage of his services, once a week on my day off.' There was a sharp intake of breath. 'And it was ever so nice.'

Lara didn't dare open her eyes in case she saw any hint of laughter in her father's shoulders. Instead she held the image of Ginny, her golden body spread out on a towel, the strong hands of a man pummelling her soft expanding flesh.

'Have you cooked for Caroline before?' Lambert asked, and Ginny said no, she'd never met her.

'But . . .' She lowered her voice. 'I've heard she's a very dignified lady.'

Dignified. There was silence in the car, and Lara kept her eyes closed for so long she must have fallen asleep because when she woke they'd left the flatness of the plain and were climbing along twisting roads into the hills.

Ginny was chatting again. She was quite well known among a certain circle for her green tomato chutney. 'If you'd be interested,' she said, 'I could add you to my list for orders.'

'Yes.' Lambert was unusually gallant. 'I would be interested. Thank you, very much.'

It was late afternoon when they came to a stop in a shaded driveway, and were greeted by the sound of water trickling. Ginny climbed out and stretched and walked round to open the boot.

'Darling Lamb,' Lara heard, as her father eased himself out of the car.

A tall, slim woman was standing in the doorway. 'You actually came.'

24

Lambert put his arms out and they embraced. Caroline was wearing a pleated skirt, belted at the waist over a cream blouse, and Lambert had to stoop only very slightly to kiss her below the brim of her straw hat.

'Well done,' she said, eventually stepping back. 'You made it.' And she looked towards Lara.

'Hello,' Lara nodded. 'It's very nice to be here.'

She waited while Caroline appraised her, looking from Lara to her father, checking for a likeness, trying to square the Lambert Gold she knew with the man who could suddenly have produced this grown-up child.

'So we finally get to meet you.'

Caroline's gaze was not entirely friendly. It seemed she was still searching, forcing Lara to check herself against her father too. Was there a likeness? Her mother always said there was. Always said it made her laugh how Lara moved like him, made small fluttery movements of frustration, even as a child, even when she hardly saw him.

By now Ginny had all her bags out on the path. 'Hello,' she said.

Caroline turned towards her, putting out a pale and slender hand. 'Virginia. So very nice to meet you. Thank you for collecting my guests.' She looked at her multitude of bags. 'If you're ready,' she said, 'I'll show you your room.'

Ginny stood up straighter as if she'd remembered she was there as staff. 'Right then.' She waved. 'Toodle-oo.' And she trotted after Caroline down some steps and around the side of the house.

Lara stood on the path, watching the tiny bubbling fountains of the irrigation system, as Caroline's cool voice floated away on a list of instructions. She breathed in deeply. It smelt so good here, the air, rich enough to drink, scented with rosemary and lavender and the cool smell of watered stone.

She thought of her back garden at home, in a dilapidated row above Finsbury Park station, and how their tangle of lilac acted as a shield against the flat, burnt air of the main road. Three weeks! She gulped down another mouthful, and she followed her father into the house.

The house was tiled and new, inside at least, with pale-wood doors and creamy sofas. It was built for summer with a small stark kitchen lined with cupboards and a tall, loudly humming fridge. One wall of the living room was made of glass, a section of which slid back on to a terrace where a round table stood scattered with Caroline's correspondence, peach-coloured sheets with 'La Forestella' printed across the top. *I'm sorry to have to tell you this*, Lara read, she couldn't help it, *but I didn't want you to hear it through some idle gossip, which as it turns out you are . . .* She looked round quickly in case she'd been observed, and finding she hadn't she glanced back down. *They say fresh air and sunlight . . . and I say what the hell, may as well throw in the odd cigarillo . . .*

She forced herself away to join her father as he leant over the railings of the terrace. The house was built on a hill, something you couldn't tell from the front, because below them the land dropped away in a steep garden of ferns and reeds and flowering oleander, a crooked path of flagstone winding down to a flat basin below, where, like an oasis, lay a bright-blue kidney-shaped pool. Lara wanted to fling off her clothes, run down the steps and throw herself in, but just then Caroline appeared.

Her arms were slim and cool as they rested on the railings between them. 'Now.' She took a breath. 'I've told Ginny she can swim between eight and nine, so as not to disturb anyone, and I like to swim first thing, before breakfast, but apart from that, you can use the pool whenever you like.'

Lara gazed down at it, so clear and tempting, the turquoise water dazzling in the sun.

'But now.' She turned. 'I expect you'd like to freshen up.'

When Lara stepped out of the shower she could hear the telephone, then Caroline's slow, serious voice, followed almost immediately by the bubble of her laughter. The sun was still hot, beating through the open window, and anxious to get to the pool before the afternoon cooled, she began to rifle through her bag. She had a swimming costume somewhere, a bikini, borrowed at the last minute from her mother, but once she'd pulled it on and fastened it, she realised it was a horrible mistake. The bikini was striped, purple and white, the top tied at the neck with ribbon, the pants held high on the thigh with bows, but since the last time she'd borrowed it, her body had changed. 'Oh my God.' She stared into the full-length mirror, tucking in a crescent of protruding breast, adjusting the narrow strip of cloth that only half-covered her bottom.

She couldn't even blame her mother. It wasn't her fault that at the last minute she'd discarded her all-in-one black costume and started rummaging through Cathy's clothes. And anyway, she'd never actually known Cathy wear it. Maybe it didn't fit her either, although that was less likely. Cathy was slight and sinewy with narrow hips, and fine long hands and feet. She had a mass of caramel-coloured hair that she tamed with flowery-smelling products, camomile and calendula, and occasionally – accepting defeat – a headscarf. Lara was nothing like her. Taller and darker. She must have inherited her curves from somewhere else.

Ruefully she moved to the window to check the pool was still in sunshine, and there to her surprise she saw her father, naked except for a pair of bright-blue swimming trunks. He stood at the near end of the pool, his shoulders heavy with a sort of down, his legs comically white, and there on the back of his head, she'd never noticed it before, a distinct hollow in the thick grey of his hair.

She shouldn't be watching, she told herself, but the shock of seeing him, unimaginably out of his dark suit, made it impossible to look away. Where, she wondered, did he get those swimming trunks, did he get any swimming trunks at all? But these were tight, electric-blue, a pair of Speedo trunks. She was cringing. She caught herself. She was cringing at her father! She had to tear herself away, but just then he raised his arms and made a perfect dive into the pool. Lara looked back at her room. It was spare and plain. A bed, a chest of drawers, a table with a lamp. She couldn't stay in here for ever, and so wrapping herself in the largest towel she could find she made her way downstairs.

By the time she reached the pool Lambert was sitting, dripping, on a lounger, and before he'd had time to look up she'd dropped her towel and plunged in. The water closed around her, contracting every pore of her body, sending each tiny hair rigid with shock. Down she went, grasping with her feet for tiles, keeping herself under, the water, already warming, holding her body, easing out the kinks and aches in her bones. She opened her eyes, swam along the blue surface of the bottom, marvelled at the strange amphibious nature of her legs, and when she could hold her breath no longer she burst up to the surface, and lay with her eyes shut against the glare. She lay still as a starfish, legs and arms outstretched, and forced herself to see how long she could last. The sun beat through her eyelids, whisked over her nose and cheeks, scorched the white caps of her knees until she was forced to roll over and swim to the side.

Lambert was still there, reading now, making occasional notes in the margins of his book. She watched him for a while and then, pushing off with her feet, she swam, thrashing back and forth across the pool in breast stroke, pausing at each side to catch her breath.

Lambert put down his book. 'Who taught you to swim?'

'No one.' She'd swallowed some water and had to cough for several minutes before she could go on. 'I just learnt.'

'Hmmm.' Lambert was appraising her.

'We had a lake . . .' But she didn't go on.

Every year, on those rare hot Scottish days that smelt of raspberries and heather, they'd walk down the hill to the lake. It lay in a dip of land, far enough off the road to be invisible, shielded on one side by Christmas trees, surrounded on the other by fields full of rabbit droppings and mole hills. It was their lake. That's how they thought of it, although occasionally others would join them there, farmers' sons, and later, Buddhist families who'd come to the valley to be near to Samye Ling. They'd bring bedspreads and batches of home-made scones, hunks of cheese and slippery green apples, and they'd spend whole days ducking and splashing and daring each other to go in. But even on the hottest days the lake was still so cold it paralysed you, cut a ring of ice across your scalp, so that once you were in there was never time to do anything more graceful than beat your arms and legs in a frantic effort to keep warm.

'You're putting too much work in,' Lambert advised, and he got up and came and sat on the side of the pool. He placed his hands together, pointed like two leaves, and then, his muscles taut, he pushed his arms away.

Lara did the same, almost sinking as she forgot to use her legs, and when she came up she found he'd climbed into the pool beside her.

29

'Keep your hands together, then only at the last minute turn them, and push the water away.'

'Right.' She put her hands into position and placing her nose in the water like an arrow she kicked away with her legs.

'Slowly,' Lambert called, and as she floundered he waded after her and slipped one hand under her belly.

Lara froze. She tried to draw herself up and away from him but he kept his hand against her skin.

'Stay relaxed,' he said, 'hold your legs straight, concentrate on your arms.'

The fingers of his left hand were seconds from the flimsy elastic of her pants. Arms, she told herself. Arms.

Lambert was moving her slowly forward, walking beside her as one would lead a horse, urging her to point her hands, turn them, push the water away. 'Now join in with your legs,' he encouraged, and in her effort to free herself she pushed away so vigorously that she slipped out of his grasp and sped off across the pool. 'Good,' he said when she reached the other side.

It was clear he wanted her to turn and swim towards him. Lara pointed her hands, took a deep breath and with such serious determination to get it right she moved through the water like a professional, her face half submerged, every sinew in her body flexed.

'Do you feel the difference?' He was heaving himself out.

She smiled at him, the water glistening in drops before her eyes. 'Yes.' She felt quite euphoric with relief. 'I do.'

All through the early evening Lara practised her stroke until the air began to cool and she saw Caroline on the terrace above, dressed in pleated trousers, a drink in her hand. Supper, it must be nearly time, and almost weak with the thought of it she ran, dripping in her towel, up the steps to get changed.

The table was laid for three with side plates, glasses and a double setting of knives and forks. Ginny had made them a dish of thick spaghetti, heaped with basil sauce, creamy and rich with nuts and cheese. I'd eat this every day, if I could, for the rest of my life, Lara thought, the flavours mashed together, but still separate, the texture of each one intact.

Afterwards there was steak, a strip of rare meat along the centre, and a bowl of peppery salad. Lara looked down at her plate. She should have mentioned she was a vegetarian. Had been one for two years – since a trip to the zoo where the sight of the polar bear, tracing a figure of eight the length of his yard, throwing himself on the last arc into the stagnant pool, had pained her so deeply that she'd felt compelled to do something to help. But had it helped? Recently Lara had been back to the zoo and the polar bear was still there, a little thinner, even more desperate, and she couldn't pretend, even to herself, that her protest had worked.

'Is everything all right?' Caroline asked her, and she saw that she was being watched.

'Yes,' she said and, treacherous, she cut into the steak.

The taste of the meat exploded in her mouth. Chewy and tender and oozing with herbs. This doesn't count, she told herself, eating meat in Italy. It would be rude not to, after Ginny's worked so hard, and she looked up to tell her it was delicious. But Ginny wasn't sitting down with them. She was in the kitchen, preoccupied, subdued, and Lara didn't know if there was praise that should be kept in check.

'That was awfully good,' Caroline said finally when Ginny came to clear, and Lara almost knocked over her glass in her relief at being able to agree.

'Thank you.' Ginny lifted her plate.

Paralysed with indecision, Lara wondered if she was allowed, or possibly expected, to help. In the end the suspense was more than she could bear, and she got up just in time to bring in the oil and vinegar decanters in their silver holders and place them on the side.

'They go there,' Ginny told her, indicating the larder, and although Lara could tell by her tone she wasn't pleased, she had no way of knowing how she was at fault.

That night Caroline and Lambert sat up exchanging news. They mentioned a long succession of people of whom Lara had never heard and occasionally, she was sure, Caroline glanced at her doubtfully, as if maybe she was there under false pretences, maybe she wasn't Lambert's daughter at all.

'How do you two know each other?' Lara edged her way in.

Caroline laughed and glanced quickly at Lambert. 'We've known each other for ever, haven't we, darling? My mother was a cousin of Anne Holt. We met when we were children. Well, I, apparently, was never a child' – she winked at Lambert – 'but your father was a mere boy.'

'Nothing mere about me,' he smiled dutifully.

Caroline, her eyes lit up, leant forward. 'You remember that awful Peregrine? Well, I don't know why, but I was thinking about him the other day and I suddenly remembered that night when he caught us, arriving back from Paris – about a year after the war – with the most ridiculous amount of shopping. All the bags seemed to say things like *Champs-Elysées* and *Boutique Parisien* but very politely he asked how it had been, my week in Wiltshire, at my mother's.' She began to laugh. 'What were we thinking of, sneaking off right under his nose like that? God, after you'd gone, there was the most awful row.'

'I do remember.' Lambert looked at her affectionately. 'We stayed at the Crillon.'

'So we did.' She sighed. 'If only he'd known how innocent it was,' and they sat for a while in silence.

Lara excused herself and went up to her room. She took out the book she was meant to be reading for college on the French Revolution and lay down with it, but before she'd even raised her arm to turn the first page she found that she was whirling, sinking, spinning until with a jolt she heard the book fall to the floor and in the split second that followed she was asleep.

By the time Lara came down the next morning breakfast was over and cleared away.

'Where are the others?' Lara asked, and Ginny told her they had driven into Siena.

'They left early before the heat becomes unbearable, but they'll be back,' she said, 'by lunch.' Ginny was already cooking, cutting vegetables, making pastry, stewing a pan of clementines for a cake.

'Did you swim?' Lara poured milk on to cornflakes, and Ginny said that yes, she'd done a hundred lengths.

She set her mixing bowl down on the table and as she stirred she began to talk, about her garden in the Cotswolds, her mother who was insistent on living alone at eighty-seven, her admiration for Lady Diana Spencer. How beautiful she was. And pure.

'You can tell she's a virgin.' Ginny looked at Lara as if she was used to being contradicted. 'Even my mother agrees and she's beady as a hawk.'

'I'm sure you're right.' Lara had never given it a moment's thought, so instead she told her about her own mother, how they were such good friends, how they'd gone to India together on the Budget Bus from London to Delhi for £50.

'Return?' Ginny asked and Lara laughed because people always asked her this.

'One way.' It wasn't just the idea of the bargain being any greater than it was, but the idea of any of the people travelling on that bus to India knowing when, if ever, they were likely to come back.

She remembered the Welsh miners, sprawled across the back seats, swapping their clothes, even their jeans and jackets, in Afghanistan for opium and hash. By the time they arrived in Delhi they owned nothing more than their underpants and T-shirts, and their rucksacks when they hoiked them on were light as air. Were they still out there, she wondered, five years later, roaming semi-naked through the streets?

'Our driver on the Budget Bus was called John,' she told Ginny. 'He was like our dad. He found the best places to camp, always near a market, with somewhere to wash, and when the van broke down he could always mend it. Even if once it took three days.'

Lara had kept a diary with felt-tip illustrations of butter-flies and birds, tents and veiled women, and carefully written accounts of her travels to make up for missing school.

'When we arrived in Delhi, we were all so attached to our dad no one could bring themselves to leave the bus. We hovered around, making excuses to get back on, even the miners, looking for things they might have lost. All day we sat there, until he had to shoo us away.'

Lara had a sudden memory of her mother, white-faced, setting off through the city, gripping on to her arm, with people all around them thrusting out their hands, calling, smiling, teeth stained red. They climbed into a rickshaw and trotted out into the traffic, but every time they stopped they were surrounded again, the same thin hands pushed against their laps. Cathy was frightened, so frightened in fact that she abandoned her search for the friends of friends they were hoping to stay with and booked into a hotel. It was a small hotel, only half built, but the room was clean and the door had a lock, and in the morning they were brought a tray with tea and a banana. Bananas were in fact the one thing they dared to eat, sealed safely as they were inside their skin.

'How did you get back?' Ginny was leaping forward in her concern, and so Lara told her about the very different driver they had a year later, who stopped the bus only where it suited him, in back streets and corrugated yards.

'He was smuggling or dealing, and if anyone said anything, like maybe we could stop near a *hammam*, you know, to wash, he just shouted at them. In fact, the journey was so awful that once we got to Germany we got off the bus and hitched.'

'Hitched?' Ginny looked alarmed, and so Lara explained about their house on the hill in Scotland and how they would hitch lifts up and down to London every summer.

'Sometimes,' she said, although it probably wasn't true, 'we made it faster than the train.'

She told Ginny about the goat they kept for milk, the yaks the Tibetans imported, and how when they moved to London Cathy missed her goats so much she decided to keep bees. They already had a cat, but she wanted something that gave produce, so now they had two bee hives on the flat roof above the bathroom that made enough honey to last most of the year. When the bees swarmed they hovered in a great black ball of buzzing in the fork of the lilac tree at the end of the garden and someone from the Inner London Beekeeping

Association would drive round and, dressed in a white suit with a hat and a veil, would knock them into a sack.

It was easy sitting there, enveloped by the smells of food, the sweetness of the onion softening and the bitter peel of the fruit. She could tell Ginny about Clive. She thought about it, but found she couldn't focus on him here. Dusty, he seemed in his donkey jacket, and far away.

Outside the day was heating up, the air growing denser as it neared noon. Lara changed into her bikini and went down to the pool. She practised her new streamlined swimming, gliding through the water with barely a splash, and when she'd done enough lengths to feel bored, she got out and lay on a towel in the full glare of the sun. She could feel it prickle her, seal heat into her body, and when she was baked through she rolled over to feed the scorching rays into her back.

'Oh my dear!' Caroline said at lunch. 'You have caught the sun!' And it was true, there was a red stripe along the bridge of Lara's nose, and under each eye, a sweep of pink.

'Where did you go?' she asked to divert attention.

Caroline told her that they'd driven into Siena to talk to a man about a horse. 'I'm hoping my horse will be chosen to run in the Palio. It was chosen once, three years ago, but since then it's been overlooked.'

Lara looked round. 'You have a horse?'

'Not here.' Caroline raised her eyebrows in a flicker of amusement. 'It's a racehorse. My husband used to own several and I keep one, in his memory. It was his greatest wish' – she looked wistful – 'that it win the Palio.'

'The Palio,' Lambert told her, 'is a horse race that takes place in July and again in August in the main square in Siena.'

'A horse race! It's much more than a horse race!' Caroline broke in. 'It's a way of life! It's the most important event in this area; people prepare for it for the whole year. There is probably never a time when the local people aren't thinking about it. Aren't stewing over who won it last year, hoping to be the winners this time round.'

'It's been a tradition in this town since the thirteenth century,' Lambert said knowledgeably. 'It's a race between the different districts of the city. The *contrade*. There are seventeen of them and each *contrada* has a symbol, the Panther or the Snail, the Tower, the Shell, each with their own colours, and whoever wins the Palio is the King of Siena for that year.'

'The jockeys all come from Sardinia.' Caroline was flushed. 'They ride bareback round the square at the most incredible speed. Three times they go. Some fall, horses are destroyed, the people go wild. It's the most intense ninety seconds – there's nothing like it – and when it's over, you need a stiff drink.'

'Isn't it a bit . . .' Lara shivered. 'A bit cruel?'

Caroline looked fierce. 'No more so,' she said, 'than the Grand National. And the horse that wins, well, that horse is a hero. It's taken into the cathedral, blessed, and revered for all time.'

'The riders are hurt too,' Lambert said.

Lara couldn't resist, she told him what he knew. 'But no one makes the riders do it!' She looked down at her salad then, but not quickly enough to miss the amused look that passed between Caroline and Lambert, eyeing each other as if to say, 'She'll grow out of it! She's young.'

I won't, she seethed, remembering a book of photographs she'd once seen of a bullfight, the crowd jeering and bloodthirsty, the toreador taunting the poor bleeding animal with his spear. I'm so glad, she'd thought, that I'm a vegetarian, and she remembered the steak and felt a stab of guilt.

'When is the Palio anyway?' Lambert was asking, and Caroline told him it was a few weeks away, on August the 16th.

'Lara.' He leant towards her. 'You're saved. Our tickets are booked for the day before.'

'Oh, but change them.' Caroline gripped his hand. 'You have to change them. You can't miss the Palio. I'll look into it for you. Or we could ask Ginny. Ginny might even be driving into Pisa later this week. She won't mind stopping off at the train station and changing the tickets for you.'

Lambert smiled. 'I'll see,' he said, but Lara couldn't imagine he'd stay a moment longer than he'd planned.

Caroline turned to her. 'Try and persuade him.'

'Really?' Lara was too flattered to object. 'I'll try,' and she raised her eyebrows enquiringly at Lambert, who looked down at his plate.

That afternoon she and Lambert attempted a walk. They wandered out of the drive and up the lane, and then, unsure which way to go when it forked, turned left, and found themselves stumbling along beside a field, dust from the earth whitening the ends of their shoes. Each time they stopped, squinting into the distance, checking to see if they were moving towards anything of interest, they heard the rustling of salamanders, not expecting to be disturbed at this siesta hour. It was nice having Lambert to herself again, falling into their accustomed silence, broken occasionally by Lara's questions and his thoughtful replies.

The fields around were planted with olive groves, their lines, as they sloped uphill, straight as the teeth of a comb, and then as they passed them, looking back from another angle, seeming to fall into ragged disarray. With each step the sun beat down more fiercely until sweat was standing out on Lara's forehead.

'Mad dogs and Englishmen,' Lambert muttered, 'go out in the midday sun,' and when Lara opened her mouth to join in she found the air was scorching the back of her throat.

'What do you think?' Lambert glanced back along the way they'd come.

'Shall we?' she said, shuffling to a stop, and with renewed energy they turned and hurried towards the cool retreat of the house.

That evening Lara curled herself into the cream sofa, flicking through a magazine while Caroline and Lambert talked.

'Do you still see Henry?' she asked.

'Why would I?'

'Well, you used to like him.' Caroline shrugged.

'I did bump into him once,' Lambert said, 'on a bus.'

Lara looked at her father, unable to imagine the circumstance under which he'd ever caught a bus.

'Actually, he was on rather good form. He suggested I borrow some money off him and when I asked why, he looked surprised. "So that I can spend the next ten years trying to get it back, of course." I thought that was quite inspired.'

'He obviously misses you.' Caroline curled her slim legs under her, hiding a dark bruise that spread up from her ankle.

'Well, maybe, but I imagine he's got over it. That was about fifteen years ago now.'

For a while neither of them spoke and the only noise in the room was the flicking of the pages of Lara's magazine. It was a Spanish magazine – *¡Hola!* – with pictures of European royalty, interspersed with the occasional racing driver or Hollywood star. The entire middle section was devoted to speculation over Lady Diana's wedding dress, with a series of photo-fit possibilities attached to her smiling head. Lara ran her eyes over the options, slinky, puffed-sleeved, spaghetti-strapped, layered in satin, sheer with lace. There were dresses in ivory, cream and lemon, rose and icing-sugar white, but in each photo Diana herself had the same feathered wedge of hair, hanging shyly down, obliterating half her face.

'Were you terribly disappointed?' Caroline was addressing Lara now. 'To miss the big day?'

'The big . . .?' She looked up from a great froth of peachy-coloured netting. 'The wedding, you mean?'

'I hear people have already started setting up camp along the route, but I wasn't sure how you young people felt about it.'

'Us? Well . . .' How to put this politely. 'We're not really very interested, at least not the people I know.' To strengthen her stance she shut the magazine. 'It just seems a bit tragic, I suppose.'

'Really?' Caroline was eyeing her with disbelief. 'I'd have thought it was the answer to a young girl's dream. Marry a prince. Live at Buckingham Palace. Meet rich and powerful people, travel the world.'

It seemed so clear to Lara that this was not the case, that this would not make any young girl happy, but the only evidence she had to fuel her argument was that the prince in question, Prince Charles, wore his parting too far over to one side. Lara had to bite her bottom lip to stop herself laughing. Hair was obviously her only criterion for making judgements about people. She should write a thesis on it. She should give up A level history and take up work instead on the psychology of hair.

'It all just seems so old-fashioned,' she said instead and then instantly regretted it.

Caroline lay back on the sofa, lighting a cigarette, while Lambert picked up a day-old copy of *The Times*, bought at great expense that morning in Siena. On its front page it had the photograph that had sent the nation into a frenzy – Diana, standing outside the nursery school at which she taught, her legs silhouetted, thanks to the sun, and seemingly naked, against the thin material of her skirt.

'She is very handsome, it must be said.' Caroline had her head on one side and Lambert craned round to look. 'He got the wrong one apparently.' Caroline blew out a soft white plume of smoke. 'At least that's what everyone's saying.'

'But wasn't it all arranged?' Lambert was squinting at the paper.

'Well, yes, but people think she got it wrong. Pointed him in the wrong direction. He was going for one of the other sisters . . . is it Jane, or Sarah? I get them muddled up, but then the word came through – no, the quiet one – Diana.'

Lambert stared into the picture in just the same way he might scrutinise a train crash or the aftermath of a bomb. 'Quiet she doesn't look. No, she's going to be lively. I'm not sure they know quite what they're letting themselves in for.'

'The Royal Family? They arranged it?' Lara was aghast. They both looked at her.

'No,' Caroline's eyes were twinkling. 'Charles's girlfriend picked her out.'

Lara was so shocked she chose not to believe her. Surely the whole reason Prince Charles had been unmarried for so long was that he couldn't *get* a girlfriend! 'But . . . if . . .' she spluttered. 'Why . . . I mean if he's got a girlfriend why doesn't he just marry her?'

'She's . . .' Caroline looked at Lambert as if the truth might be too shocking for her seventeen-year-old ears. 'She's un-suitable.'

Lara picked up ¡Hola! again and looked with more interest at the photos of Diana. No – she scanned each identical one – she could see it in the quiet confidence of her face, in the hopefulness of her smile, even in the hair that flopped over her face: Diana had no idea.

That night Lara dreamt of Charles and his black Jamaican girlfriend searching for his trousers in her room. They giggled and flirted and made lustful, lascivious comments, some-where between Ray Cooney and Macbeth, and she had to hide under the covers for fear they would fall on to her bed.

The next morning they all drove into Siena. Caroline had an appointment with the doctor at ten. 'I'll meet you here in an hour or so.' She indicated an outdoor café and moving delicately, clutching her handbag, she walked away.

Lara stood on the edge of the Piazza del Campo and stared. They were in a medieval square, a circle really, surrounded by stone buildings, so tall and ancient they formed a shelter from the sun.

'Is this where they have the horse race?' she asked, and she stepped out from the coolness of the wall.

The Piazza, like all of Siena, was built on a hill. It was in the shape of a half-moon, or of the sun setting, its rays spreading up towards them from the bottom of the slope. All around the edge of this half-moon was a strip of flattened concrete and at its highest end was a row of cafés, their tables and chairs shaded by umbrellas.

Lara began to walk downhill, stepping between the people sitting on the ground, dodging children who ran, arms stretched, down the gullies of the rays. In every groove, between each dark-red brick, there was a scattering of confetti, and she imagined a whole spring and summer of wedding parties bursting out from some dark courtyard, followed by well-wishers, sprinkling them with shreds of colour.

Above the rooftops, beyond the square, was a striped black-and-white tower. 'The Duomo,' Lambert told her. 'It can't be far away.' Marking it with their eyes, they chose a lane that led off the Piazza.

The lane was narrow, its high walls creating alleyways of cool, with shops like caves hidden entirely from the sun. There were delicatessens, their windows decorated with packets of pasta, curled and coiled, striped like candy, formed into multicoloured bows. There was dried fruit arranged in doorways, apricots so plump Lara could hardly resist, nuts and seeds and packets of dry biscuits made from almonds and vanilla sugar, just waiting to be softened in a cup of tea. There were tiers of handbags, just as beautifully arranged, and a pharmacy, its walls covered in gilt mirrors, chandeliers hanging from the ceiling, its cabinets as ornate as a museum.

By now they'd lost sight of the striped tower, and so they hurried on uphill until they came to another square, and found they were above it, that it had somehow swapped sides. They turned downhill, glancing into stone alleyways that sliced between tall buildings, their windows strung with washing, pastel-coloured Vespas parked below, until eventually they came into an opening, and there it was before them, a cathedral of such beauty that its tower now appeared only to be a detail, the tail of an animal, tacked on behind. The front of the cathedral was striped as well, but paler, pink and cream, the columns and turrets picked out and moulded like elaborate decoration on a cake. At the top was one round window and above that a mural set against gold leaf.

'The Duomo,' Lambert murmured, as if it were a half-forgotten friend, and they climbed the steps to the main door.

Inside it was completely dark. Lara had to clasp her father's arm to stop from stumbling. 'Sorry,' she said, when she realised what she was doing, and she let go. They stood side by side waiting for the dark to lift until, like a negative developing, the cathedral slowly flickered into life.

'Oh my God!'

The whole interior was striped in black and white, the pillars, the arches, the walls, and above them the vaulted layers of the ceilings were scattered with gold stars. The floors were tiled in black and white and red, in some places so intricately that whole areas were roped off, and there were statues, carvings, heads of cardinals lit up with gold.

'Oh my God!' Lara said again more quietly, and then laughing she realised that this was exactly the reaction that was required.

Around the pulpit was a seething mass of carvings, Jesus Christ himself, dying, nailed to the cross. There were dogs with puppies hanging from their teats, lions devouring long-necked monsters, snakes and people that looked like slaves.

'Dad?' She was hoping for answers, but when she looked up he had gone.

Lara walked very slowly around the cathedral, hovering on the fringes of groups of tourists listening to their guides, but even when she came across a guide talking in English, she realised she was too restless to stop. She found herself in an ante room where one man was praying, kneeling against the railings, lit up, as if he had arranged it, by a shaft of light from a high round window above. The man was oblivious, his face closed, his lips pleading as he clasped a rosary between his hands. He was too absorbed to notice Lara, and she was sure, just from the shape of his body, that he was praying for someone on the brink of death.

Outside this room there was a bank of candles, all flickering hopefully in the gloom, and quickly Lara took one herself. Who was she lighting it for? She held the wick against a flame while she decided. She was lighting it for someone – the wick had caught and she'd have to hurry – someone she was going to love.

'Lara?' She jumped, blushing, as if she'd been caught out, the daughter of a Buddhist and an atheist Jew, caught in the act of being superstitious, but when she turned to Lambert he smiled and said gently that they'd better go.

For a moment they stood on the steps, once more unable to see, and when their eyes eventually adjusted they stood there for a minute more, watching a group of nuns attempting to take photographs while three boys threw a rugby ball from one to another, bouncing it at unexpected angles on the cobbles, forcing the nuns to jump and scowl.

They were almost back at the Campo when Lara slowed to look into the window of a shop. Inside there were swimming costumes of every kind. Some hung from the ceiling, caught up with string, while others were pulled tight over cotton torsos, their chests thrust forward, the Lycra of their briefs stretched flat.

'Is there something you need?' Lambert asked.

Lara pointed to a black-and-brown polka-dot bikini, a demure version of the one she already had.

'Why don't you try it?' he offered, and waited while she stood in a small cupboard, walled in by bags and boxes, and hurriedly tugged it on.

Yes. It covered her. That was all she needed to know, and eager to rescue him from the indignity of standing with gussets and bra straps brushing against his head, she quickly pulled it off.

'Thank you so much,' she said, as Lambert took out the necessary lire, and the shopkeeper, a woman, held the door for them with a disapproving look.

Caroline was already at the café. She was drinking black coffee and smoking a long thin cigarette.

'How was it?' Lambert kissed her under the shadow of her hat.

She blew out a plume of smoke and laughed. 'Much the same.' But even so she looked suddenly exhausted. Lambert pulled his chair close and sat beside her, but when he took her hand she pulled away. 'Don't fuss,' she said. 'Really. You of all people.' And she clicked her fingers to the waiter and ordered more coffee. 'Just a cold lunch, I think, when we get back.' Caroline took out a powder compact to examine her face. 'And then of course tonight we'll be dining out.'

Lara looked around at the other tables, couples chatting amiably, families sprawling, taking up several tables' worth of space. What would they talk about, the three of them, for an entire night, and she wondered if it would be inconceivably rude if she asked to stay behind.

'Dining out?' Lambert raised an eyebrow.

Caroline inhaled hard on her cigarette. 'I said we'd go up to the Willoughbys'. You know they're only up the road at Ceccomoro. I thought it might be amusing for Lara.'

'Andrew Willoughby?' Lambert opened his mouth as if to say more, and then shut it again.

'Oh for God's sake, Lamb,' Caroline tutted. 'Don't be such

a . . . It's all so long ago, that miserable business, and whatever you say about him, he's been a help to me out here.'

Lambert looked out over the square. 'Of course,' he said coolly, and he said nothing more.

Upstairs, in front of the long wardrobe mirror, Lara tried on her bikini. It fitted perfectly, something she'd been too rushed to properly check when she'd tried it on before, and for the first time since her body had begun to change, since, at the age of twelve, it had appalled her by thickening and developing breasts – small lopsided breasts she'd never asked for – for the first time, really, in five years, she looked fine. She twirled around in a little loop of pleasure, admiring herself, so sheer in polka-dot, the square of her back between the straps turned from pink to brown, her legs smooth, her stomach flat. Her nose still looked a little sunburnt but the stripe below her eyes was darkening, turning to freckles, throwing light up into her eyes.

She took her towel and a bottle of suntan oil and skipped through the house.

'Don't forget to use it,' Caroline called as she ran across the terrace. 'I know you think you're immortal but one day, when you have skin like wrinkled leather . . .'

'OK.' Lara glanced back at Caroline, creamy in her pleated skirt, her hat pulled down a little, her legs pale. 'Thank you,' and she went more carefully, treading with bare feet down each hot step of stone.

It was worth not having swum that morning to feel the anticipation of it now. Very slowly Lara waded out from the shallow steps, sinking inch by inch, watching the water creep over the edge of her new costume, darkening it until she was submerged. She swam underwater for as long as she could, watching her hands form into their leaf point, feeling her muscles flex and tense as she pushed the water away. She rose up at each end, shaking her head, glorying in the shower of drops, swooping back under, pushing off hard, gliding towards the other end, her body bursting with pleasure, her mind free from any thought. When her eyes became sore she flipped over, going more slowly, slicing the water with her arms, kicking back and forth.

Eventually she pulled herself out and sat for a while on the scorching stone at the side of the pool, feeling it sizzling against the wet material, marvelling at how quickly she dried. She glanced up at the terrace and in case Caroline was watching she collected the boiled brown bottle of Ambre Solaire and moved into the shade. She rubbed some into her face. It smelt of coconut, of Bounty bars and advertisement beaches. She dribbled it along the length of her legs and arms, and when it was rubbed in, squirted a splash over her shoulder and stretched an arm around to rub it into her back.

'Would you like help with that?' It was Lambert.

Lara spun round. 'No. It's fine.' She was seized with fear he might be about to touch her skin. She took the bottle and slid it under the seat. 'I'm going to lie on my back anyway,' she said, and smiling at him, hoping to disguise her panic, she arranged herself on the towel and closed her eyes.

Not long after she heard a splash. She opened one eye and saw the ripples on the smooth blue pool. She rolled on to her side. She could see him under the surface. He swam a length, turned, took one professional gulp of air and swam another. Where did he learn to swim like that? Who taught him? But more than that she wanted to know how he'd managed to resist the pleasure all these years. All the summers of her childhood when he'd stayed leashed to his desk, his only exercise a walk through Kensington Gardens and then back.

It was obvious from the way Caroline talked that he must have had another, livelier life, but whenever Lara asked him if he was going away, taking any time off from his work, his answer was always the same. 'Time,' he'd say, 'there's too little of it as there is.'

Lara got up to drag the lounger further into the shade. She scooped up the suntan lotion and began to smooth another layer into her legs. Lambert heaved himself out, and wrapping a towel round his middle sank down on to the other seat. She smiled at him and slid over the lotion, watching, she couldn't help herself, as he poured a pool into his hand and dabbed it experimentally into the thick hair of his chest.

'I wouldn't mind,' she told him, 'if we just stayed here tonight.'

'Oh, no.' He shook his head, as if whatever reservations he'd had that morning about going out were now forgotten. 'You have to come. See all the young people. I think it's why Caroline arranged it. She's worried you'll get bored.'

'I won't get bored.'

'Well, if you really don't want to then . . .' He frowned, as if this was just one more complication.

'Oh . . .' She was regretting everything now. 'I mean. I don't mind.'

Lambert lay back with his paper. 'It's an interesting house, apparently, Ceccomoro. It was originally a village, well, a hamlet, I suppose, but Willoughby bought each family out, it took him years, and he turned it into his hilltop empire. They're our nearest neighbours here, the Willoughbys, and Andrew, he lives out here all the time, well, however many days you have to live abroad to be a tax exile.' There was a flicker of his earlier, disgusted tone, and then, after another minute or so, half lost in a distracted yawn, he added, 'I used to know his wife, long ago.'

'Oh really? Will she be here?'

Lambert laughed. 'I doubt it.'

'Does he live out here alone then?'

'That seems unlikely.' He flipped the pages of the paper. 'But I expect we'll find out.'

Lara looked up at the sky. The deep blue bowl of it. As bright as a postcard of the sea. There were so many questions she wanted to ask: how many children does Andrew Willoughby have, what are their ages, how far away are they, their nearest neighbours? She looked around but could see nothing but the dust-grey leaves of olive trees, and the hills rising up out of the valley, thick with pine.

'The great tragedy about Lord Willoughby . . .' Lambert was talking, she assumed to her, 'is that he was rather promising as a young man. He was the second son of Lord Montague and he was training to be a lawyer – you could do that if you were a second son – had already become a lawyer, quite brilliant, I think. But then, his elder brother died and he was expected to give up his career and take over the estates. But he just wasn't up to it. He squandered the family money, as much as he could get his hands on, and instead of banishing himself to Yorkshire to look after the estate, he spent his every waking hour chasing after girls.'

'But I thought you said he was married. I mean . . . that you knew his wife?'

'Yes.' Lambert frowned. 'Yes, well, he was married. Still is. Poor girl. Anyway, eventually his father gave up on him, disinherited him, passed on the title and all that went with it to Willoughby's son, Kip, who at the age of seven became the new Lord Montague. Poor boy. And Andrew Willoughby, his tail between his legs, abandoned all his duties and disappeared out here.'

Lambert rifled through the paper as if he might find more

news of it right there, and forgetting she still didn't have cream on her back, Lara rolled on to her front and entertained herself by watching the ants, so busy as they worked, pulling pieces of dried grass bigger than themselves across the tiles.

That night Lara tried on every single item of her clothing, and found each one somehow not to be quite right. There was a pair of pink-and-white-striped trousers she'd bought in Oxford Street, but as she examined them she saw why they had been so cheap. At home, when she'd tried them, she'd been standing on the bathroom chair, checking them section by section in the narrow oblong mirror above the bath, but here, in the full length of glass attached to the back of the wardrobe door, they didn't work at all. She pulled them off and tried a skirt, but she didn't seem to have a shirt to go with it, and very soon she'd run out of combinations and so opted for the jeans and cotton shirt she'd travelled in, which had appeared, washed and ironed almost beyond recognition, on the end of her bed. She put on her high heels and swept her lashes with mascara, noting with pleasure how white the whites looked, how blue the blue, against the stripe of tiny freckles on her cheeks.

When she finally came down Lambert and Caroline were waiting for her on the terrace, and as soon as she saw them all the pride she'd taken in her appearance fell away. Lambert had on a light suit, and Caroline was as perfect as a film star in a gauzy jumper crocheted from silk.

'Shall we go?' Caroline, just for a moment, appraised her, and then she smiled and they walked out to the car.

No one spoke as they set off. It was just beginning to grow cooler and the shadows cast by the bushes seemed to add a hint of restlessness to the wakening night. Caroline drove, her back straight, her hands almost translucent on the wheel, a spectacular cluster of jewels on each ring finger, forcing you to think of whoever it was that had slipped them on. They glided down a hill, up another and then curved round in a semicircle through open fields until they turned into a chalky white drive, the start of which was marked by two stone lions. They continued more slowly then, the shards of white rock snapping and splintering beneath their wheels, and then they turned a corner and Caroline slowed the car.

'There it is.'

To one side, set in against a hill, looking out over a valley, was the house. It really was a village, the cluster of tiled roofs, the gardens falling away from it, the low walls and terraces and the outbuildings on either side. Above it, set into the hill, was a chapel with a bell tower, steps cut into the green hill, at least a mile long.

'It's beautiful,' Lara said, because it was, and also because something was expected, and Lambert shook his head.

'I told you.' Caroline put a hand on his arm. 'He's happy to be Lord of the Manor here.'

She drove on then, letting the car bump along the drive, slowing when they reached two giant pots of oleander like sentries on either side of the road. She turned the car, pulling into a yard, and parked between a Mercedes and a jeep.

'This way,' she called and walked ahead of them, making her way up a small flight of steps and through an opening in a wall.

They followed and found themselves looking down into a courtyard. There was a long bank of roses and beyond that a swimming pool edged in tiles, one side protected by a high stone wall, the colour of honey in the falling light. In the centre of the courtyard, which once must have been the village square, was a long table covered with a cloth and as they stood, admiring, several women, Italians in head-scarves and aprons, appeared around the corner of the house with plates and candles and small jugs of flowers which they began to arrange along its length.

'Hi!'

They turned at the shout, and there was a girl in a bikini standing with her back against the wall, a girl of such voluptuous beauty, her body bronzed, the white scrap of her costume only just supporting the deep weight of her breasts.

'Caroline!' She waved, then rose up on her toes and in a perfect arc dived into the pool.

'Who is that!?' Lambert asked, but almost immediately the girl had risen to the surface, and, her hair slicked back, her eyes glistening, she climbed out.

'I'll tell them you're here. She smiled and grabbing a towel she ran up some steps and into a house.

'Remind me,' Lambert said, his voice more careful now, 'which one is that?' and Caroline, keeping him waiting, lit a cigarette and blew the smoke into the still air.

'Lulu? Oh . . . she's not one of Andrew's. That's Pamela's girl.'

Lambert put his head to one side as if to read her. 'I see.'

Just then a woman in a Japanese kimono came out to greet them. 'Caroline.' She looked askance at the cigarette in her hand. 'Doctor's orders. Surely not!'

'Pamela' – Caroline ignored her – 'you know Lambert, of course, and this is his daughter Lara, who has very kindly come out to keep us old folk company. She's been here for three days now and she's most horribly bored.'

'No,' Lara protested. 'Really.' But other guests were streaming through into the courtyard and both Caroline and Pamela turned away.

Lara hovered beside her father as people began to gather. Lambert took out his Gitanes, and began to smoke nervously, and Lara, feeling herself examined, stared at the roses in the garden with unnecessary scrutiny, testing the soft velvet of their petals, stooping down to breathe in the lemon sweetness of their scent.

And then Andrew Willoughby was there, small, with a sand-and-speckled beard, thin hair below his ears, but unmistakably the owner of the house, in a hat and a sequinned waistcoat, calling from the head of the table for everyone to sit down. Lara hurried back towards Lambert, stood as close to his side as she dared, but Andrew had spotted her, was calling out and waving.

'Lara. Lara Gold. Come up here and join our end of the table. What are you thinking? You don't want to sit down there with the old and the dimwitted.'

Lara glanced round at her father, who had turned away, and seeing no alternative she walked reluctantly towards Andrew Willoughby, who was holding a chair for her, the empty one beside him, and as she sat down he began to introduce her to the young people who sat around.

'Lara, this is Pamela's daughter, Lulu, a great actress, just honouring us with a few weeks of her time.' The beauty from the swimming pool smiled at him. 'And this is May, who is . . . what are you? My fourth daughter?'

May was fair-haired and olive-skinned with the perfectly tilted nose of a doll. 'Hello,' she said, and Lara saw if she hadn't been sitting beside Lulu she would have been considered beautiful in her own right.

'And Piers, her fiancé.'

Piers, sitting on Lara's other side, took her hand and shook it as if he were on best behaviour, was showing his future father-in-law just what a good upstanding citizen he was.

'And of course, my son, Kip. Kip!'

But Kip ignored them. He was stretching across Lulu for the breadsticks, which he managed to knock over as he prised one out. 'Sorry,' he said, and his hand brushed against her cleavage, displayed to its best advantage in an off-the-shoulder top.

'Fuck off.' Lulu swiped away his hand indulgently. 'Or when supper's over I'll find you, and I mean it' – she was grinning – 'I'll sit on your face.'

'So, Lara Gold.' Andrew had turned back to her. 'Tell us about yourself.'

'I . . . um.' Lara felt herself blushing. 'I'm Lara Riley actually. I got my mother's name.'

'Are you the O'Riley they speak of so highly?' Andrew leant in towards her:

Are you the O'Riley of whom I've heard tell?
Well, if you're the O'Riley they speak of so highly
Cor Blimey, O'Riley, you are looking well!

Andrew finished with a flourish and just then someone kicked Lara under the table.

'Sorry.' Kip looked up with genuine concern, his eyes meeting hers, his face growing serious for a second.

'It's all right.' Lara tried to smile, but something in his look made her feel as if she'd been hit. She put a hand up to her chest. She could hardly breathe. It was as if all the wheels on a fruit machine had come to a sudden stop. 'I um . . .'

'Don't be shy,' Andrew was demanding. 'Tell us something we don't know.'

'How old are you?' May offered helpfully.

Lara turned away from Kip. 'Seventeen.'

'And what are you going to do when you grow up?'

Andrew's eyes were twinkling, and feeling sure it was a trick question, she racked her brains for something witty and urbane.

Finding nothing, she fell back on the truth. 'I'd like to work in the same area as my mother . . .' She hesitated, but seeing they wanted more she carried on. 'She works with adult literacy students, people who never got a chance in life, you know, to basically learn to read and write, and with the support of the local council my mum set up a writing group for women who arrive in Britain with no skills. Last year they produced a book . . .'

She'd forgotten to be self-conscious and was really trying to let him know, let the whole table know, how truly amazing it was. To see these women, who not so long before could hardly read and write, search through the index of a book and find their names. 'The book is full of poems and stories about their lives, where they came from, the things they've suffered, the terrible things they've seen, and it's on sale in the local bookshop and so far sixty-five copies have been sold.'

She finished speaking and looked around, at Piers who had blushed a mulberry red, at May who was making some kind of sculpture from her napkin and at Kip who was crumbling up his breadstick, making an anthill from the crumbs. Lulu had pushed her chair out from the table and was mouthing some information to another girl further down.

Only Andrew Willoughby was looking at her. 'So we have a guest in our midst with a social conscience,' he said. 'What are you doing for your A levels, or have you given up on this elitist system of education?'

'No, I mean . . . English and history and –'

'History . . .? I see. Always a sign of danger.' He looked along the table at Lambert. 'So we've got a little Bolshevik in the making, have we? You'd better watch out' – he turned to the others – 'watch out she doesn't infiltrate with her ideas.'

Just then a ruddy-faced, blond-haired man squeezed in next to Lulu. 'Too boring down that end,' he said. 'What's all the excitement up here?'

'A communist,' Andrew told him. 'A communist with blue eyes and a sunburnt nose. The most dangerous kind. Be warned.'

'Roland.'

The blond man put out his hand and when Lara took it, protesting that she wasn't a communist, he slipped his thumb against her palm and stroked it. Startled, she pulled back. He laughed and Kip, presumably aware of the trick, laughed too.

To Lara's relief Andrew turned his attention to Lulu, to a film she'd been cast in, and Andrew began teasing her about a sex scene she would have to do. 'But I haven't given my written permission,' he said. 'How dare these Yanks come and take advantage of our most beautiful girls!'

'Sorry to disappoint you,' Lulu said. 'One, you're not my father and two, I'm not doing any sex scenes. There's just a snog.'

'Not true,' Andrew insisted, but Lara didn't know which piece of information he was refuting.

The food came then, and there was an excuse for her to duck out of the conversation as she tried to find a way of pulling apart her prawns, peeling back the slippery shell, scraping off the soft slush of the eggs.

Occasionally she looked up and whenever she did she found Roland's eyes on her. 'Like this,' he said, 'Comrade Lara,' and he sucked at the belly of a prawn, made a slurping noise with his tongue, and winked.

During the main course, Roland described a waterfall he had heard about, '*La cascata dell'amore* – the Love Falls.' It had a pool below it into which you could jump. 'It'll only be fun if we all go,' he said expansively. 'Except my fat wife, of course. She can stay behind,' and although Lara took an audible intake of breath, and looked round for some response, the insult was ignored and it wasn't until later in the evening when a tall woman, heavily pregnant, came up behind him and began whispering in his ear that Lara understood this had been meant as a joke.

People began to drift around, swapping places, squeezing on to others' chairs. Andrew stood and stretched, and visibly giving up on the young crowd moved down to the far end of the table, where immediately great gales of laughter rose up as if he were relaying some anecdote he'd been saving just for them. Lara felt the atmosphere at their end of the table lighten and for the first time, in a tone of genuine conversation, May turned and asked her where she lived.

'Finsbury Park,' she said.

'Where the Rainbow is?' She'd caught Kip's attention, and they all looked at her, mystified, impressed, as stunned as if she'd said she lived on Mars.

'Have you seen any bands there?' Kip asked.

'I saw Peter Tosh once.' She didn't mention she'd gone with her mother. 'And you?'

'I was thinking about it,' he said. 'I wanted to see Peter Tosh but I was away at school.'

'He was good,' Lara said, remembering the reggae star's tall dark dancing frame, and it gave her confidence, the way Kip looked at her. 'So, have you got other brothers and sisters?' She wanted to hand the conversation back to them. 'Or are you all here?'

'Sisters,' May corrected, and she explained that apart from Kip there were only sisters. Tabitha, the pregnant woman, and another, older girl, Antonia, who had a place among the grown-ups. 'Then there's Katherine who's in America and Fifi who's . . . not well.'

'And then, finally, me.' Kip looked up.

'Yes, you.' May poked him. 'Our poor mother. Papa was never going to let her stop breeding until there was someone to inherit.'

'And is she . . .?' Lara remembered too late her father's assurance that the mother of all these girls, the mother of Kip, so disconcertingly handsome she could hardly trust herself to look, was unlikely to be here.

'Shhhh.' May had hold of her arm. 'She's never been here. Papa won't let her come. And if you see her, whatever you do, never mention Pamela.'

'Of course,' Lara agreed blindly, and she nodded her head as if it was likely she'd see Lady Willoughby any time soon.

Later, while the grown-ups and the older girls sat around drinking small shots of grappa with their coffee, Lara sat with May, Piers, Lulu and Kip along the edge of the swimming pool, their feet in the water, drinking cold beer, smoking Marlboro, flicking ash from their cigarettes into the roses behind.

Lulu talked. She looked even more beautiful, if that were possible, than she had in her bikini. Her low-cut top showed up the flawless beauty of her skin, her chest and neck so smoothly gold it looked as if she had sat with a copper plate in her lap to reflect the sun. Her arms hung cool and luscious and her legs, bare from the knee down, were golden too. She talked and the others listened, aware that next year she would be gone. She was only an honorary teenager, just gracing them with her company, playing with the small fry before she jumped. She told them about Los Angeles, about the actors she'd met, about the film she had a part in, about the classes she'd taken and what had been said about her talent. Occasionally she brushed her hand against Kip's leg as she stretched and flexed her body and Lara noticed with surprise that he didn't take any of the opportunities she gave him to respond.

Lara sat on his other side. She could feel the tension of his shoulder, the heat of his leg. Once, when Lulu momentarily leant against him, he turned and caught Lara looking, and she had to cough to cover the sound of her nervous gulp.

'So Kip' – Piers sounded earnest – 'what are you going to do now you're set to fail so spectacularly in your A levels?'

Kip shifted uneasily. 'Same as I was going to do before. Nothing.' And he raised his eyebrows and smiled.

'What about your guitar?' May coaxed him. 'If you keep practising?'

'And what about you? What are you planning to do?' he said accusingly.

'I'm getting married, you know that.' She looked quickly at Piers. 'There's lots to arrange.'

'Well, maybe I'll do that too' – he shrugged – 'get married.'

Just as Lara was about to cough again, someone crept up from behind and pushed her into the pool. She flew in sideways, awkward, her mouth open in a scream, so that with a throat full of water she plunged down towards the bottom, and she couldn't somehow find the strength to propel herself back up. She was choking, struggling, and then as if a tide was turning, she started to rise back up.

'You bastard,' she spluttered when she finally surfaced, looking along the row of grinning faces. 'You bastard!'

She settled on Roland, who had squeezed in between Lulu and Kip and was grinning at her even more widely than the others. She threw the stub end of her cigarette at him, the one she was still holding, and then seeing she wasn't expected to be angry she tried to smile as she swam to the side. She climbed out and with her back to them she began to wring out her wet clothes.

'I'm soaking,' she moaned, to give herself more time, and she began to twist the water out of her shirt, which had become transparent, sticking to her body, outlining her breasts, clinging to the dark points of her nipples.

She stood there, mortified, refusing to give Roland the pleasure of seeing her turn round, until eventually May took pity and brought over a towel.

'Are you all right?' she asked, and seeing that she was shivering she offered to lend her some dry clothes.

'Thank you.' Lara tried to keep the tremble from her voice, and with the towel held around her she followed May into the house.

'Why did he do that?' she asked pointlessly, and May laughed.

'Oh, he's always like that. Don't take it personally. It's nothing to do with you.'

They padded with wet feet along a path lined with lavender and then up a flight of old stone steps.

'This building used to be home to a family of sixteen,' she said, and they stepped into a high-ceilinged room with several doors leading off it. May opened one on to a room filled almost entirely with a high wooden bed. 'This is where I sleep.'

There were two dark-wood cupboards bulging with clothes, drawers and hangers dense with clean, ironed cotton. May tugged at a lower drawer which sagged almost to the floor, and after rifling through she found a pale-blue vest and a pair of shorts. Gratefully Lara pulled them on, kicking off her wet things, rearranging the towel round her shoulders for warmth.

'Right,' May said, and led her out along a narrow corridor,

past a bathroom into which she slung her wet clothes, down several steps until they passed the half-open door of another bedroom. There were plates and books strewn across the floor, clothes and magazines and torn packets of Marlboro jumbled on the bed. 'Actually, hang on,' and running in, May pulled an ash-grey jumper off the bed. 'Kip won't mind,' and she hurled it to Lara.

It was soft as satin and crumpled, but the creases fell out when she put it on. Lara folded the sleeves over and watched it fall against her thighs.

'Thanks,' she said, but when she looked up May was watching her. 'What?'

'Nothing.' It was as if she was shaking out some thought. 'You just reminded me of someone,' and frowning May flung the towel into another bathroom as she led Lara out of the house.

The party by the pool had broken up and everyone along the candlelit table had changed places again. A plate of chocolates was being passed around, and Kip, who was sitting in his father's old place, legs draped over the edge of the table, grabbed at it, taking as many as he could before it was passed on.

'I'm so sorry.' Roland's wife Tabitha sat down beside her. 'I hear my dreadful husband's been up to his old tricks again. Anyway' – she smiled sweetly – 'you look ravishing in that outfit. Rollo,' she called, 'you're an absolute disgrace.'

Of the three sisters that she'd met Tabitha looked the most like Kip, with dark hair falling silkily against her face, a wide mouth and those blue eyes, so clear, the whites with a shimmer of blue too. She was wearing a cotton dress, gathered below the bust to fall over the mound of her stomach, sticking out so separately from her it seemed rude not to acknowledge it was there.

'When's the baby due?' Lara asked, and Tabitha took her hand and placed it on her belly. It was an odd sensation, so hard and hot, but pleasant, so that Lara had to force herself to let go.

'At the end of the summer, six more weeks,' and Tabitha glanced over at her husband, talking to Caroline, bending close in to her, his eyelids lowered, using all his skills to draw her in.

Lara noticed an empty chair beside her father, and before it was taken she sidled along the table and sank down.

'Hello.' He looked at her quizzically, unsure what it was about her that had changed, and seeing them together Caroline stood up, leaving Roland unceremoniously mid-sentence, and asked if they were ready to go home.

'Yes,' they said together, and not wanting to break up the entire party they murmured their goodbyes to Pamela only and walked slowly to their car. Caroline, her face white in the moonlight, stumbled a little on the step and Lambert took her arm and held her close as they climbed through the door in the wall.

'Shall I drive?' he offered when they reached the car, but she turned on him fiercely.

'I'm perfectly all right.'

Back in her room, Lara looked at herself in the mirror, swathed in the soft grey cashmere of Kip's jumper. She pulled it up to her nose and breathed. It smelt faintly of cigarettes, of chlorine and the damp dust of stone. She breathed in deeper, pressed the cuffs against her face, and still chilled from her unexpected dip she climbed under the covers with it on.

She woke in the early hours of the morning, her heart racing, the terror of an unremembered dream pulsing through her blood. It's just because I'm too hot, she told herself, unpeeling the jumper, and she got out of bed and went to the window for air.

She didn't notice it at first – she was too taken up with the lingering fear of her dream, but once she'd leant out of the window she heard it clearly, the sound of music coming from the hills. It was gypsy music. Lilting and dangerous. She opened her window wider. It reminded her of the first summer she'd spent with her grandparents in Dublin, and the ceilidh they'd taken her to where she'd fallen so much in love with the sound of the accordion she vowed she'd learn to play it when she grew up.

As she watched, a light flickered – fire or torchlight, she couldn't tell. It flickered on and off several times and then went out. She waited but although she stood there for half an hour, breathing in the rich scents of the night, listening to the music drifting towards her, the hills stayed shadowy and dark.

Eventually Lara got back into bed. She closed her eyes, took a breath and let herself relive the moment when Kip had looked up and fixed her with his stare. It happened again, the shock and the exhilaration, the spinning, wheeling jolt as if she recognised him, although she knew it wasn't possible that she'd seen him before.

Next morning everyone was subdued. Caroline was weak, too tired even for her morning swim, and Lambert, in a sudden fit of restlessness, had decided to work. He sat at the table on the terrace, his notes held down by paperweights, sighing and wincing as he scratched away. He rose every so often, as if to reach for a book, and then, remembering where he was, he shook his head and sat down.

Lara lay in the shade and read. It was too hot to swim, and her head ached anyway. Eventually Ginny called them in for lunch, serving it in the kitchen so that Lambert wouldn't have to move his notes. She had made a sort of baby food for them, ravioli with a filling of pale cheese, soft salad and an oily mash of spinach. For pudding there was a lemon tart, so sweet and bitter that it stung the inside of your mouth, and as soon as you'd recovered made you long for more.

Afterwards Lara went back to bed, and spent all afternoon reading and dreaming, staring at the square of sky outside the window, watching for some clue that it had cooled. She must have slept, if only for a moment, because she was startled awake by the tyres of a car, the rasp of brakes and the sound of voices below. She jumped up, straightening her clothes, and ran down to see who was there.

'I'll tell her,' Ginny was saying through the open door when Lara squeezed past her.

'Hello.' There was May with a white-paper carrier bag and behind her the jeep from Ceccomoro, its canvas top rolled back, Piers sitting in the front alone while Roland and Kip lounged, smoking, against the garden wall.

'We brought your clothes back,' May said, and Kip kicked a stone across the forecourt.

Lara took the package and looked inside and there, neatly folded, were her washed and ironed clothes. 'Thanks so much.'

She glanced up at the closed shutters of Caroline's room. She didn't know if she had the right to ask them in. She looked at Ginny, but she was simply nodding and smiling, and not able to think of anything else to say Lara watched as they climbed back into the car.

'Oh,' she remembered then, 'I've still . . .' but the jeep was turning round and her voice was drowned out by the screech of tyres as it picked up speed. 'Bye,' she called, waving in a sudden burst of friendliness, and Kip smiled at her out of the open back and flicked out his half-smoked cigarette.

'I didn't give them *their* clothes back,' she told Ginny, and feeling at a sudden loss she followed her into the kitchen.

Ginny poured her a glass of pear juice, which she drank slowly, feeling the ice-cold thickness of it sinking to the bottom of her stomach.

'Don't worry,' Ginny smiled gently, 'you'll get another chance,' and then a moment later, colouring, her voice rising, her face creasing into an uncontrollable smile. 'So that's Lord Willoughby's son, is it? Lucky lad must take after his mother.'

'Yes.' Lara gulped down the last of her juice, and then Ginny, laughing, leant over to ruffle her hair. 'I hope you know he's just about the most eligible bachelor in town, even if he wasn't gorgeous.'

No, she wanted to say, irritable, and she realised she'd hoped no one had noticed. That it was just possible Kip's beauty might only be visible to her.

Ginny turned away to grate some cheese, her fingers firm and capable as she turned the Parmesan into a cloud of froth. 'Lady Lara Willoughby.' Her throat was full of laughter. 'Doesn't that sound lovely?' and blushing furiously Lara told her to be quiet.

The first time Lara fell in love it was on the Budget Bus. His name was Sam and he was blond and lanky with a wide, white-toothed smile. Lara saw him before they'd even started, while they were still in Tottenham waiting for the journey to begin. People were milling around, stowing their bags into the boot, checking their names with the driver, choosing the seats that would be theirs for the next six weeks. There were fifty-two seats, one for each week of the year, and within a few days they would become as familiar as home.

'Hello,' Sam smiled at Lara and Cathy as they climbed on, only an hour after the appointed time for departure, and when they chose two seats on the left-hand side, about a third of the way back, he slipped into an empty one behind.

'Hello,' Cathy smiled back at him and he leant forward and told them he had a sister about the same age as Lara who was under orders not to grow up until he got home.

How long will that be? Lara wondered, but she felt self-conscious suddenly, and shy.

An hour later, as they made their slow way through London, he asked if she wanted to play cards. 'All right,' she agreed, and she watched him shuffle, admiring the way he flipped the cards, bent them, let them scatter together in a spray. They played gin rummy, endlessly, altering and elaborating the rules. They moved on to cheat and then to racing demons where the cards had to be spread out like patience in the gangway of the bus where Sam and Lara would crouch, slapping them down, screaming in a frenzy to anyone who might want to pass.

The Budget Bus was famous. The magic bus it was sometimes called, but mostly by people who hadn't caught it. Lara and Cathy had referred to it as magic while they'd waited in Scotland for that last primary-school year to be finished, and Lara realised after ten days or so of travelling that she really had imagined it would fly – spread its wings and rise over the tops of mountains, dip down to rest on the edges of lakes. But in reality the Budget Bus trundled slowly across Europe, through Turkey and into Iran. It broke down in Afghanistan and then again in the Khyber Pass where the gears failed on a stretch of flat. Soon after a small boy hurled a stone through its back window, spraying shards of glass over the bare shoulders of the miners, leaving little pin-pricks in their already tender skin.

Lara and Cathy made another friend, a pale, red-headed woman called Jennifer, and at night the four of them would venture out into the towns they stopped in. They bought fruit in the markets, packets of biscuits and flat bread, and the further east they went, the more attention they attracted. Men in turbans and long cotton dresses, men from *The Arabian Nights*, followed them and stared, at Cathy in her jeans and headscarf, at Jennifer with her blue-white skin, but mostly at Lara who had plaited her dark hair into pigtails and tied the ends with pink and orange bands.

'You're the right age for marriage,' Sam told her, 'in this culture,' and on more than one occasion money and even camels were offered in exchange.

'Keep close,' Cathy warned her, and so she'd slipped her hand into Sam's.

It was after midday, and Lambert stood, a pile of papers in his arms, and watched disapprovingly as the table he'd been working at was shifted by two workmen to the far end of the terrace.

'No, this way, over here!' Ginny was directing them, high-pitched, swathed in a professional apron, her hands dripping from the sink.

'I suppose I'll go upstairs and work,' Lambert said.

'Oh for God's sake,' Caroline snapped. 'Couldn't you just forget about your work this once? After all, when did you last take a holiday?'

'The thing is,' Lambert explained, 'I'm not getting any younger. And the century, you may have noticed, is rather long.'

'Yes,' Caroline said, subdued. 'I see.' And softening, she went over and kissed him on the forehead.

Lara watched him as he went upstairs. What, she wondered, would happen if he didn't make it to the end? How would the book work if he died before it was over? It was 1981 and he was already nearly sixty. There were still nineteen years to go. More than the span of her life again, and by then – it made her shudder – he would be seventy-seven.

'Work well,' Caroline called after him. 'And don't forget, they're all coming at one.'

Lara didn't dare ask who was coming for fear of disappointment. There were three tables on the terrace now and Ginny was covering them with thick white linen cloths.

'Can I help?' she asked her, and Ginny said she could count out sixteen knives and forks, small and large. And sixteen spoons.

Lara began to count. Besides them, that meant they were expecting thirteen guests. If it was the Willoughbys, that meant three daughters, Antonia, Tabitha and May. Then there was Kip, Roland and Piers. Pamela and Lulu, and of course Andrew, but that still left four. Maybe they'd bring their own guests, or maybe it was thirteen other people entirely.

Having laid the table she spent the rest of the morning in the pool, swimming swift lengths until she felt lean and strong and hungry and her mind was soothed. She changed, keeping her bikini on under her clothes in case Roland repeated his idea of a joke, and finding it was still early she went back to the kitchen.

'I suppose you'll want to know who you're sitting next to?' Ginny nudged her, handing her a bowl of flowers to set on the crease of the white cloth. 'Caroline has already done the placement so let's keep fingers crossed and see where she's put you.'

Even as they spoke Caroline was there with a tiny basket of white labels arranging them at the top of each plate. 'And how are you today?' she asked, as Lara followed her along the table, staring, gratified, at each hoped-for name.

'Oh I'm fine, thank you.' She hesitated. Could you ask after the health of someone who was ill? Was it polite, when they were trying so hard to pretend that they were fine? 'Who's Isabelle?' she asked instead.

'Isabelle?' Caroline looked flustered as if she had only just realised that she'd put her beside Lambert. 'Hmmm.' She looked as if she were about to swap him, and then, with a shrug of her shoulders, she walked back into the house.

Restless, Lara hovered around Ginny, watching her stir dressing, artfully scoop avocado pears out of their skins, slice and arrange them against white rounds of mozzarella, hoops of tomato, green sprigs of basil.

'Scoot,' Ginny said when the doorbell rang. 'Wash your hands first!' and she ushered her towards the bathroom as Caroline appeared to answer the door.

'Was it a frightful journey?' Caroline was saying. 'You poor dears. It's so good of you to make the effort,' and she heard the clatter and race of feet across the room.

Lara dried her hands and looked into the mirror. 'Hello,' she practised. 'Yes, I'm fine.' And she tilted her head this way and that, smiling so that the smile reached her eyes.

When she came out she was introduced to a woman, Isabelle, and her husband Hugh. They had two children, already dashing out towards the pool, a girl of about twelve and a boy, as lively as a dog, of seven or eight.

'I'd better chase after them,' the woman said, brushing light strands of hair out of her eyes, and she set off anxiously into the garden. 'Allegra, stop him.'

Lara shook hands with Hugh, a big shambling man with surprisingly thick hair above a battered face.

'So nice to meet you.' He bent over, whispering unnecessarily into her ear. 'So very nice.'

They walked out on to the terrace and looked over the railings to where Isabelle was frantically trying to stop her boy from hurling himself into the pool.

'No, Hamish,' she kept saying, her voice travelling up, as he tugged at his clothes. 'No. Stop it. NO!'

'Oh just let him do it,' Hugh mumbled.

Caroline, taking a deep breath, shouted down, 'Do let him swim, we won't eat for at least an hour!'

Isabelle looked up at them, her hands raised to the sky, as if to say thanks. Thanks a lot! Beside her the child grinned, stuck out his tongue, and plunged into the pool. Allegra, who'd been squatting by the deep end, her long hair trailing down into the water, stood up slowly and, pulling off her sundress to reveal a silver costume, tested the water with a toe.

'Do you have brothers and sisters?' Hugh asked, as they watched his two children, one serenely swimming, the other flipping and diving as he hurled his body back and forth.

'No, I'm an only child,' and as always she didn't know whether to be grateful or sad.

'Lara is Lambert's daughter,' Caroline said, passing Hugh a tumbler of whisky.

He stopped, his arm outstretched. 'I thought . . . I didn't know.' He frowned.

Just then, in a great flurry of noise, two carloads of Willoughbys arrived. They stormed into the house, kissed Caroline hello, were introduced to Hugh, although some of them obviously knew him already, and then waited eagerly while drinks were poured.

'This is Ginny,' Lara said when she came out with a bowl of cheese straws warm from the oven, and, with exaggerated friendliness, they greeted her. Roland even took her hand and kissed it, but Ginny didn't seem to mind. She blushed and giggled and went to the fridge for more wine.

Eventually Isabelle came up the stone steps, pulling a squirming Hamish, his hair all spiked with wet, and followed languorously by her daughter who'd slipped her dress back on.

'Thanks.' She glared at Hugh as if to say it's all very well for you, but Hugh, who had already been poured a second whisky, put his head imploring on one side. 'Hey,' he murmured and his eyes seemed to say what did I do?

Caroline began to seat everyone, the young and old interspersed, as far as Lara could see, for maximum discomfort, although cleverly she put Hamish beside Kip, who immediately began a game of paper, scissors, stone with him, adding the welcome agony of a Chinese burn for anyone who lost three times in a row. Hamish squealed with delight the first time the skin of his arm was twisted, and Isabelle, smiling wearily, accepted a large glass of wine and sank back in her chair.

'Are you having a nice holiday?' Pamela asked her.

Isabelle flicked the hair out of her eyes. 'Well,' she said, and she sighed.

Just then Lambert appeared. He looked ruffled as if he'd been far away and there was an ink stain across the fingers of his right hand. 'So sorry,' he nodded apologetically, 'I lost track of the . . .' and everyone at the table looked up at him. He had a splash of ink under his right eye too, as if he had literally been wrestling with his pen.

'You're just in time,' Caroline called, gracious, and she motioned to the empty seat beside Isabelle.

Lambert sat down. He poured Isabelle a little more wine, himself some water, and then he leant in to her and murmured something, too quietly to be overheard.

'How very funny.' A smile crept across her face, and she turned in to him and lowered her voice too.

She had pale-brown hair, the colour most women dye blonde, and light-brown almond eyes. Her hands, folding and re-folding her napkin, were unusually worn, the skin along the index finger splintered and cracked, the nails cut square and short. But all the same she exuded glamour, as if those hands, among all the others, oiled and buffed and painted, were the only hands to have.

'So . . . um . . .'

Someone cleared their throat and Lara realised that it was not just her but Hugh who was watching Lambert and Isabelle.

'Are you on holiday here as well?' She turned to him.

Hugh swallowed. 'We've got a house near by, an hour or so. We come here every summer and at Easter too and if the weather holds, sometimes in the autumn. Issy is passionate about it. She'd live here all year round if she had her way.'

They couldn't help it. They looked back at Lambert and Isabelle, and it seemed, even in the moment that they'd looked away, Hugh's wife's face had changed. The creases had smoothed out, her eyes had brightened and even her hair was streaked with fine splinters of gold.

'Dad?' Lara felt she must at least try and save Hugh from his agony. 'Dad?' she tried again, but Lambert, so unused to being addressed as anybody's father, failed to look up.

Mercifully Ginny appeared with two huge plates of salad from which everyone could help themselves.

'Please let me.' Hugh grabbed at one, holding it at an alarming angle so that Lara had to slide off her portion before it fell to the table in a mess of olive oil. 'Bread?' He passed it round, holding the basket obstinately across the table to his wife, although she had shaken her head curtly at the first sign of it.

'Thank you, no,' Lambert said when he continued to dangle it, and, their voices lowered still, they carried on their talk.

Lara looked along the table. Kip was piling bread on to his plate as if he hadn't eaten in a week and Hamish, eager to replicate him in every way, piled his plate too.

'No.' Hugh leant over at least two people, a note of hysteria rising, and removed all but one slice. 'Sorry,' he said then, and as if in apology to the people he'd half squashed, he offered round more wine. 'Go on,' he insisted when Lara declined, and he looked so mournful that she changed her mind, although her head was already spinning with the glass she'd just gulped down.

By the end of the main course, she'd drunk so much that she was talking quite merrily with Tabitha on her other side, asking her what it felt like to be pregnant, to have something moving about inside you, to feel it kick. How would Tabitha know when it was coming? Was she afraid? She had to stop herself from asking how she could bear it, being married to a man like Roland, when there he was, squatting down between their seats, sweating slightly, holding a cigarette.

'Anyone coming for a swim?' he asked, and Tabitha ran her fingers through his hair.

'You'll sink if you swim now, you great oaf.'

'Looked in the mirror recently?' His eyes narrowed, and he blew a cloud of smoke up into her face.

Tabitha laughed. 'Go on, swim with him, Lara, or he'll sulk.'

Not wanting to add to the game of insulting her, Lara followed him towards the steps. She looked back once, to

74

check for disapproval, but everyone was taking up their cups of coffee and moving about the table, everyone except Isabelle and Lambert, who stayed where they were.

As soon as they reached the pool Roland, with one fluid movement, tugged his shirt off over his head. He tossed it on to a chair and unfastened his belt, unbuttoned his trousers, began to pull at the zip, and then, as if he knew she would be watching, he snapped his head up.

'I don't charge,' he grinned. 'Come closer,' and he stepped with his muscled thighs out of his trousers.

Underneath he was wearing trunks and as if solely for her entertainment he walked very slowly round the pool. He had an athlete's body, naturally strong, as if without effort he'd been the hero of his school. But his hair, although blond, had the slightest tint of green, and this green was there too in his skin. He dipped one toe in, and then, without warning, he leapt into the air, flipped over into a somersault, and plunged in. She couldn't help it, she grinned.

'It's not a spectator sport,' he shouted, flicking the water from his fringe. 'Come in!' and he lay back in the water and watched as she removed her clothes in the most matter-of-fact way she could.

Tentatively she walked to the edge, stepping back a little whenever he swam near, feeling as if she were standing on the edge of a tank of dangerous fish. I'd get in, she thought, if I could be sure he wasn't about to attack me, and then as if reading her mind, he swam away from her and began to do lengths in backstroke, to show that really she had nothing to fear. Lara sat down on the edge and dangled her legs in, and then, to her relief, Kip, followed by Hamish, came running down the steps.

Roland ducked under the water and burst up beside her just as they appeared. He draped one arm over her legs, his hand on her thigh, so that she had to slap him away, her eyes shooting towards Kip to show him this wasn't how it had been, wasn't why they'd crept away. But Kip didn't meet her eye. Instead he tugged off his clothes, left them where they fell, and divebombed into the deep end of the pool. Hamish tried to copy him, landing on his belly, flailing for a moment before he caught his breath.

A moment later Allegra appeared, silent on bare feet, and slipped off her blue sundress. She sat beside Lara, her slim legs hanging down into the pool, her face inscrutable as she dripped patterns of water over her skin. In silence they watched Kip and Roland racing and wrestling, while Hamish, swimming like a puppy between them, begged to be picked up and flung into the air. Lara copied Allegra and scooped up handfuls of water, flicking the cold drops against her face, trickling them over her burning head. The sun was beating down now and the sky was dense with blue. But rather than get in Allegra splashed herself with bigger handfuls, wetting her costume, her neck and her long hair, so that it stood back from her face. For the first time Lara saw her properly, her wide mouth and high forehead, the delicate colours of her skin. She was long and thin and coltish, must have been told a thousand times she was going to be a beauty.

Slowly the whole party descended to the pool. They brought coffee cups and miniature glasses of liquor and Hugh a full bottle of red wine. The adults arranged themselves in the shade, and Andrew Willoughby picked up the most recent copy of *The Times* and began to read.

'Who's coming up to Ceccomoro to watch the wedding tomorrow?' he asked, and when no one answered he let the paper slide to the ground. 'Suit yourselves,' he said and closed his eyes.

'I'll come.' Allegra raised a hand, but Isabelle, from where she sat on a lounger, shook her head.

Lambert took up the abandoned *Times*. 'The English papers.' He held the newsprint to his nose. 'It almost makes up for being away from home. The one reliable pleasure.'

Andrew, his eyes still closed, spat back, 'It depends on whether one is in them or not.'

'Yes,' Lambert murmured. 'And what is being said.'

The party didn't break up until early evening and slowly, sleepily, everyone staggered away.

'We'll see you tomorrow?' May asked as she was leaving. 'Come early or you'll miss it.'

Lara looked round at Caroline. 'I'd love to. If I can get there.'

'Well, if there's any problem, Kip can walk over and get you, can't you, Kip?'

Kip, who had Hamish in a headlock, looked up. 'What?'

'You can walk over and get Lara, show her the shortcut?'

'Help!' Hamish screamed. 'Mercy!'

'She wants to see the wedding,' May insisted.

'If I'm up.'

Hamish was kicking out at him in an attempt to loosen his grip, and just then Lulu who had spent the afternoon chatting mostly to the grown-ups put her hands under his shirt and tickled him so that with a groan he released Hamish and turned to grab her wrist.

'Can't catch me,' she shrieked, and she dashed away, running just out of his reach around the drive, screeching and laughing so that the whole party turned to watch them as together they crashed into the back seat of the car.

May shrugged and rolled her eyes, and Lara turned to say goodbye to Hugh who was gulping down a mug of black

77

coffee, while his wife, with crossed arms, watched from beside the car.

'I said I'd drive,' she told him, but he ignored her and smiling blearily at Caroline, at Lara, even at Lambert, he swung into the car.

When everyone had gone they turned back into the house, already clear and tidy as if the day had never been, and Lara lay down on a white sofa, and once more leafing through the pages of ¡Hola! listened while Caroline and Lambert dissected the guests.

'Sorry you got stuck with poor Isabelle Whittard. She used to be rather lovely, but marriage has turned her into a bit of a bore.'

Lambert looked amused. 'How odd,' he said. 'I used to find her rather plain, but now I see that I was wrong.'

Caroline raised her eyebrows. 'Well, the poor husband certainly looks exasperated by her. Shouldn't wonder he was trying to drown his sorrows. Very pretty the young girl, though.'

Lara looked over the top of her magazine to see her father put his head on one side, unconvinced. Good, she thought, but she couldn't erase the image of Allegra, her wide rose mouth, her honey-coloured hair falling forward as she watched Kip leap out of the water.

'And as for Andrew Willoughby . . .' Caroline stretched.

'Yes,' Lambert agreed. 'Always was a shit.' And a shadow fell over his face.

Lara took the newspaper up to bed with her and studied the painting of Lady Diana reproduced on its front cover. It had just been unveiled at the National Portrait Gallery – *The first royal woman*, it said, *ever to be immortalised in trousers.* The artist, apparently, was poised for flight, having once before been forced to go into hiding for three weeks when his painting of Princess Margaret failed to meet approval. Royal or public, it didn't say. On the inside page was a photograph of Charles and Diana at a garden party, posing under umbrellas in the torrential rain with a quote from Diana saying she didn't mind anything at all, but it mustn't rain on Wednesday. It mustn't rain on the day of the wedding. It just absolutely had to stay dry. Lara got up and looked out at the night sky. She could hear the music again, waltzing, catching on the current of the wind, and as she watched, she saw the bright flickering of a fire. Was it a code? she wondered, when after a minute or two it went out and then flickered on again, and she opened the window further and leant out.

Lara wasn't the only one to fall in love on the bus. A teacher from Birmingham become besotted with a stained-glass maker from Kent and before they'd even crossed the channel they'd already asked their neighbours if they wouldn't mind moving so that they could reorganise the seats. That first night when they stopped to camp – in ex-army surplus tents provided by the bus – they sneaked away from the fire where supper was being prepared, and when they came back they were bleary-eyed and weak. They hardly ate, and all the next day they sat together, stroking and kissing and whispering in each other's ear.

'Oh for God's sake.' Cathy shook her head, but Lara, whenever she got the chance, just stared.

That night, when everyone had settled down to eat, they heard a thudding, juddering noise coming from the abandoned bus. 'What is it?' At first they were alarmed but then they realised it was the lovestruck couple having sex in the boot. It was hard to ignore it, the clanking of the suspension and the odd eerie echo as they moaned, but it went on so long that eventually a guitar was tuned and voices raised and within a week, although they started spending whole nights in the boot, no one bothered to mention it at all.

'Strangely quiet tonight,' Lara and Sam would joke if there happened to be silence, and they'd set off to explore the town, invariably heading for the market to buy coloured thread with which Lara had taken to decorating people's clothes. She embroidered flowers and leaves and rows of children holding hands and in exchange the passengers gave her Coca-Cola, or failing that, soapstone carved into religious charms.

Kip didn't call for her the next day. Lara never really believed he would, but all the same she got up early and spent much of the morning in her room listening for the sound of him, slouching across the gravel in his trodden-down shoes. Eventually, just before eleven, she wandered downstairs to where Lambert was working and Caroline was writing some kind of list and asked if anyone else was thinking of going over to Ceccomoro to see the wedding.

'My dear.' Caroline looked amused. 'I thought you were entirely uninterested.'

Lara hesitated, remembering how only a day or two ago she was. 'Well, I sort of promised.' She blushed, and Caroline with a slow smile went into the kitchen where Ginny was peeling the thin bubbled skin from roasted peppers and asked if she wouldn't mind giving Lara a lift.

Ginny was quite skittery with excitement. She climbed into the 2CV, forgetting at first to shut her door, then stalling the car as she attempted to reverse, so delighted was she to get a chance to talk about the wedding.

'It's like a fairy tale,' she breathed, and Lara saw that she was close to crying.

All the way along the road, past the stone lions and along the chalky drive, Ginny talked about her admiration for Lady Di. Lara kept quiet, her lips pressed together, fearful that she might betray her own ambivalence, wishing she could offer Ginny her place. But Caroline would miss her when lunch was to be served, and what would the Willoughbys say if she invited her in? Eventually they pulled up in the yard.

'You know something?' Ginny said. 'I nearly didn't take this job. I was planning to be there. To camp outside St Paul's Cathedral, but I couldn't afford to, not really, turn down a whole month of work.' Ginny smiled and shrugged her shoulders. 'I would have done it though, if I could, for her.' And, sniffing with emotion, she waved Lara away and began to turn the car around.

The television room was dark, the stone floor covered in rugs, cushions from the sofa pulled down to make extra seats. Everyone looked up as Lara pushed open the door, some smiling, some startled, others as if they'd never seen her, or if they had, never expected to set eyes on her again. Carefully she stepped over lounging bodies, searching out a space, until she came upon a spare cushion, the empty flank of a sofa behind. It wasn't until she sat down that she realised her shoulder was leaning up against Andrew Willoughby's leg, and beside her, the nearest body was Kip's. He looked at her and nodded, smiling just minutely, and then he turned and glanced at the doorway, where Lulu stood, staring at the space Lara had just filled.

'Oh.' She struggled to get up. 'I'm sorry.' But everyone hissed at her to shhhh and Lulu shrugged and kicked at

Roland to move over so she could drape herself across the arm of his chair.

Lara wasn't late. Italy was an hour ahead, and the Prince and soon-to-be Princess were still to enter the cathedral. It was a beautiful day in London. Thank God, she thought, laughing at herself for getting so drawn in. But just the sight of London, of Buckingham Palace and St Paul's, made her nostalgic and she found that she was missing her mother, as if she might be somewhere in the crowd. Unlikely as it was, she scanned the faces of the people waving their Union Jacks, enlivened with happiness and patriotic fervour, almost hysterical with the luck of a fine day.

'His Royal Highness' – a voice cut through the babble of the crowd – 'Charles, Philip, Arthur, George, Prince of the United Kingdom of Great Britain and Northern Ireland, Prince of Wales and Earl of Chester, Duke of Cornwall, Duke of Rothesay, Earl of Crick and Baron of Renfrew, Lord of the Isles and Great Steward of Scotland, will shortly be married in St Paul's Cathedral to . . . Lady Diana Frances Spencer.'

Lara thought how inadequate Diana's name sounded beside his. Couldn't she have more, an extra title or two, just for today? Baroness of Nursery Schools, Hairstyle Trendsetter to the Outer Nations of Knightsbridge and World's End. Earlette of Sloane Square, Loafer to the Court of Sunday's *Mail*. Princess of the Pure and Hopeful, Beloved Especially of Ginny.

Just then they caught sight of the royal carriage. Prince Charles was arriving, the shape of his head unmistakable from above, even in his hat. His hair, Lara was sure, parted for the occasion even further to one side. But where was she? It was Diana the crowd wanted to see. Will she be late? She'll have to be. Three minutes. Is that the traditional time allowed, before everyone gets jumpy? Charles was inside the cathedral, as were the Queen and the Queen Mother, both in blocks of colour, the same from top to toe. There was Prince Philip, Princess Anne, the Princes Andrew and Edward.

The camera scanned the crowds, and then there she was, in her coach, her face veiled, her father redder than ever beside so much white. 'As commoners,' the commentary informed them, 'they are not entitled to a military escort but must make do with police on horseback.' But the crowd didn't care about the uniforms of the Spencers' escort. What they longed for, even more than a sight of Diana, was a sight of Diana's dress. The coach was stopping. They were going to see it. There was an intake of breath in the room as Diana uncurled from the carriage. And there it was. Hideous. More hideous even than anything dreamed up by *¡Hola!*. Lara shot a quick look round, but everyone was transfixed by the fairy-tale sight of someone transformed from shy and awkward into a princess. Diana was moving now, ignoring her train, leaving her bridesmaids to do battle with it, attack it like an unruly sheet. She pulled away, determined, gliding up the steps, disappearing through the doors of the cathedral, her train following finally until it was out of sight.

'Fuck.' Tabitha's voice yawned up from the sofa. 'Help me up, someone. I need a wee.'

Roland stayed where he was but, once his wife was on her feet, he watched her go, moving precariously through the crowd of her family, swaying as she reached the door.

'Piers,' Roland hissed, and when Piers turned round, he winked at him. 'You'll be next.'

Piers turned back to the screen where Charles and Diana were now standing side by side, Charles, scrubbed and gleaming, Diana hiding in her shroud of white.

'Yes,' Piers murmured, refusing to be drawn in, and he squeezed May's hand.

There was silence again while the marriage ceremony began and not a word was said until Diana was asked to repeat the list of Charles's names and managed to mix them up.

'Noooooo,' they all shrieked, and they heckled her, giggling and smirking, relieved to have someone to break the tension for them. By the time everyone was quiet Charles and Diana were married.

'Well.' Andrew Willoughby yawned and stretched. 'He's gone and done it now.' And giving Pamela a pinch on the bottom as she stood up, he said that was enough of Great Britain for this summer; he didn't want to hear another word about it until next year at least.

One by one everyone stood up and wandered outside. Lara wasn't sure what she was to do without the official right to be there bestowed by Caroline, so she followed the others out, walked towards the car park, stood in the stone doorway, peering out as if she owned a car. She looked back, thinking she should at least say goodbye, or thank you, when Kip came out of the house and called to her, 'You'd better stay for lunch or there'll be trouble.'

'OK,' she agreed, and seeing her puzzled look, he came closer.

'She thinks everyone hates her, that's all.'

'Who does?'

'Pamela. The big P. I mean we do, but it's too hot for a row today.'

They stood there looking out over the countryside, over the dark clumps of trees, the dry stone walls that edged the fields, the steep slope of them, falling and then rising into hills.

'Where's the short cut?' she asked. 'If I wanted to walk home, I mean?'

'Oh that.' He grinned. 'You mean the sexy path?' and blushing unexpectedly he seemed to forget what she had asked him and ambled off towards the pool.

That afternoon everyone was subdued. It was as if the sight of Britain had made them self-conscious, reminded them of who they usually were. Lara lay on the sun terrace, feeling the stone scorch into her skin, listening idly to the lull of conversation. Piers was asking everyone where they would choose if they had to plan a honeymoon, and the answers came back Scotland, a floating palace in India, Egypt, Bali, Devon. Charles and Diana were spending three days with the family of Lord Mountbatten, killed two years before by an IRA bomb, and then, as if to erase the memory, they were off for two weeks on a Mediterranean cruise.

'If you come to LA, you could visit me,' Lulu said languidly and Andrew, who was reading in a deckchair, asked when she was deserting them.

'Darling!' Pamela looked hurt. 'I've told you already. She's going tomorrow. I'm taking her to the plane. So *I'll* be gone all day.'

Andrew pulled his hat further down over his face and humphed. He looked tired, his nose bobbled and red, his legs almost comically thin under his plantation-owner shorts. 'Well,' he said, 'who's going to cheer me up when she's gone?' He flicked his magazine irritably, and his eyes lighted on Lara. 'Miss Riley,' he said, 'I'm relying on you. You can keep us amused.'

'Me?' Lara smiled, hopeful that she'd misunderstood, but Andrew held her gaze, as if waiting, right then and there, for her to come out with something witty. 'I'll try,' she said, because she had to say something, and seemingly satisfied,

Andrew Willoughby went back to his paper, while Lara searched her memory for the existence of even one amusing thing.

'Lara.' Someone was prodding her with their foot.

'Yes?' She sat up, her vision blurred with so much squinted worrying at the sun.

'What do you say?' It was May, her tawny hair pulled up into a topknot. 'Supper in Siena to celebrate Lulu's last night?'

They were all looking at her expectantly, everyone except Lulu who was lying reading on her stomach, one bare leg stretched out a little at an angle, just lapping over on to Kip's towel.

'OK.'

'So.' May was counting, her eyes alight with organisation. 'You, me and Piers, Lulu, Roland, Kip. That's six. Tabsy, will you come along?'

Tabitha threw a look at her husband. 'I might come in for supper, but if you want to go on . . .' She yawned. 'I'm usually finished by ten.'

'Oh Tabs,' Roland said, 'don't be a spoilsport. If you come, we'll have to take two cars.'

Tabitha's face fell. 'Fine. It's all the same to me.' But not long after Lara noticed that she gathered herself up and as daintily as she could stumbled into the house.

They stopped at Caroline's on the way, their car sending out sparks of gravel as it skidded to a stop.

'You're back!' Lambert was at the door, so pleased he put an arm out and gave Lara a hug. 'I was beginning to wonder . . . how long can a wedding last?'

'She's only come to change.' Roland strode forward. 'We're all off for a night out.'

'Oh.' Lambert seemed to droop a little and he let go of her arm.

'It's Lulu's last night,' Lara explained. 'We thought we'd go into Siena, eat pizza in the square and then go on to a club. There's a club apparently – the Purple Pussycat, behind the Duomo.'

For a moment Lambert brightened and then he understood that he was not being asked. He looked at the crowd of them, quiet suddenly under his penetrating stare. 'I hope you have a good time.'

But couldn't we? Lara thought, couldn't we ask him? But nothing was up to her.

'Hurry up!' Piers shouted from the car. 'If you're going to get changed . . .' and without looking at Lambert again she ran upstairs.

Today, she realised, was the first time that they'd been parted since she'd arrived at his flat a week before, and as she tore through her clothes, hoping for something to materialise that wasn't actually there, she weighed up the idea of staying. She could curl up on one of the white sofas, listen to Lambert and Caroline swap slices of their past, but she knew she couldn't resist the lure of the night out, the thrill of driving through the early evening, of eating pizza in the dark.

Lara glanced out of the window and saw Kip, shuffling back and forth, his hands in his pockets, the nape of his neck dust-brown against the white collar of his shirt. Quickly she pulled on a pair of jeans, slipped her feet into high-heeled sandals, and with only the most cursory glance at her flushed face in the mirror flicked on a smudge of eye liner, bit her lips together for more blood, and ran.

The others had filed into the sitting room, were lounging against the furniture, restless, fidgeting, talking to Caroline as she sat, her feet on a stack of cushions, her legs wrapped in a mohair shawl so light it hardly touched her skin. Lambert stood to one side, his hands in his pockets, his head bent.

'I'm ready,' Lara said, and as one they turned and bounded for the door.

'Bye, Dad.' She leant up to him and felt the soft touch of his lips against her hair.

'Bye.'

It was unfamiliar – being the one with something to dash off for, when for so long it had been him who was always too busy to stay. Usually within half an hour of meeting he was already restless to get back to work, and if not, then it was only because he had a drink, long overdue, with a publisher, or a meeting with a researcher who'd unearthed a document of such magnitude and significance it couldn't wait. Once he'd left her to attend a party at the French Embassy where the Ambassador was a particular admirer of his work, while she climbed down into the bowels of London to catch the underground to Finsbury Park.

'Bye, I won't be late,' she said, knowing, as they both did, that she would, and even though he smiled encouragingly she could hardly bear to look out of the open back of the jeep as they sped away.

Siena at night was magical, the sandstone of the walls softened to honeycomb, the Piazza del Campo glittery with lights. Smartly dressed couples wandered arm in arm, their hair glossy, their clothes so perfect, so pressed and crisp they looked as if they must have an army of Italian mothers working at home just for this moment, to send them out into the evening with pride. There were tourists too, enthused by the rules of Italy, dressed in their best, sitting at tables, watching the young people saunter by while old men sat inside, drinking dark coffee and tall thin flutes of beer.

A waiter moved two tables together and pushed into place six chairs.

'Can anyone speak Italian?' Lara asked.

Kip laughed. 'More cheeps, more beer.'

'I'm learning,' May said, and so they all pointed to their choice of pizza, while she read it out to the waiter, accompanied by the occasional cry from the others of 'Don't forget, more cheeps, more beer.'

Lara sat facing the restaurant with her back to the square, her chair tilting very slightly, so that she had to lean forwards with her elbows on the table for support. Lulu, Roland and Kip sat opposite, leaning back, arms folded, making comments on the passers-by.

'Bloody hell,' Roland gloated. 'Look at that!' And in spite of herself Lara turned to stare.

The girl Roland was looking at had a large nose and narrow forehead, but she was dressed in a tight white T-shirt, nipped in at the waist, which showed every seam and contour of her bra, even the shape of the clasp that dug into her back. Beside her strutted a man in a cap-sleeved T-shirt and a chest that bulged like a bull.

'You in the mood for a fight?' Piers laughed at him, and then as Roland began to flex his muscles May reared up as if she'd been stung.

'Kip! If you want to play footsie, play it with someone else!'

'I wasn't,' he mumbled. 'Christ, I was just moving my legs.'

'Lara?' May wasn't letting it go. 'I think that was meant for you.' And she made a doe-eyed expression in Lara's direction.

'Fuck off!' Kip threw a slice of bread at her, and then his leg really did brush against Lara's.

She froze, her eyes on the tablecloth, only looking up when

it was safe again, and later, when she caught Kip's eye, amid the clatter of arriving food, she thought she saw the smallest smile of gratitude crease the corner of his mouth.

By the time they left the restaurant everyone was drunk. For a while they stood in the square and argued lazily over whether it mightn't be just as much fun to sit in the middle of the Campo and watch the people come and go.

'No.' Both Lulu and May were insistent. 'We can't miss the Purple Pussycat!' And with shouts of 'Follow us,' they headed in the direction of the black-and-white spire.

The others ambled after them, down lanes and alleys, heaving themselves up hills and hurtling down again. Lara was the only one wearing high heels and her shoes kept catching and grating on the cobbles, small slices of colour shaving off along the way. After twenty minutes they found themselves once more in the square.

'For God's sake.' Roland was sweating, his hair darkened almost to brown, but the others were doubled up with laughter.

'Let's just stay here,' Kip suggested, but May began accosting people.

'*Per favore.*' She smiled her sweetest smile. '*Dov'è il Purple Pussycat?*'

Mostly she was met with blank stares and shrugs of the shoulder, but then a man in a checked jacket and aubergine-shined shoes stopped to explain, and seeing them all looking so idiotically hopeful, he beckoned for them to follow.

They would never have found it without him. The Purple Pussycat was behind an arched door, sunk into the wall, with only the smallest strip of neon to show that it was there.

'*Molto, molto genitale.*' May clasped his hands, and the man shrank back from her and dashed away.

'Oh my God!' May's face flooded with mortification. 'I

meant to say thank you, you are most kind . . . *molto gentile*, but instead I think I said he had large genitals!'

They all fell against the wall, snorting and choking, coughing and screeching as if their lungs might burst and then Piers wheezed out, 'I told you it was dangerous to learn Italian.'

'I thought he looked a bit shocked.' Roland staggered up. 'Anyway, we'd better go in, or he'll realise his mistake and come back to show you whether or not you were right.'

Still laughing, they pushed open the door and stumbled down the red-carpeted stairs to a small vestibule where, for millions of lire, they were admitted into the club. The whole place was padded in velvet, floor, walls, stools, even the bar, the underside of it lined with material, soft and grimy to the touch. Behind the bar there were tubes and swirls of purple light, just enough to see the long array of drinks by, but the rest of the club was in almost total darkness, the outlines of the tables just visible, a little rectangle of dance floor lit up by spotlights planted in the ground.

Roland took Lulu's arm. 'Dance with me!' he crooned, and looking back over her shoulder at Kip, she shrugged and sashayed away towards the far end of the club, where very soon they could be seen, their dark and perfect silhouettes thrashing about to the slow music.

May disappeared to the loo, Piers offered to buy drinks, and Kip and Lara were left alone.

'Shall we sit here?' Lara suggested, and she slid along a velvet bench so that there was room for him. For a moment they sat in silence and then Lara noticed they were wearing the same clothes. 'Look,' she said, 'we're twins.'

Kip looked down at himself, and then at Lara, at her denim legs and up over her white-shirted body and then slowly to her face. She got the full dazzle of his attention then, the dark round of his pupils, the sphere of blue, and the lashes, long as a girl's, as long as hers, glinting against his skin, tanned only lightly, the stamp of luxury, knowing there was the whole summer ahead.

'Just give me one of your shoes,' he said, 'and we'll be impossible to tell apart,' and he moved his leg against hers and touched her foot.

A spark shot through her. 'No,' she laughed, 'you'll wreck it,' but all the same, his foot began to prise away her shoe. 'No.'

She was wrestling with him, her leg almost entwining his, and then his arm was across her, pressing her down against the seat. They were panting, their faces close, his lips seconds from her ear. She could smell his breath, still fresh through the sweet smell of the beer.

'Stop scrapping, you two.' It was Piers, slamming the drinks down on the table, small clear glasses of liqueur, 'or they'll check and find you're under-age.'

They pulled away, too quickly, Kip's elbow almost knocking over a glass.

'I'm eighteen,' he hissed, 'so shut the fuck up.'

Lara chose a drink. 'What is this?' She took a gulp. The white hot liquid scorched her throat.

'Grappa,' Piers said. 'Go easy.'

And although her lips were numb and her eyes were stinging, she was fuelled with a new courage and she slid her hand across the inches of the seat between them and pressed it against Kip's. There was a dangerous chasm of lost time when she felt nothing, and then his fingers crept over hers and very gently squeezed them. Her heart soared. Her mouth swept up into a smile and, if it had been anyone but Piers sitting opposite, they would have asked what on earth was going on. They sat like that, not looking at each other, their fingers red hot, passing messages, a whole coded conversation, back and forth between them.

'Budge up, you two.' It was Roland, a sheen of sweat glistening on his forehead. And then May appeared from the ladies, her hair newly brushed, her eyes glittering with fresh make-up. Lara inched closer to Kip, hiding their hands with her body.

'I need a seat.' Lulu was rumpled and glowing from her dance and the splash of water she must have thrown over her face. 'Make space!' and she squeezed herself in between them.

Lara couldn't even see Kip now. Just the shadow of him over Lulu's shoulder. Instead she sipped her grappa, keeping the heat in her alive, half following the conversation, which was never about anything she knew, until eventually it turned from talk to rambling and even Roland admitted they were in danger of losing consciousness in the over-padded cell of the room.

It was worth having spent an hour or two inside the Purple Pussycat just to emerge again into the night. It was a miracle – so jagged and cool, the stars as they walked through the darkened town like a spray of glitter across black.

'This way, children.' Roland herded them, gentle suddenly as a grown-up, and Lara's shoes clacked and slipped as she hurried to keep up. 'Come on, you,' he called over his shoulder.

They were walking up a hill, a sloping narrow lane between tall houses, when Lara heard music. Cellos and violins, the low hoots of a flute. She looked up. The sound was coming from a building on her left. There was a high arched door, and above the door, a sign: *Accademia Musicale*.

'Listen.' She breathed in, but when she looked round the others were racing on. She could see them disappearing round a bend. All the same Lara couldn't move, the music was so beautiful in the silence. She walked forward into the doorway and let the music wash over her as the conductor must have raised his arms, stuck out his chest and urged the mass of musicians to swell the music out. She opened her own arms, floated back her head.

'What are you doing?' Kip was staring at her.

'You've got to look at this.' The courtyard was half covered by a frescoed ceiling, pale-blue sky, cherubs reclining against clouds. There were olive trees in pots, the undersides of their leaves silver, and ahead of them in an unexpected gap between buildings, hung a perfectly round moon. The music swooped and wept from the room above as Kip came towards her. Oh my God, Lara thought, as he took hold of her shoulders, he's going to kiss me. In this magical place. She took a quick breath and held it.

'This is so corny.' Kip frowned. 'I feel like I'm in a bad musical.'

'Yes.' Lara gave a high, forced laugh, and she watched him back out through the courtyard and into the street.

'Come on,' he called. 'Or they'll go without us.'

'OK.' Lara took her shoes off. 'I'm coming,' and she raced after him, scooting up the slowly curving lanes, catching him up, so that they arrived breathless and together at the waiting car.

Lulu made a space for Kip on the jeep's hard bench and as soon as he was settled she leant her head against his shoulder and let her hand trail the length of his leg.

'Oh for God's sake, Lulu,' May murmured. 'Leave him alone. Don't you know it's illegal to marry your step-brother?'

'Of course it's not,' Roland shouted from the front. 'And anyway, it's not everyone who's obsessed with marriage. Your father doesn't think it necessary to marry all the women

94

he goes to bed with. He doesn't even think it necessary to marry the old P.'

'Only because he's married to Mummy!' May hissed back.

And Lulu swung one long leg over Kip's knees and nuzzled her mouth against his ear. 'Marry me, Lord Willoughby,' she crooned.

'Honestly!' May rolled her eyes, but everybody else, even Lara, laughed.

Lara woke to find her joints were made of tin, the hollows in her body full of smoke. Slowly, painfully she got out of bed, and saw through the half-shuttered window that the day was overcast. Kip's jumper was still lying on a chair. She pulled it on and went down to sit with Ginny over breakfast. But Ginny was out. The breakfast was cleared away, so instead she poured herself some juice and went out to the terrace where her father was already working, scribbling furiously, scratching down notes, flipping over the pages of books, reeling off sentences that seemed to flow, comma-less, line after line.

Lara pulled up a chair and, careful that the glass shouldn't risk touching even a corner of one page, she waited for him to look up. She waited for some time, coughing very slightly, shuffling a little, even traipsing inside to peel and eat a fig, the steamy richness of its flesh making her look round, self-conscious. But it was worth it – the gritty pulpiness that tasted of its smell, and fortified with it, she went back out and brushing against Lambert's shoulder she asked him how he was.

'I thought we'd go to Florence.' He looked up, as if he'd been waiting all morning to give her this news.

'Florence?' It had never occurred to Lara that they'd go

anywhere else. She'd imagined that her father had used up all his zest for travelling by coming here.

'Just for a few days. It seems a shame not to see the Pitti Palace. We can catch a mid-morning train from Siena and we'll arrive in time for lunch. I thought we might try Harry's Bar.'

There was a Harry's Bar in London, and now she thought of it, of course, despite its name, it *was* Italian. They had a dish, a spaghetti, fine as noodles, covered in a cheese cream sauce, which although Lara knew was far too rich for her, she'd once eaten so much of it she'd actually been sick.

'Have you been before? I mean to Florence?'

'Yes.' Lambert stretched as if this were the most normal question she could ask. 'I spent a summer once travelling through Italy. I stayed in a wonderful hotel, by the Ponte Vecchio, but according to Caroline it's no longer there.'

'A whole summer . . .'

She wanted to ask him where else he'd been. When, and how, and who with. And why he had stopped travelling. But, as if guessing her thoughts, he picked up his pen again and began to read through what he'd just written, his eyes flicking over the words as if he were only now understanding what they said.

When Lara returned from India she imagined she'd tell Lambert every detail of her year away. She'd tell him about the pilgrimage they'd made to the temple at Bodhgaya where the Buddha had found enlightenment. She imagined she'd tell him how they'd travelled there by train from Delhi, relieved to be moving again after their one night in a hotel – safe in a compartment, watching the countryside stretch out around them, thinking they'd never get over the sadness and relief of being off that bus. They spent a night in a room with two benches to sleep on, a wooden table with a chair where Lara wrote, conscientious, in her diary, and the next morning they found a rickshaw to take them to the temple.

The temple was beautiful, with a gold Buddha at the front, and inside, on the walls, the story, in pictures, of the Buddha's life. It surprised Lara to learn the Buddha had had a life. She'd thought until then that he was a god, like Krishna or Shiva, but here she learnt that he'd been born a prince, five hundred years before Christ, out of his mother's side, in a beautiful palace, in beautiful grounds.

'His parents loved him so much that they never wanted him to know sorrow,' Cathy told her, as they looked at each painting, 'and so they kept him in the palace, constantly entertained, served with the most delicious food and the sweetest drinks, surrounded by the dearest friends until he was in his twenties.'

By then the Buddha was growing restless. The palace was beautiful. The gardens were scented and full of birds, but what he wanted was to see outside the palace walls. His parents pleaded with him not to venture out, begged him to be satisfied with what they could provide for him, but in the end they could not keep him a prisoner and eventually it was decided that he could leave the grounds, but only if he went in a procession. On the wall of the temple there was a picture of this procession. Silk-patterned saris, elephants and canopies, servants waving banana-leaf fans.

Once he was outside the first thing the Buddha saw was someone very old. 'What has happened?' He was greatly shocked. It was explained to him that this was what life was. People grew old. Their skin wrinkled, their backs bent. Then a little further on the Buddha saw someone who was ill. He was outraged. How could this be? Is this what life is? Then by

97

the side of the road he saw a bier on which a dead body lay, surrounded by grief-stricken relatives. What does life mean, he asked, that it contains so much suffering? He returned to the palace and for a long time he sat and thought.

By now the Buddha had a wife and a baby, but all the same, after much thought, he decided to leave again. He took nothing with him, and for many months he stayed with a group of poor ascetics in a forest. They ate almost nothing and thought a great deal, and there were many pictures in the temple of a starving Buddha, dressed in rags, impossible to recognise without the cheerful round of his belly.

He left the forest and walked as far as Bodhgaya, where he stopped and rested. He ate and slept and regained his strength, and then he found a Bodi tree of great beauty and sat under it. For three days and nights he sat there, tormented by every mental anguish, until on the third day as the dawn broke all became clear. He was enlightened. With no one to tell his revelation to, he touched the ground to mark the moment of his enlightenment.

On the wall of the temple there was a large picture of the Buddha, a trickle of earth running through his fingers, a serene look on his already serene face. In the garden of the temple, at the exact spot where the Buddha had sat and touched the earth, there was a monument. Pigeons perched on it, but Cathy was doubtful that the tree that grew close by was the original Bodi tree that had been there two thousand years before. All the same, they settled under it and ate their lunch.

'Many people came to talk to the Buddha about his enlightenment,' Cathy told Lara. "Please teach us," they begged, but the Buddha replied, "It is too near. It is too simple. It is too unbelievable to be taught." But eventually he relented and what he taught them were the four noble truths.

Suffering. The causes of suffering. The path of suffering. The cessation of suffering.'

Lara and Cathy spent the whole day at the temple. They threw crumbs for the parrots and peacocks who roamed the gardens, and bought two bangles and a little carved-stone Buddha from a woman by the gate.

'Did he ever go back and see his baby?' Lara asked. 'You know, Buddha, once he found enlightenment?'

'Hmm.' Cathy thought for a while, but she had to admit that she didn't know.

Lara had tried to talk to Lambert about her travels, even gave him a demonstration of the dancing that she'd learnt in Bangalore, her knees bent wide, her feet slapping down against the floor, her wrists circling, her neck long, her eyes making their own dance from side to side, but it seemed incongruous and boastful to talk of palaces and temples, of bright colours and tinkling bells, camels and family bicycles while he'd spent every day of every week of every year in the small close confines of his Kensington flat.

'Dad?' She tapped him on the shoulder, and he looked up from his page. 'When were you thinking we should go?'

'Sorry?' Lambert was lost somewhere in the century. 'Oh,' he remembered, 'Florence. Tomorrow. We'll catch the morning train.' And with a frown of determination he went back to his work.

Lara wandered down to the pool and sat on the edge, her feet in the cool water, the soft wool of Kip's jumper collecting heat as the sky began to clear. Her head was throbbing, mildly at first, but soon so painfully that she had to go up to the house, rummage through the kitchen, and then trailing out again into the garden down to the half-hidden door to

Ginny's room. But Ginny still wasn't there. She checked the drive and saw her car was gone. Caroline's car too, and so there was no one to ask for aspirin except Lambert, and from the tilt of his back, his shoulders, the tautness of his neck, she knew he was not to be disturbed. Instead she put on her bikini and went for a swim. It hurt. The cold water forcing the pain up through her body, cracking as it reached her head.

Will Kip miss me? she asked herself, safe under the water. Will he notice that I've gone? And then with a smile that threatened to let in water she remembered the feel of his fingers as he'd pressed them against hers in the club. Lara came up, her headache forgotten, and reached for the jumper, drops of water falling on to it, rolling like mercury across the wool. She patted herself dry with it, held it up to her nose, breathed in the smell of him still collected in its mesh.

And then Ginny was leaning over the terrace railings, a finger to her lips, reminding her Lambert was still working, before she waved. Lara pulled the jumper on over her bikini and ran up to where Ginny was already unpacking shopping, piling apricots into a bowl, rinsing nectarines in a colander.

'How was it?' Ginny asked, her whole face bright with anticipation. 'Tell me every detail.' She set a pan of water on to boil. 'Tell me about the dress.'

'Oh . . . oh yes.'

The wedding seemed so long ago, and to make up for having nearly forgotten, she re-created for Ginny the spectacle of Diana stepping down from the carriage, walking up the steps and into the cathedral, her ridiculously long train gathered up by bridesmaids of every size. Ginny listened intently, dropping tomatoes into the boiled water, letting them sweat there, before she pulled them out to be peeled.

She cut basil, a great sheaf of it, the smell, so sweet, filling the room, its whiff of cat's piss only a breath behind.

Lara told Ginny about the inside of the cathedral, the candles and the flowers, the hats, the faces, the echoes and the music, told her more, really, than she'd noticed at the time. Ginny broke eggs into a bowl of flour, mixed in water and a pinch of salt, and then when it was moulded rolled out a sheet of dough. She cut it into squares with a metal cutter, the edges frilled, and as Lara talked she filled each square with a pulp of ricotta and then sealed the edges with a lick of egg and the pressure of her thumb. Lara recited the vows for her, stumbling, just as Diana had, on the list of Charles's names, and Ginny, her face paling, looked up sharply, to show that she was not amused.

'He was so serious,' she explained in defence of herself and Diana. 'The Archbishop. He never once smiled.'

'Yes,' Ginny nodded. 'But marriage is a serious thing.'

By the time Charles and Diana were in their golden coach, alone together finally, waving dutifully at thousands upon thousands of people, Ginny had a pile of ravioli parcels and a pan of bubbling tomato sauce.

'That's it,' Lara said, as Ginny dropped each parcel into the wide pan and together they watched the steam rise up as the ravioli sank, swelled and then floated to the top.

Caroline arrived home with a bunch of flowers and a newspaper, a silver rain of fireworks, the night before the wedding, showering down over the front page. Ginny looked longingly at it, but Lambert, having cleared away his work, opened it hurriedly, going first to the obituary pages, and then flipping backwards until he'd reached the front. Ginny waited, they all did, for the pages to flutter shut, and then she served the food. As well as the ravioli there was salad and a plate of cold meat, and instead of pudding the dish of apricots, almost too beautiful to disturb in their green bowl.

'If the food's this good at Harry's Bar . . .' Lambert looked up at Ginny as she set down a tray of mint tea, and she blushed and hurried back into the kitchen for a plate of petits fours.

'I nearly forgot.' Caroline reached into her bag and slipped an envelope along the table. 'Here are the tickets for tomorrow. Your train leaves at ten-thirty-two.'

'Thank you so much.' Lambert gently touched her hand, and Lara saw the power of his gratitude, so welcome that even a woman in failing health would do what she could to earn it. 'We're looking forward to it, aren't we, Lara?'

'Oh, and Lara.' Caroline turned to her. 'I don't know what time you came in' – her face was flooded with sudden disapproval – 'but you left the porch light on.'

'Oh.' Lara was mortified. 'I'm so sorry.' And suddenly she was happy that they were going, could hardly wait another moment until they were gone.

The hotel in Florence was on the top-two floors of an old house. It was elegant, with chaises longues, rugs and paintings, the dining room hung with mirrors that reflected the pale green of the tablecloths, the napkins matching exactly the dark green of the walls.

A man in plum-coloured uniform showed them to their rooms. They were connecting, although the key, Lara noticed, was on Lambert's side. They looked at his room first, admiring the wide bed, the pale curtains, the bathroom, the tiles so thick they looked edible, the decoration like white icing, piped on. Lara's room was identical, except the bed was smaller, but it had an armchair, long and low, the kind that lured you down into it, made it difficult to get up. Her bathroom was the same, but more beautiful because it was hers. She wanted to run a bath immediately, squeeze in the contents of the tiny bottles, lie in it for an hour, wrap herself in the sheet-sized towels. But Lambert was checking his watch.

'We should go,' he said, and he slid the porter a tip.

The man inclined his head and backing out he shut the door.

'Do you want to change?' Lambert scrutinised her flowered dress, her sandals, the heels so badly chipped, and then as if thinking better of it he shook his head. 'No, you're fine as you are.'

'Are you sure?' She glanced back into the bathroom, ran her fingers through her hair.

'Yes,' he insisted, and he looked again at his watch.

'Signor Gold!' The *maître D'* at Harry's Bar welcomed Lambert with expansive arms. 'Please come this way. Your friend' – the man sank his voice to a whisper – 'is already here.'

Lara laughed and looked at her father to see how he would react to this mistake, but Lambert was walking ahead, sliding eagerly between the tables to where, half hidden by an overflowing vase of flowers, a woman sat alone. She had light-brown hair and almond eyes, and one hand was clasped around the stem of a champagne glass. As they approached she raised the glass and took a sip, as if taking courage before standing up.

'Isabelle.' Lambert slipped an arm around her, and for just one moment he pulled her up against him so that her skirt rucked.

'Hello.' Lara looked round quickly for Hugh, for Hamish or Allegra, knowing as she did so that they wouldn't be here, and then to cover herself she kissed Isabelle, once on each cheek, before they all sat down.

Lambert and Isabelle did their utmost to include her in their conversation. They helped with her order, urged her to try a Bellini – a glass of peach juice and champagne – even asked what she'd most like to see in Florence, but it was clear that for all their efforts they were having lunch alone. Lara humoured them, nodding politely, joining in occasionally, laughing at their jokes, but eventually she allowed them to give up. She turned her attention to her meal, draining her glass, ordering another, finishing up every last rich morsel, frowning with the effort of ploughing her way through it, forgetting, as she'd promised Ginny, to notice whether the food at Harry's Bar was as good as hers or not.

'How long have you got?' Lambert leant in close to Isabelle.

'Till tomorrow night,' she told him conspiratorially.

They grinned at each other, their faces lanterns of delight, and Lara saw her father reach under the table and rest his hand on her bare leg.

'Do have pudding,' they both urged, indulgent, as if she were their child, and so although they were declining she ordered a marmalade sorbet and spooned her way through it, letting it numb her from the mouth down.

'Lara?'

'Yes?' Her mouth closed round the ice-cold spoon.

'The Uffizi or the Pitti Palace? We can't decide.'

'Or *David*?' Lambert suggested. 'Did you know Michelangelo's *David* is right here in Florence?'

No, Lara thought miserably, I don't know anything, but instead she nodded knowledgeably and said she'd like to see that.

Outside in the street it was staggeringly hot. Not the harsh bright sun of Siena, but a muggy, damp and overwhelming heat that made you want to lie down. They walked along beside the River Arno, glancing into the enticing cool of the boutiques, pushing against the flow of tourists, swiping away the gnats and flies that hovered above their heads. Lambert lit a cigarette and waved the smoke around, and then, giving up, they stopped at a hotel and ordered a taxi. The Accademia was a cool white building, unusually modest, where at the end of a long corridor, flanked by rows of Michelangelo's slaves attempting to free themselves from the constraints of their still-clinging stone, they found the figure of David, waiting to be admired. Waiting, Lambert told them, since 1504.

They stood in silence, jostled occasionally by others, listening to the comments in every conceivable language as they stared up at the statue. His body was perfect, his eyes held the surprised look of one who finds he's just stood up to a giant, so why then, Lara wondered, were his genitals so small? She glanced furtively at Isabelle, at Lambert, at the pressing crowd of Germans, French and Japanese, convinced they were all thinking the same thing. It wasn't as if she had a vast experience, or any experience at all, but even a child could tell . . . And then, at the same moment, she and Isabelle yawned.

'What next?' Lambert ushered them out. 'We're not far from the cathedral, or we could walk back towards the river and see how long the queue is for the Uffizi.'

'Yes,' Lara said, and then although she was sure he had despised them both for doing so, Lambert also yawned.

They stood out in the narrow street, the sun beating down, the air so thick and dense it was hard to breathe.

'I don't mind.' Lara pressed herself back against the

building, hoping to take some cool from the stone, and when she looked up it had been decided, they were going back to the hotel.

They were silent in their lift, standing as far away from each other as they could get, three perfect strangers going to their rooms. But in the hushed and polished hall they couldn't pretend. Lara turned her key, clicked open her door, and then unable to resist she turned to look across at Lambert, catching him just as he slipped his arm round Isabelle and steered her into his room.

Lara lay in her bath, the water frothing around her, thinking how different life would be if every day were divided in two by a siesta. Whoever achieved anything worthwhile in the afternoon? And she thought of those dragging college lunch hours by the end of which they were all ready to go home. It occurred to her then that she'd stopped thinking about Clive. She closed her eyes and pictured him leaning up against a wall, pulling on a roll-up, his shoulder bent to shelter the spark of his lighter from the wind. But where as before he was looming, his image fiercely black and white, now she could only summon up a pale and shadowy version. Another week and he would cease to exist at all. Lara stayed in her bath until the water was cold and the bubbles had subsided, leaving a slick blue film of oil. Would Kip have noticed that she'd gone yet, and what would he think when he did? It pleased and unsettled her to think he might imagine she was being cool. Her best friend Sorrel would be impressed, at any rate. 'The more you like someone,' Sorrel had advised her, 'the less you let it show!'

Slowly Lara climbed out and stood naked before the mirror. She was so brown that the slim stripes of her bikini glowed. She turned and twisted, inspecting herself from every angle, and then, with an exhilaration she'd never experienced before at the sight of her own reflection, she realised that for the first time since puberty she didn't have a single spot. She flipped her hair and bound it into a turban, rubbed her body with three kinds of lotion, and massaged her feet. She inspected the dry skin of her elbows, painted the nails of her toes pink, and lay down on her bed.

It was then that she heard them. An indistinct sound of movement and murmuring, nothing to force her imagination too strongly, but just loud enough to remind her they were there. Her father and Isabelle, together, in the room next door. Quickly Lara switched on the television and with the burbling of Italian, so light and optimistic turned up loud, she climbed under the sheet.

'Are you ready?'

Lambert was changed, and smart enough for dinner in a pale linen suit. Isabelle was pressing the button for the lift, her hair still wet at the ends, flicking prettily against the collar of her dress.

'Yes,' Lara said, and she slipped on her shoes.

This time they had no plan. They walked through the city, admiring buildings, traipsing across squares, until they reached the Ponte Vecchio with its ancient shops, propped up by beams, clinging to each side of the bridge.

'Did you know,' Isabelle said shyly as they walked across, 'that in the Second World War this bridge was due for demolition, but it was too beautiful. Even the Nazis couldn't bring themselves to blow it up.'

They both glanced at Lambert to see what he would say. 'Well, it is too beautiful.' He looked back the way they'd come, and there was no flicker in his face of the other things, more beautiful, that they hadn't spared. Instead he cleared his throat. 'This bridge was built in 1354,' he told them, 'and until the sixteenth century it was lined with butchers' shops, but Ferdinando I, who had a private corridor that ran above the bridge, from the Pitti Palace to the Uffizi, couldn't stand the smell of the meat, and he evicted them. Since then the street's been full of gold- and silversmiths.'

'Can you imagine,' Isabelle murmured, 'that kind of power?'

They walked slowly, stopping at each window, staring in, until Isabelle gasped and put her hands up to her mouth.

'My mother used to have something just the same.' She pointed to a brooch – a silver butterfly, made from a mesh of tiny wires. 'When she died I looked everywhere for it, but it didn't seem to be there.'

Lara looked at her father to see what he would do. But he was gazing out through the back window of the shop at the water beyond.

They walked until it was dark, with nowhere particular in mind to eat. They crossed and re-crossed the river, meandering along each bank, listening as Lambert explained the architecture, the dates and history of each bridge, as if he'd spent his whole life in Florence, had been born and raised in Italy, had lived a thousand years and been instrumental in the city's design. Every so often they passed a restaurant, and they stopped and stared at the menu, reading it together just under their breaths. But always without discussion they'd move on. What they were after Lara didn't know, and then they saw it. The perfect place. A restaurant built into the wall. It was bathed in golden light and from it came the warm smell of cooking, and the gentle clatter of laughter, glasses, knives and forks. There were steps that led up to it, and as if drawn by magic, hardly bothering to look at the menu pasted up outside the door, only wanting to be part of that golden galleon, floating above the water, they walked in.

As soon as the starter came they knew that they'd been fooled.

'This is tourist food!' Isabelle was distraught. 'Everything here was made on Monday and they're dishing it out till the end of the week.'

It was true, the food was tasteless, the salad wilting, the portions mean. It wouldn't have seemed so disappointing in England where people were used to buying sandwiches reminiscent of old foam, but here, in Italy, it felt like a disgrace. The second course was no better, oily and half cold, and unable to finish it, they asked for the bill.

Lambert paid it, leaving the money on a plate, and then, just as they stood to leave, his eyes lit up. '*Porca Madonna*,' he hissed, just loud enough to be heard, and knocking over a glass of wine in his excitement he called to them to run.

They ran until they were down the steps, and halfway along the street, by which time they were laughing so hard they had to stop and lean against the river wall. Eventually they turned towards their hotel, feeling the heavy food disperse with each half-mile, sucking in the still-hot air, leaving the taste of the wine, the stale bread behind, still laughing occasionally, bound together by their sinfulness and bravery, not bothering to avert their eyes when they climbed into the lift, but standing huddled together as they sped up to the top floor.

'It must have been the food.' Lambert was apologetic at breakfast. 'You don't mind, do you, if you go off and look around the city on your own? I just think I should stay with her. In case . . .'

'Of course.' Lara hated the thought he might be lying, and as soon as she could she cut him off. 'It's fine.'

She set off shortly after breakfast with a map, the location of the hotel marked by the concierge in red. She found her way to the river, and from there headed towards the Ponte Vecchio and the Pitti Palace behind it. The Pitti Palace was not small, as she'd imagined it to be, but a huge imposing building of grey stone. She bought a ticket and went up the wide stairs where she found a room of statues, carved in white marble, the men, without exception, their penises lopped off. Why? She peered closer, how and when did it happen? And she looked round to see if there was anyone she could ask. But everyone else was gazing at the paintings, the portraits and still lifes, the sombre and ecstatic scenes of Old Testament cruelty and death.

She walked on through the rooms, but found herself distracted by the ceilings, carved and modelled out of gold, and by the walls hung with intricately designed paper, the detail of the tiles on the floor. In the royal apartments there were carpets, crystal chandeliers and four-poster beds and she felt too dazzled by their splendour to give more than a brief glance at the paintings.

By the time she emerged into the open, she was ready to lie down. She sat on a bench in the courtyard and let her eyes rest thankfully on the plain stone. Two cats appraised her for the likelihood of food.

'Go away, shoo.' She couldn't unbend her heart to their filthy coats and motheaten ears, and she thought of her own cat, Berry, with her dainty walk and luminous white bib.

'I'm sorry,' she said, remorseful, wondering since when she'd become so hardened, and she went into the café and bought a packet of biscotti and some milk, and pouring the milk into a saucer she watched them snuffle it up.

There was a fountain thick with water lilies at the back of the courtyard, where stone cherubs fought each other playfully in the water. The bottom was lined with coins, a year at least of wishes, and so Lara threw in a coin of her own. She watched it arc and spin, splash through the water, and just in time, before it reached the bottom, she wished for her life to begin. Was it too much? Too greedy? To wish for her whole life? But in the streets where she lived she'd seen too many people made desperate by ill health, by poverty, by broken windows and drunk men, that she knew how it could go. She thought of her mother, how she'd carved a bright space for them both, painted the rooms of their small house white to make them larger, painted the fridge, second-hand and stained, bright-blue. She felt an ache in her heart, so sharp she retreated to her bench, but she didn't know who it was for. For her mother, she decided, although Kip's name was in her palm, ready to throw in the form of a new coin. Kip. She allowed herself to think it, but she was too cowardly to wish for more.

Lara wandered through the streets, bought herself a slice of pizza, gazed at the teenagers larking about for photographs. They looked so well cared for. How, she wondered, had they managed to stay children when she'd been grown-up for so long?

Later she knocked on Lambert's door. 'I'm back,' she said through the glossy painted wood, but there was no reply.

Lara was almost asleep when Lambert called for her. 'Are you ready? We need to leave soon.'

Isabelle was standing a little way behind him.

'Do you feel better?' Lara asked, and it was true, Isabelle did look a little pale.

They travelled to the station together and Lara waited, gazing around at anything that might distract her while Lambert and Isabelle said goodbye. But she needn't have made such a pretence of blindness, because they only kissed, a little peck on each cheek, waving once before the train pulled out.

'Bye, Lara,' Isabelle called and Lara had to spin round and wave before she missed her.

They had half an hour before their own train left, and to make up for their previous journey they bought enough supplies for a week. *Panini* and crisps and brown bags bulging with fruit, newspapers, magazines and sweets. They sat opposite each other, flicking through glossy scented pages, munching their supplies, swigging back luxurious amounts of water, and when after an hour Lambert slipped off his shoes and put his feet up on her seat, Lara didn't flinch or move away.

Ginny and Caroline were both waiting on the platform at Siena. Lara saw them as soon as she stepped down from the train.

'Well done,' Caroline said when they came near. 'You made it back,' and she looked at Lambert with an amused eye.

Ginny couldn't help herself – she gave Lara a hug. 'How was it?' she asked.

With even more pleasure than it had given her at the time Lara described for her the wonders of Florence. 'You really should go,' Lara urged her.

But Ginny began murmuring anxiously about her mother and her tomatoes and Lara saw that she'd already made up her mind to go straight home.

'That reminds me,' Caroline said as they climbed into the car. 'I've got to know, are you staying for the Palio or not? Tickets are virtually impossible to come by, so if you are . . .'

'Yes,' Lambert said without hesitation.

'Lara?' Caroline's eyes were sharp. 'You'll stay?'

'Yes,' she nodded fervently. And she imagined the murderous racing of those hooves, the shrieking people, but mostly the opportunity of those extra days.

'Well' – Caroline was smiling – 'whatever made you change your mind, I'm glad.' And she steered the car towards the sweet cool air of home.

Kip's jumper had been washed and pressed and folded with her own clothes into the wardrobe. Lara took it out and sniffed it, but there was nothing left except soap suds and fresh air. I'll take it back to him tomorrow, she thought, and just then Lambert appeared at the door.

'Should you ask your moth –' He coughed over the unaccustomed word. 'Your mother, about staying? Or at least let her know?'

'Yes.' She realised she was still holding the jumper and in her confusion she put it on. 'I'll do it now.'

They went downstairs together to where the telephone sat on Caroline's desk. Lambert helped her through the code and then idled away towards the terrace, lighting up a cigarette, while Lara rang her own number and listened to the familiar ring. She could hear the echo of it on the green hall table, shrilling up the stairs, sounding through into the kitchen, where, likely as not, her mother would be sitting, reading the paper, a pan of rice, some soup maybe simmering on the stove.

'Mum? It's me.'

Her mother gasped, as if to hear her voice was painful. 'Lara?'

'How are you?' Lara was teasing, stalling, because of course she knew Cathy would be too concerned with the reason for her ringing to answer she was fine.

'Is something wrong?'

'I just wanted to let you know, I'm staying for a bit longer.' She could feel her mother's breathing change. 'Just for another five days, just so you know not to expect me back at the end of next week.'

'All right . . .' Her mother was listening for clues now. 'Is that what you want?'

'Yes. It's a horse race. The Palio. Apparently we'd be mad to miss it.' Lara knew this was a language of indulgence Cathy had no wish to understand.

There was a silence.

'Well . . .' she said at last. 'Have a good time.'

'Yes.' There was a pause where people in American films would have declared their love. 'Bye then. See you soon. Bye.' And with nothing left to say they both put down the phone.

Lara knew that for her mother the telephone was a dangerous machine. You could pick it up, dial, lose yourself in conversation and then, some months later, the ruinous cost of it would drop through the door. There was a radiator like that in the hall. A plug-in electric radiator they used only in deepest winter when the insides of the windows frosted up. Cathy would switch it on, and just when the hall, with its rug and its bare boards, would start to thaw she'd lose her courage and switch it off again. Lara used to eye it sometimes, its red light winking, its sharp edge pulsing heat, and imagine pound notes burning just above it, shrivelling and falling to the floor.

'Oh by the way.' It was breakfast time and Caroline was spooning sugar into hot black coffee. 'Your Ceccomoro lot came calling for you.'

'Really?' Lara studied the apple she was slicing – widthways to admire the star of its insides. 'When?'

'Yesterday. Or the day before. Let me think now.' She closed her eyes to conjure up the date. 'They were going on some expedition, wondered if you'd like to come along.' Caroline smiled, helping herself to a soft white roll. 'But I told them you were away.'

'I've umm, I . . .' She looked down at her plate. 'I was wondering if there was a way to walk over there. I've got something . . . I should return.'

'Oh, don't worry. I've got to go up and talk to Andrew. I'll take it for you, if you like.'

Lara bit into her lip. 'Thanks.' She saw her chances disappearing. 'I'll get it for you. It's just a jumper. Actually, it might be Kip's.'

'But is there a way?' Lambert looked up from his paper, news of the Royal Wedding finally replaced with the headline that one more Irish hunger striker was dead. 'Is there a way to walk to Ceccomoro? It might be nice for Lara to try it, before it gets too hot.'

'I've really no idea. I can't imagine.' Caroline looked at her. 'But have a lift, if you're determined to go.'

An hour later, they were driving along the road to Ceccomoro, Caroline behind the wheel, her face dappling in and out of shadow as they passed under trees, her skin bleached white in the open scorching stretches between fields of sunflowers and maize.

'Did you enjoy Florence?' she asked, and too eagerly, like a girl guide, Lara replied, 'Oh yes.'

'It must have been terribly busy, rushing about, seeing everything . . .' There was a pause and Lara knew, for certain, that she was hoping to find out more.

'Yes,' she said more tentatively. 'And it was incredibly hot.'

'You mean too hot to visit galleries?'

'No.' She'd already told her, last night at supper, about the splendours of the city, the queues at the Uffizi, the serene beauty of *David*, while Lambert interrupted occasionally to add his comment as if he'd been with her all along.

'Just so hot, walking about. The air is so muggy. It makes you tired.'

'Siesta weather . . .' she murmured.

And remembering the luxury of that white bathroom, Lara relaxed. 'Yes, it was hard to leave the hotel.'

Caroline took her eyes off the road and looked at her, just for a second, and she was sure, although she couldn't imagine how, that she'd given something away.

In silence they curved around the edge of the valley, slowing at the point where the village of houses that was now Ceccomoro nestled against the side of the hill.

'There were people who lived there until not so long ago,' Caroline told her. 'Old people who'd lived in that village all their lives, who'd never left these hills. Can you imagine? Never even been into Siena.'

Caroline turned off on to the narrow white road, past the stone lions, and pulled up in the yard. Lara clutched Kip's jumper as if it were a ticket. She noticed that the jeep was not there, and as she followed Caroline that the swimming pool was empty, the rose garden deserted.

They stopped in the cool stone hall of the main building, climbing a few stairs into an elaborately decorated room, vines and flowers and diamonds painted straight on to the plaster, and there, as if he'd been watching for them, was Andrew Willoughby, dressed in slippers and a cravat, holding a file of papers under one arm.

'Darling.' He pressed his lips against Caroline's bone-china cheek. 'So punctual. And who do we have here?' He turned to Lara and raised his eyebrows, 'A young secretary?'

There was so much sex in the word secretary that Lara had to look down at her feet. 'I'll wait out in the garden,' and still clutching the jumper she turned and walked back out.

Lara meandered around the rose garden, scooping up the fallen petals, thinking how as a child she used to sprinkle them with sugar and leave them out on the window ledge all night, hoping that by the time she woke they would have crystallised into sweets. She could even taste their odd half-mouldy sweetness, and remember how they never quite looked like the picture in the book.

Beyond the rose garden was a gate, and a path that swept down and then up into the hills. There was a statue at the top of it, a figure with wide-open arms, and unable to resist she walked through. She was in another garden, scattered with trees, thick with the smell of pine and acorns, of dust and dried-out streams. She walked slowly at first, not sure if she was allowed to be in here, and then, the longer the path ahead of her stretched, the faster she walked until she broke into a run. Maybe this was the path that led back to Caroline's? Or one of the smaller paths that opened off it, and she stepped into the undergrowth, shielding her eyes for fields, for hills or a distant, familiar road.

Instead she stumbled against something down by her feet and almost tripped. It looked like a white rock, but when she bent down she saw it was a pair of breasts. Just sitting there, with no body anywhere in sight. The breasts were beautifully carved, perfect in their curve, the nipples even slightly different from each other, just like her own. Lara looked back the way she'd come and noticed other mounds she'd assumed to be stones lining the path down which she'd run. Slowly she walked back, inspecting each one, more breasts, some buttocks, and a penis that would have put Michelangelo to shame.

By the time she'd inspected them all, the sun was almost overhead, drying the grass so that it cracked and sizzled along the edge of the white path. Her head was spinning, her ankles stung where they'd been scratched, and the jumper she was still carrying was damp from the sweat of her hands. Ignoring the last slack penis, lying against its cushion of stone balls, she pushed back through the gate, skirted the edge of the garden and walked slowly into the shade of Ceccomoro. There was the pool, so cool and inviting, and Lara kicked off her sandals and sitting on the side dipped her feet and legs in.

'Oh. It's you.'

Pamela was standing on the other side, looking over at her. She was dressed in a pink-and-black kimono, the sleeves almost hanging to the ground, her hair swept up into a chignon, but her face gave her away. It was swollen, streaked with tears. She pulled a tissue out of her pocket and turning away, quickly blew her nose.

'Are you all right?' Pamela sniffed. 'Out here all on your own?'

'I'm fine. I'm . . .' Lara hesitated, and then relieved to have something to do, picked up the jumper and splashing up out of the water handed it to her. 'I borrowed this ages ago, I thought I'd better bring it back. I think it's Kip's.'

'I see.' Pamela took the jumper and held it against her. 'They've all gone out.'

'Oh yes, that's fine. I wanted to walk home anyway, but Caroline didn't know the way.'

Pamela scanned the fields around them. Her eyes were bloodshot, mascara smudged into the fine damp lines below. 'You want the escape route?' She laughed drily, and pulling her kimono around her, started down the lane that ran behind the yard. 'I'll show you.' She strode ahead, her bare brown legs only a little less beautiful than her daughter Lulu's, her shoulders and sunbleached hair identical from behind.

'From here . . .' She stopped and pointed. 'You head for that field, walk along the edge to the corner, where you'll see a path between the maize. Just follow that and you'll come out, after twenty minutes or so, on the road above your house.' She must have caught Lara's look of wariness, because she gave a rousing smile.

'You'll see where you are. And don't forget – beware the wild boar.'

'OK.' Lara smiled back, hoping it was a joke. Then, more to convince herself. 'I'll be fine.'

It wasn't until she'd traipsed halfway across the field that she remembered Caroline. She turned round to shout a message for her, but Pamela was gone. For a while she stood, undecided, and looked back at Ceccomoro, the white-painted sides of the houses, the red steps and rooftops, the grey shutters, and below it, dug into the side of the hill, the blue streak of the swimming pool, bordered with laven-der, so dense she imagined she could smell it from here. And then she heard the distant drift of a shout, the unmistakable sound of a splash. Was it them? But if they'd come back, then surely she would have heard a car? And knowing anyway it was too late to return, she walked on.

There was the corner of the field, just as Pamela had promised, and a high mass of bright-green reeds that looked like corn on the cob. They were so lush and soft they made her think of water and she realised that, thirsty as she'd been, she'd forgotten to ask for a drink. Lara walked more quickly now, consumed with only one desire, to get back to what she considered suddenly to be home. In front of her was the path.

She swelled with the success of it, her abilities, her fearlessness and navigational skills, but within minutes, as if to punish her, a second path appeared, running off at an angle, neither one giving up a single clue as to where it might come out.

Now what am I going to do? And not wanting to dwell on it, she chose one indiscriminately and began to rush along, the reeds waist-high, the white earth of the track dwindling to a trickle as the foliage became denser, her legs and arms scored with blunt scratches, her eyes stinging with the dust of jostled stalks. She pushed on, even though it seemed impossible that this was the right route, and then, finally to answer her doubts, the path stopped altogether. She was in the middle of a field, surrounded on every side by maize. Lara stood still. Her throat was parched, her head hummed with the heat, a tender spot on the crown growing more tender with each bolt of the sun's rays. Slowly, reluctantly, she turned around, and pushing her way back through the already trampled reeds, she arrived surprisingly quickly at the point in the path where it had forked. She didn't trust herself even to look across at Ceccomoro, to imagine the swimming pool, the table laid by now for lunch, so instead she plunged into the other path.

The grass was lower, soft as banana, soothing her torn arms. The path wove and twisted, widened and wound through a little wood where the trees bent over to create a den of shade. Lara stopped, drinking in the cool, pressing her sore limbs against the trunk of a granite-coloured tree, letting the molten boiling of her head settle and become still. She couldn't be far now. She peered into the dark entrance to the path that dipped down into a rust-red trickle of dried swamp, and saw to her dismay that leading off from it was another path, narrower, but straighter, the flickering light of sunshine just visible at the end.

She went back to her tree. Her mouth was so dry she could hardly swallow and a great flare of misery rose up inside. She'd be here for ever, lost in this wood, eaten eventually by wild boar. She had to laugh then as she sank down against the tree, and what made it worse was knowing she could so easily go back. If she ran, she could be at Ceccomoro, plunging into the pool, glugging down a glass of ice-cold juice, in ten minutes or less. But even as she thought it, she knew it was out of the question. A wild boar would have to eat at least one of her arms first.

'For God's sake,' she said aloud, and she stepped down into the dip of the stream. The earth was crumbly and, as she reached out to pull herself up by a tree root, she heard a noise, the swish of grass, the tramping of feet. A sheen of sweat broke out over her, and her heart pounded so loud she could hear it in her ears.

'Who's idea was this?' It was a male voice, low and grumbling.

And then irritable, a girl's. 'Yours!'

'Well, she's either a medal-winning sprinter or she's been kidnapped by the communists.' She recognised the voice as Kip's.

'Don't joke.' It was May. 'Really. They could have mistaken her for someone important.'

Lara looked down at her legs. There was one long trail of blood where a stalk had caught a vein. Her hands were grey with dust and she could feel the grit of husks against her scalp. She swallowed and tears pricked dangerously against her eyes.

'Let's get back.' May was close now. 'Or the P will murder us.'

Lara held her breath as first Kip in his trodden-down loafers, his ankles brown below his jeans, and then his sister

121

in khaki shorts and flip-flops traipsed by, swiping at the grass.

Lara hardly dared breathe until they were out of sight, but as soon as it was safe she scrambled up the other bank into the mouth of the path from where they'd come, and ran without stopping until she reached the road. She burst out on to it, so dizzy with relief that at first she couldn't get her bearings. Where was the house? To the left or right, up or down the hill, but when a car swept past, the three men inside all craning round to stare at her, ragged in her sundress, her sandals torn, she remembered, and she raced along the road, only slowing to slip through the door, up to her room where she waited until she was safely in the bathroom, under the shower, before she allowed herself, for one brief moment, to sob.

'You missed a very enjoyable lunch.' Caroline eyed her over tea. 'And those poor Willoughby youngsters, traipsing off to look for you.'

Lambert glanced up.

'I just wanted to find the path,' she said, but she could tell Caroline disapproved.

'I think it would be polite,' Caroline continued, 'if you gave them a call to tell them that you're all right.'

She wrote down the number and, once Lara had dialled, gracefully retreated to the terrace where Lambert was working in the shade.

The longer the phone rang, the easier Lara breathed. Who would be inside on such a beautiful afternoon? And looking round to see that Caroline had noticed her attempt, she moved to put the receiver down.

'*Pronto?*'

She'd left it too late. Lara cleared her throat. 'Hello. It's . . . Lara.'

'Lara.' It was Roland's unmistakable drawl. 'We were just wondering about you, and now I can ask you myself. Do you, or don't you, want to come out with us tomorrow on an outing?'

Lara hesitated, looking back at her father, remembering how uncomfortable it had been the last time he'd been left behind.

'We're going to the Love Falls. You know.' He put on a fake Italian voice. '*La cascata dell'amore.* Now it's all very well saying you'll come, but what about the other day, making promises and then disappearing without a word?'

'I . . . we went to Florence!'

'Lara . . .' He was laughing. 'It's only a joke.'

'But seriously.' She lowered her voice. 'Could my father come, it's just. . .'

Roland's laugh turned to a snort. 'Of course, bring anyone you like. Bring your mother, your sister. Bring the cook!' He almost choked as if the idea was hilarious, and still laughing he put down the phone.

Lara and Lambert were ready the next morning by ten, their towels rolled into sausages, their costumes flat inside. Ginny had packed them a bag of supplies, great melting slabs of sandwiches, thick with ham and mozzarella, glued together with olive oil, and a basket arranged with half a dozen different kinds of fruit. Caroline had found a newspaper in Siena, a copy of *The Times*, which Lambert, leaning up against the door jamb, was flicking his way through now.

'Well, have fun!' Caroline called as the first of two cars pulled into the drive.

Piers climbed out and, seeing Lambert, nodded courteously to him and opened the passenger door, offering him his arm as if he were an old man.

'Lara!' Roland called, his bare torso at the wheel of the jeep. 'Jump in the back, and we'll race them.'

Lara looked over at Lambert to show she had no choice and, throwing her bag and towel in before her, she climbed over the metal door into the back.

'Hello.' Kip was in the front, and he turned and just for a second caught her eye.

It was a sensation like melting. Burning and dissolving all at once. 'Hello,' she mumbled, and she felt so dizzy that she closed her eyes.

'Are you all right?' It was Tabitha, sitting opposite in a bright-red dress, its scallop sleeves and scoop neck showing off the beauty of her upper body, helping to distract from her legs, which even since last week had swollen, the calves veined and heavy, the ankles gone.

'Yes.' Lara pinched the underside of her knee where no one would notice. 'We went to Florence for a few days, that's all.'

But Tabitha was too tired to concentrate any further. She let her head loll back, her hand on her high stomach.

'Ready?' Roland said, and he roared out of the drive.

'Careful,' Tabitha whispered, but it seemed that no one heard.

It wasn't long before they passed the others. They were driving more sedately, Lambert in the front, two girls Lara didn't recognise in the back. She caught her father's eye as they sped by, forcing herself to wave cheerfully when she caught sight of his alarm. Soon after they turned on to an unmade road, but rather than slow down Roland forced the car on, flinging and bumping it over the ruts of the ground.

'Wooaaa there,' May cried out involuntarily as her sister

was thrown up nearly to the roof, and Antonia, who was on Tabitha's other side, asked, shouting over the noise, if she didn't think she'd be better off in the front.

Tabitha only shook her head. 'It's fine,' but a sheen of sweat stood out on her brow.

Up and down hills they drove, swerving round S-bends, falling against one another, hanging grimly for dear life on to the metal and canvas walls. Dust blew in from the open back, and cars, the ones they narrowly missed, hooted furiously while Roland, choosing to misunderstand their recriminating tone, hooted joyously back. By the time they stopped in a grove of trees where several other cars were parked Lara was so angry she could hardly stand. She wanted to run at Roland, gore him with her fists, show her outrage at his behaviour, but she knew any flicker of feeling would be met with hilarity and delight.

'Made it!' Roland stretched, pulling his stomach in, thrusting out his chest. '*L'Amore* Falls!'

He extended his arms, his muscles flexed, his hair slicked down with sweat. He stayed like that longer than was necessary, as if enjoying the sheer power of his body, the lucky golden glory of being him, alive. They couldn't help it, all five of them, they looked at him, a lion, the leader of his pride, and then, to show she'd seen it all before but unable to control a small proud smile, Tabitha picked up a straw basket, and began to pick her way down towards the water – the roar of which was so loud that until now Lara hadn't heard it, it had so entirely filled her ears.

The waterfall was spectacular. It fell in a froth of foam, clearing quickly to a shoot of clear green water, tumbling into a pool below. The pool was banked by flat warm rocks, as if nature had formed it for no other reason than for fun. There were people swimming in this lower pool, letting themselves be pushed out by the tumbling water, clinging to the rocks to stop them floating off downstream.

Tabitha was spreading out a blanket in the shade of an overhanging tree. Lara unrolled a towel beside her and watched as May, lean and brown in her kingfisher-blue costume, waded into the river. Lara looked round for the others and saw Roland, followed by Kip and then Antonia, climbing the rocks that led up to the top. The rocks were huge, with splits and dents for footholds, and Lara could tell just by looking that there was no easy way down.

Eventually all three reached the top and turned and one by one they stepped out along the slippery stones until they stood just above the lip of the water as it came crashing down. Roland raised his arms, gave out a war cry, and then, instead of jumping, he put out a hand and pushed Kip off the ledge. Lara's blood rose, her hands formed into fists, but beside her Tabitha was laughing.

Kip fell, half-drowned by the spray, his arms and legs curved out to miss the rocks. She thought she saw his mouth open in a roar, and then he hit the water and was gone. She could hardly bear to wait. More than anything she wanted to look away, but she didn't dare until he was safely up. And there he was. Triumphant, spouting water, eyes gleaming wet.

'Your turn now, you slimy bastards,' he shouted up to where Roland and Antonia were still standing at the top. He tipped on to his back and kicked himself towards the river mouth.

Lara pulled on her costume, tugged off her dress and ran down towards him. Thank God, she wanted to say, you're all right, but not a single word came out. Instead she smiled and slipped into the water and, swimming away from him, she closed her eyes against the sun and waited for his touch. She could almost feel it. His underwater embrace, their secret conversation re-established with no need for words, but instead of Kip she found herself seized by a stranger. He was stocky and strong. The sinews of his arms bit into her flesh. Lara struggled to swim free, but as she tried to shake him off she felt the water sucked down around her and the bomb of a teenage boy hit the surface with such force she was forced out of his grip and under by the pull. When she came up, the man glanced over at her and shook his head. '*Stupida*' she heard him mutter, as, still choking, she thanked him. *Molto genitale*, she said, but not aloud.

From then on Lara kept close to the rocks, idling in the shallows, clinging to the bank. The water was so clear at the edges that she could see swarms of minnows just below the surface and larger, browner fish, so close she was sure she could reach out and touch one, tickle it like salmon until it dozed into her hands. She sat on a half-submerged stone and watched Roland jump, legs straight as a needle, his gold skin flashing in the glare, and then Antonia, who, after a long suspenseful wait, leapt into the waterfall with a shriek. When she surfaced, her eyes were gleaming and she heaved herself out, and with a scornful look at both Roland and Kip, who'd rewarded themselves with cigarettes and lounging, she re-climbed the rock, and after an equally hair-raising wait threw herself off again.

By the time Lambert arrived Lara had forgotten he was coming. She'd forgotten the other car, Piers at the wheel, slowing sensibly on an S-bend. Lambert was carrying their straw basket of fruit and a long, furled-up umbrella. He was followed by two identical girls who trod shyly on to the rock beside Tabitha and settled themselves down.

Lara pulled herself out of the water. 'Hello.' She touched her father on the arm and he turned and introduced her.

'Lara, this is Nettle, and Willow. Their mother is a friend of Pamela. She's coming out in a few days.'

'Willow and Nettle,' they corrected him, and they looked up at Lara, the bewildered look of years of boarding school stamped across their bony, rounded backs.

Just then Roland hurtled down from the rock above, leaping out dangerously from the waterfall, clasping hold of his bent knees in mid-air and falling like a star.

'My God,' the girls gasped, and they watched him admiringly as he swaggered out.

'You have a go.' He splashed them, but they sat folded in on themselves, knees drawn up, stomachs hollow as greyhounds.

Lambert sat down beside May. 'So.' He sounded awkward. 'What are you reading at university?'

'Oh,' May replied, equally awkward, 'I'm not bothering with university. I've been in Paris, doing a cordon bleu cooking course, and next spring . . . actually I'm getting married.'

'I see.' Lambert cleared his throat. 'Of course, I remember now. So you are.'

Lara lay in the sun, half reading the paper while she watched Kip leaping down the waterfall, his sleek skin, his lovely awkward body. Occasionally Lambert's conversation drifted over to her. He was telling May about the history of Siena, how for many years, long ago, it was at war with Florence. Lambert described for her the battles between the two cities, and the weakness in Renaissance politics that eventually allowed the French to storm in and seize power.

'They still pay homage, at the Palio, as I'm sure you know, to the cities that gave them shelter when they were in exile. It's a wonderful thought, isn't it, a whole city going into exile, and then,' he added wistfully, 'returning home again.'

May murmured that it was. 'That's so interesting,' she said with just a little too much enthusiasm. 'I didn't know.'

Eventually Lambert stood up for a swim, and as soon as he had slipped into the water May moved her towel over to lie beside Piers.

'I've had a thought,' she said. 'Maybe, as well as wine and champagne, we should have cider at the wedding. You know, for all your awful rugger friends.'

'Hmmm, whatever you say,' Piers said sleepily, and he took her hand.

'So, tell me, girls.' Roland was squatting down beside the twins. 'What's the news with you this summer? Is your mother still in that bloody awful play?'

'Yes,' they told him hesitantly.

Roland lay down beside them, his back to his wife, and leant up on one arm so that his muscle bulged. 'So what's the gossip and scandal then? Come on. Tell me something I don't know.'

'There's nothing,' they squirmed. 'Nothing.'

Tabitha ignored him. She took out a magazine and balancing it on her bump she leafed through its sumptuous pages.

By the time Lambert rose up out of the water there was no place for him. He stood for a moment, unsure what to do, glancing up at Antonia and Kip on the cliff above, urging each other on to increasingly dangerous jumps. He looked at Piers and May holding hands on their blanket, discussing their wedding, arguing in the most amiable way over the names of babies they hoped to have.

'Sit here,' Lara called, patting the towel beside her, and Lambert sat down.

It was up to her now. She would have to entertain him, but she couldn't think of anything to say. She looked round anxiously. How could they ignore him like this? Gossiping and giggling when they should be taking this opportunity to talk to him, but even as she blamed them she struggled for anything to say herself. Lambert opened a bottle of apricot juice and offered it around. But no one wanted any.

'So . . .' She took her cue from the news. 'What will happen, will the hunger strikers all be left to die?' She'd been reading in *The Times* how terrorists had fired shots over the coffin of a twenty-five-year-old man who'd died after seventy-one days without food. She felt her eyes well up with pity, her heart thump with anger on his behalf. 'Will no one do *anything*?' She thought she heard Roland groan, but she didn't look round.

Lambert narrowed his eyes as if he'd seen something new in her. 'It will make a difference,' he said, 'but only when no one's looking.' And he explained how important it was that the government must never seem to be talking to their enemies, even if the only way to move forward was to talk. He began to explain to her about the history of the Troubles, the birth of the IRA, the Tory Party's policies, and Lara listened so hard she found she'd drifted off and was watching Kip wrestling with his sister on the rock above. 'Is that any clearer?' Lambert asked, and she had to swing her attention back to him, and just in time to catch Roland in a gaping yawn.

'Yes.' She nodded earnestly. 'I think it is.'

Lambert picked up the paper and Lara read over his shoulder about a little boy who'd been missing since the day of the Royal Wedding. He'd been wearing dark trousers and a blue-and-white-hooped T-shirt and he'd last been seen by his nanny and his younger sister when he'd bought sweets in Kensington High Street before setting off ahead of them for home. A week. Lara thought. He's been missing for a week, and the boy who'd re-enacted his last steps, a boy called Sunil, had worn the hooped T-shirt too and bought exactly the same sweets.

Eventually it was time for lunch. The Willoughbys had brought a feast. Lara pushed their own basket of fruit to the middle and unpacked their sandwiches, which looked meagre and faintly disrespectful beside the tray of chicken, roasted vegetables, salads and cake that May and Tabitha unloaded from the car. But eating was a relief. There was something unanimous about it; it was something they could all join in. Even Kip and Antonia dragged themselves out of the water and came, chilly and dazzling, to the edge of the cloth.

'Let's play a game,' Piers suggested, and it was decided that everyone must take a turn at saying something that they'd never done.

'I've never had sex with a goat,' Roland started, his mouth still full, but he scored nothing, because nor had anyone else.

'You only win points,' May chided him, 'if everyone else has done it. You need to be the only one who's resisted the lure of the goat.'

'I've never had sex . . .' Antonia sounded pleased. 'With a man!'

But she only won meagre points because Roland, Kip, Piers, Lambert, Willow and Nettle all put up their hands. 'Nor have we!' they chanted.

'Piers . . .' May nudged him. 'Be honest. What about school?'

'Does that count?' he asked, eyes widening, and he was told it did.

Roland grinned and lowered his arm too. 'They were only boys.'

Lara's heart was thudding. Did her one night count? Her one night spent fumbling and apologising and keeping her eyes tight shut while a boy from Turnpike Lane attempted to make love to her? Yes, she decided. It had to. And she was glad now she'd gone through with it.

'Lara!' the circle were calling. 'It's your turn!'

'OK. I've never . . .' What could she say? 'I've never had a fringe.' There was silence for a moment as they took this in. 'I mean, I've always had a side-parting. I've thought about it . . . but . . .'

'OK, OK, you nitwit. Next.' There were groans and laughter and it was Tabitha's turn.

'I've never seen a wild boar.'

'Nor me. Or me.' Almost no one had. The game went on.

'I've never taken cocaine,' Piers said, triumphant, as if he'd known his abstinence would prove to be useful in the end. And he was right. Hands stayed down, except for Lambert. Even Nettle and Willow kept their arms by their sides.

'I've never seen my mother naked.' It was May, and for a moment she looked sad.

'I have,' Kip said gloomily.

'But you were spoilt. The baby. The only one she loved!'

'You should have been there. It wasn't that much fun.'

'OK, enough bickering.' Antonia sighed. 'Kip, it's your turn.'

Kip thought for a minute, and then he looked up. 'I've never been in love.' There was silence as his eyes travelled the circle. For a brief moment they met Lara's and she looked down.

Of course she'd been in love. Her whole life had been lived out in degrees of adoration. What else was there to do? She looked across at Willow and Nettle, blushing, scratching patterns in the earth, at Antonia – a woman of experience, just not with goats, or men. Then there were Piers and May, officially in love, and the one married couple, surely they must have been in love once. Roland's hand flickered and was slapped down. And then slowly, out of the still circle, Lambert raised his hand.

Lambert and Kip looked at each other.

'Damn.' Kip shook his head.

And Lambert smiled, rueful. 'Damn indeed.'

'Lara wins,' Roland said, and he stood up and stretched.

It was late in the afternoon when they arrived home.

'How was it?' Caroline looked up from a letter she was writing.

'It was good.' Lara had to force herself to smile. She felt tired suddenly, her skin dry and dusty from so much sun.

'It was interesting.' Lambert was himself again in his white shirt and polished shoes, and he sat down on the sofa as if he'd just conducted an experiment, which could now be put safely to one side.

As soon as it was polite to do so Lara went up to bed. How could he, she asked herself, say he'd never been in love? And she didn't know who she felt more bitter towards – her father or Kip.

Only Ginny noticed anything was wrong. 'A touch of sun-stroke, could it be?' and she made Lara a drink of iced water and lemon and cut two slices of cucumber to put over her eyes.

'It could be,' Lara agreed, hopeful that it was, but she felt heavy-hearted and despondent.

She lay by the pool, swam, sat up in her room, even wrote

the postcard to her mother she'd had for more than a week. *It's great here.* She let her writing grow large. *I'm having a really good time. Swimming, eating and sunbathing. Has Berry had her kittens yet? Hope you're well.* She could imagine her mother reading it, flipping it over to look at the picture on the front – the Palio, horses streaming round the Piazza, their legs so delicate and brittle it would take one fall for them to snap. She could see her turning it back over, frowning at the lack of information, and before she was tempted to add more she scrawled a row of kisses and her name.

After lunch Lara went out for a walk.

'Careful,' Lambert warned her, but she didn't invite him and he didn't offer to come.

She walked down the road, turned the bend and found herself at the mouth of the path that led to Ceccomoro. The escape route. She thought of Pamela's sad face, and she walked on down the road. It was hot today. Mad dogs and Englishmen, she remembered, and she wished then she hadn't set out alone. A car sped by and she shielded her eyes against the glare. Heat bounced off the road, shimmering silver against the olive leaves, beating down painfully on her exposed toes. She should turn round, she knew, but ahead of her was a layby with an empty car parked in the cool of some trees.

Lara reached it and found the stump of an old gate-post on which to sit in the shade of the wood. It smelt good. Pine and dust and the hot tar of the road. She gulped the air down. There was silence here except for the reedy shrill of crickets that she already had to listen for to notice they were there. And then a white car slowed on the bend. There were two people in it, talking, and it pulled up just beyond her and stopped. The engine stayed on, the exhaust pumping out hot fumes while the two heads came together and kissed. Lara could see them silhouetted against the windscreen, the wisps of the woman's hair and the man, half-bald, half-curls. You see, she found herself thinking, even they're in love, and then the passenger door opened and Andrew Willoughby got out. Lara looked away.

'*Au revoir*,' she heard him say. 'And let it be sooon.' He eased out the word with longing.

'Soonimento,' the woman replied, and Andrew laughed.

Lara looked back in time to see them kiss again, Andrew leaning into the car, the woman – a screen of light-brown hair falling forward to obscure her face.

'*Arrivederci*.' Andrew straightened up. 'Bye now,' and the car screeched out on to the other side of the road.

Lara looked away again but it was too late.

'Can it be our young communist?' Andrew called, straightening his clothes, 'waiting for a revolutionary to come by and whisk her away to the hills?' He fished some keys out of his pocket. 'But seriously, my darling, if you want to meet up with your pals you've come the wrong way.' He unlocked the door of his car. 'Get in,' he said. 'Go on, I'll give you a lift.'

Obediently Lara got in. The seats were hot and sticky, despite the shade, and she had to squint to look at him.

'So.' Andrew drove slowly, one hand on the wheel. 'Are you having a good time?' He glanced at her bare legs burning into the leather of the seat. 'Is it living up to your hopes? Italia?'

'Yes,' she said. 'Oh yes.'

'Good.' He sounded magnanimous, the host of all of Italy, as if he'd sort it out for her if that were not the case. 'You went to Florence, I hear. With your dear papa.'

'Yes.' It was only then she realised they'd passed Caroline's turning and were on their way to Ceccomoro. 'Oh no,' she gasped. 'I . . . they'll be worried if I don't go back. I only said I was going out for a walk, and anyway I saw everyone yesterday.'

'You think they'll be disappointed to see you again?' He laughed. 'You've no idea how many distractions my family need.'

'Exactly,' she said. 'They probably need someone new.'

Andrew looked at her. 'True.' His eyes narrowed. 'But there is no one else.' He smiled as if to take the sting out. 'So buck up. You'll have to do.' He slapped her lightly on the leg and drove through the gate of lions, along the avenue, and drew the car up in the yard. 'I'll ring Caroline and tell her we're keeping you here. Until tonight.'

It was only later as she stood in the cool stone study, soft with rugs and tapestries, waiting while he dialled, that she had time to wonder what he'd been doing leaving his car in a layby and driving off with someone else. Who was she? Lara frowned, and she had the uneasy feeling the woman was familiar, with her curtain of brown hair catching the light as she leant out to pull the door.

There was no one by the swimming pool, or in the garden. 'Yes,' Andrew Willoughby had said into the telephone. 'Someone will bring her home.' And then, his duty done, he'd wandered off, his footsteps echoing over stone, and left her alone.

Slowly Lara walked through the narrow web of streets that ran between the houses. She looked up at each building, expecting to hear the hum of voices from one window or another, but the air was thick with quiet and there was no one there. Eventually she went back to the main square. There was the table under its double canopy, the countless chairs ranged around it. Not far away, just up the hill, was the kitchen in an old stone building so shaded it was actually cool. Lara peered inside. There were two tables for chopping, a range, a tall white fridge, but everything was orderly and deserted, the surfaces empty, the floor swept clean. She tiptoed through it and out into a breakfast room on the other side.

From there she walked along a corridor, and was surprised to find herself once more in the main part of the house. A bedroom with a white-painted bed, a state room with a wooden table and some sort of giant dark-wood throne. Beyond that was a room with nothing in it but two tall pale cupboards and a sewing machine on a table, the pedal for turning it built into its frame.

Further along she recognised the door to the television room. Lara pushed it and found herself in almost total darkness. She could sit in here, she thought, and when it was cooler walk home, and she let the door fall shut behind her. A figure shifted in the corner, and Lara jumped. It was a man, she could see him now, his legs slung over the arm of a chair.

'I hate the sun. Couldn't it just go behind a cloud, just once?' And she realised it was Kip.

Lara stepped nearer. Kip was wearing jeans and a dark shirt. He had on shoes and a jacket.

'I'm holding out for a bit of rain,' he said. 'I thought it would help if I was prepared.'

Lara chose a chair and sank down into it. She wanted to laugh but he sounded so serious. 'Do you get homesick?' she asked instead, swinging her own legs over the arm.

'For where?'

'For . . .' She wanted to say home, but she caught herself in time.

'I won't miss school. If that's what you mean.'

'For England?'

Kip shifted in his chair. 'Do you get homesick for Finsbury Park? For the Rainbow . . .?'

'No.' She laughed. 'Well, I might, if I stayed away long enough.'

They sat in silence.

'I expect I'd miss my mother,' she said eventually. She tried to summon her up, but for some reason all she could manage was the sweet face of the cat.

Kip swung his leg and for just a second their feet touched. Lara felt every nerve in her body fizz. She gulped, and they both heard it.

'So what will you do?' she said. 'You know . . . I mean, did you really do so badly in your exams?'

'They're sending me away.'

'Where?'

'At first they said I could go anywhere. But when I suggested Las Vegas, they said they meant . . . anywhere in Africa.'

'Oh.' Lara felt light with shock. He was going away. But she was relieved too. He'd be safe in Africa. Away, not just from her, but from everyone. From Lulu, from his sisters, from the sisters of his friends. 'How long will you be gone?'

'A year or so. It's to keep me out of trouble. Form my character. Give me a chance to experience life.'

'A bit like a year off before university?'

'Yeah, but just without the university.'

They both laughed, and then, frowning, Kip stared at the floor.

'When will you go?' Her voice was almost a whisper.

'In a month or two. I'm not sure.'

He swung his legs down and pushed himself up out of the chair. He seemed unsure what to do next, because he hovered there, still frowning, as if he'd forgotten what had propelled him to stand. Lara put out a hand to him. He took it, and as if it were the most natural thing in the world that he should help her, he pulled her up. She straightened against him and still holding her hand he slid her arm inside his jacket. She felt the warmth of his ribs through the cotton of his shirt, the silk lining of his jacket. Kip wrapped his other arm around her.

'Is *this* too corny?' she asked.

'I don't know.' His mouth was close. 'But I think it might be all right.'

They turned and surveyed the room. There was a sofa with its throw half-dragged on to the floor and an ashtray full of the butts of cigarettes.

'We're safe . . . no violins . . . no moonshine . . .' and he bent his head and kissed her.

His lips were cool, his breath as fresh as summer, and as he pulled her to him she felt her heart leap up like a flame.

'You're so . . .' she tried to tell him.

'What?' he murmured.

She ran her hands along the shirted stretch of him. 'Nice,' and she kissed him through his smile. 'You're meant to say you too,' she laughed, but instead he kissed her again, and again, until they were drunk, and without letting go of each other they lay down on the floor.

Kip pushed off his shoes, fumbled with the buttons on her shirt, but she wound her arms around him, and pulled him on to her. She wanted to feel his weight, his knees, the buckle of his belt dig in.

'I'll squash you,' he warned, and it was true she wanted to be squashed.

By the time the bell for dinner rang her face was sore from kissing, her clothes rumpled, her hair ragged with heat.

'My God, what time is it?' She sat up. She felt as if she'd been in that room for days.

Kip looked round for his shoes. His jacket was half under a chair and the buckle of his belt was loosened. He'd taken her hand and eased it down the front of his jeans until she'd felt the hardness of him straining against his shorts but they'd done nothing more. Anything more would have involved talking. Contraception, a lock for the door. It was easier to just go on kissing.

Kip flicked on the light.

'Ow.' Lara covered her eyes. She turned away to pull her shirt closed, ran her fingers through her hair and turned to face him. 'How do I look?'

Kip put his head on one side. 'Fuc . . . fine,' he said and he took her hand and led her out.

Lara sat at dinner and pressed a cool glass against her face.

Andrew Willoughby was seated with the twins on either side of him, and he was amusing the top half of the table by interrogating them, asking them which girl at school they most admired. 'Was it on the same girl – your pash? Come on, you can tell me. Isn't that how it works with twins?' He stopped then to see which one was blushing the brightest scarlet, but it was impossible to say.

Lara hid behind their despair, watching them, relieved, as they sent occasional beseeching looks down the length of the table to Pamela who was bright and smiling again, her face aglow with sun and make-up.

The main course was cleared away, ice cream was served, and as soon as it was safe to do so Nettle and Willow slipped away and with their departure the table was freed. Places were swapped, coffees topped up with spirits and Lara, May and Tabitha retreated to the pool, dipping their legs in, lighting up cigarettes while Tabitha sucked hungrily at the wisps of smoke.

Kip ambled over. Lara looked up at him and he reached down and clasped her hand.

'Come with me,' he said, and his sisters watched her as she struggled up. 'And you,' he said to them, grinning, 'come on. Roland's got an idea.'

May jumped up, but Tabitha stayed where she was. 'I think I can resist.' She yawned, and reaching out she whipped the cigarette from between May's fingers.

They followed Kip through the dark of the gardens, round the corner of the main house, across the car-park yard to where a stable block had been converted to make more bedrooms for guests. There were lights on here and when they knocked Roland opened the door and put his finger to his lips. He came out, and tiptoeing elaborately he led them along the length of the block to a door at the far end. Then very formally he knocked.

'Your entertainment, madame.' Roland bowed when Nettle looked out and he pushed open the door.

The girls were both wearing pyjamas – sprigs of pale-blue flowers and girlish white collars. They looked appalled to see their visitors, and as if she was naked Nettle crossed her arms over her chest.

'Lights out!' Roland ordered and nervously Willow started to giggle. Roland snatched up several sheets of paper and began scrawling the alphabet around the outside. 'Get a glass,' he told Piers who'd just arrived, and everyone was urged to sit cross-legged on the floor as he spread out the square of paper and set the tumbler in the centre. 'It's time for the séance to begin.'

At first it seemed too dark to make out anything, but the curtains were open, the moon was bright, and once they'd become accustomed to it, the room was alive with shafts of light and shadow. Everyone put out their hands and touched the top of the glass.

'It's not me,' Roland promised when after a still minute the glass began to move.

'Someone must be pushing it,' Kip murmured, and they all looked suspiciously at each other.

Lara rested her hands even more lightly than she had before, but even so the glass moved away from her, sometimes slow, sometimes faster, from one letter to the next. P. Z. H. B.

'It's not working,' May complained.

'Shhhh.' Roland shifted. 'It may be warming up.' He set the glass back in the centre. 'You have to concentrate. Give it your power.'

'Shut up, you idiot,' Piers said, but he put his hand on the glass all the same.

Slowly it began to move. M. U. It stopped for a moment, and then, as if it was unsure, it set off again very slowly until it stopped at T.

'Mut?' Willow suggested.

But it raced on, swirling round the board, settling back on T.

'Mutt!' Nettle flashed her sister a smile but before she'd finished speaking it had moved to I.

They all craned forward to stare.

'*Mutti*?' Piers sighed. 'What does that mean?'

'It could be German,' May offered. 'If it were a German séance it might be saying Mummy.'

'*Donner und Blitzen*. Ve have a German spirit visiting us.' Roland picked the glass up and blew into it. 'English, please,' he ordered and even Nettle and Willow laughed.

Once again they waited, their arms outstretched, their eyes

pinned to each other's lightly hovering hands. I'll be able to tell from the pressure of the fingers, Lara thought, vowing not to let her eyes drift away from the glass, but after a while she couldn't resist stealing a quick glance round the circle, hoping for clues as to who was and wasn't pushing. It wasn't her. That was all she could be sure of, and then there was a rustle, and the glass was moving – sliding away across the paper, taking their fingers with it, losing some as it reached the letter S. It stopped there for a moment and then more slowly moved to I. Lara felt her skin grow tight and the silence in the air was stifling. D, the glass was travelling towards D, and then without pausing it moved to V.

'Sid V . . . Sid Vicious!' Kip shouted and at that moment the window, which had been shut, slammed open and a vase crashed to the floor.

Everyone screamed, at least the girls screamed so loudly it was impossible to know if Kip, Piers or Roland had uttered a sound. May flicked on a light, and with the rush of brightness the screams turned into laughter.

'Let's do it again,' one of them suggested but the light stayed on and no one moved to play.

It was after midnight when Lara got home to Caroline's. Roland had driven her, and Kip had come too, squashed in beside her in the front seat of the jeep. She'd closed her eyes as they'd roared through the dark night and she'd felt so happy she didn't even mind that Roland was risking all their lives. The porch light was on.

'See you tomorrow,' Kip called, and without asking where or when, she darted inside.

The stairs were dark, but her head was too full of shrieks and love and laughter to give in to fear. She lay in her bed and imagined the weight of Kip's body squeezing the breath out of her. She twisted and turned and then to still herself she slid her hand between her legs. 'You've got to practise in case you ever meet someone you actually like.'

She thought of Sorrel and her theory of virginity, and how eventually when she was almost sixteen she'd spent the night with a friend of Sorrel's boyfriend, in that flat in Turnpike Lane so filthy she was sure she would catch an incurable disease just by lying on his bed. He'd groped and prodded for what seemed like hours, and when it was over he'd lain back and lit a cigarette.

'So,' he'd asked after an awkward silence. 'How many orgasms did you have?'

Lara was so embarrassed she could hardly speak. 'I don't know,' she'd muttered, her eyes still tightly shut. 'I can't remember.'

When he got up, shortly after, to put on his mustard-coloured briefs, she realised she'd got through the whole thing without seeing his willy. Willy! Was that what she'd called it? But what else was there? Cock and dick were pornographic somehow, and prick too close to an insult she didn't intend. Penis was a foreign word. As ugly as vagina and all wrong. Fanny. That's what she and her mother had called hers, but so long ago, and for years now it had gone unnamed.

She'd read once in a magazine that you were meant to stand naked in front of a mirror and examine yourself. Your thighs, your breasts. Your vagina. Lift one leg and peer inside. Or better, turn around, swing your head down and take a look. 'Meet and Greet', the article was called. It must have been an American magazine. But they had no full-length mirror in their house and it was impossible to stand on the edge of the bath and keep your balance.

Lara flicked on the light. There was a mirror here built into the wardrobe. Tentative, blushing even, she pulled off her nightdress and bent over. There was so much more of it than seemed polite. A long gash of hair and flesh, a maze of pink leading to a pinpoint at the centre, and at each side two small pendulums like tonsils hanging down. Is it beautiful? Are you? she asked. Remembering not just to meet, but greet. Could something be beautiful if it didn't have a name? Pussy, minge, cunt. The blood was beginning to throb in her head. I'll name it, she thought, quick, then I can stand up, and in a flash it came to her. She'd call it Iris. Iris. She pulled her nightdress back on and pleased with herself, feeling somehow different, she climbed into bed.

Lara woke late, and when she got up she saw a white car parked in the driveway. She ran to the other window that looked over the pool but there was no one there. She dressed and went downstairs. It couldn't be Kip, could it, already? But instead of Kip, Isabelle was sitting on the sofa, turned towards Lambert, talking quietly, the fingers of one hand trailing over his.

'Hello!' Lara said, and then remembering she was only meant to have met Isabelle once, she stepped back a little even though Caroline wasn't there. 'Is Andrew here . . . I mean, I thought . . .' she said in her confusion, realising she associated the white car with the layby, and then seeing in a flash her mistake, recognising in that instant the fall of Isabelle's hair, she sat down and told them, much too fast and without waiting for any sign that they were interested, the moment by moment events of the séance.

'How terrifying,' Isabelle said, her eyes kind, her cheeks red, but Lambert said nothing.

'Is that right, Dad?' she asked him. 'Is it German for Mummy?'

He looked at her as if there was no earthly reason why he should know. 'Yes,' he said then. '*Mutti.*' The word sounded different when he said it. As gentle as a stroke.

'I think I'll get some breakfast.' Lara swallowed, and she tiptoed out.

She poured a glass of apricot juice and cut a slice of bread, so springy it squashed almost flat under the knife. She peered into the fridge, her stomach hollow with hunger. She took out cheese, and peeled away a wafer-thin slice of ham which she crammed into her mouth. She put the kettle on and once she had her tea she went outside and sat at the far end of the terrace with her back to them. Much as she wanted to she resisted looking round. Was there a row? She chewed as quietly as she could, straining for raised voices, half expecting Isabelle to storm out in tears, but instead she was disturbed by Caroline.

'You left the porch light on again.' Her voice was acid, her face white. 'Mightn't it just be more convenient if you stayed out all night?'

Lara almost choked. 'You could switch it off,' she stammered. 'Please switch it off when you go to bed.'

But Caroline was walking away, ramrod straight, around the corner of the house.

Lara retreated to the kitchen where she cut herself another slice of bread, spooned it high with blueberry jam, but when she carried it out to the terrace she glanced, without meaning to, in through the windows and saw her father and Isabelle standing by the bookshelves, their faces so close their noses touched. Quickly she sat down at the table, and realising there was nowhere for her safely to go she turned to the crossword in a three-day-old paper and stared at the impossible clues until she was saved by Ginny coming back from the local market laden down with food.

Lara lay on a lounger and thought about the boy from Turnpike Lane. She regretted now, more than anything, that she hadn't looked. Sorrel had seen men naked. Any number of them. She'd described their 'tackle', as she called it, thick, thin, curved, once even square. Square? Yes, I promise. Short and stubby. Horrible it was, like a box. Lara had been with her the first time. Waiting for a train at Edgware Road. She'd just put money into the vending machine and, although she knew it never actually worked, she was tugging at the metal drawer, trying to get at the bar of chocolate that was rightfully hers. Bastard, she hissed, punching it with the side of her fist, when Sorrel rushed towards her, eyes wide, face flushed.

'It was out, all huge and red.' She pointed to a man stumbling away along the platform.

'What was?' Lara asked, although she knew.

'His Thing,' Sorrel said and she shook her hands as if she'd touched it. 'Arrrhhhh.'

'Should we tell someone?' Lara looked round, but just then their train pulled in and they couldn't resist it, they got on.

'You were so lucky!' Sorrel turned to her. 'He didn't flash at you.'

But once they were home, Sorrel's mother made such a fuss of Sorrel, that Lara began to feel as if it was she who had missed out. If only she'd seen it, she thought. If only the man had flashed at her, and then it occurred to her that maybe he had and she'd just been too busy hammering on the vending machine to notice. 'It happened to me too once, well almost . . .' she wanted to tell them, but she resisted disclosing the promise she'd made to the Tibetan monk.

It was in India on the way home from the cinema. They'd seen a film about two lovers, divided by caste, who could only meet in secret. They attempted to kiss through doorways, windows, holes in walls, even once through bars when he was wrongly imprisoned for another man's crime. The audience was in a frenzy. Just to have them embrace. Please let that happen! But they were kept in suspense until the very end when it was discovered the man was from a high caste after all and they were married in a blaze of red saris and dancing.

On the way home the monk, who was from the Purawala refugee camp where Cathy and Lara were visiting His Holiness, said he wanted to show her something. They stopped on a deserted path.

'Can I?' he said, so serious and polite that she couldn't possibly have said no.

'Yes,' she answered, and once she'd promised solemnly not to tell, he slowly lifted up his orange robes and there, below them, billowing out, was a pair of boxer shorts made from the American flag.

Kip didn't appear until the middle of the afternoon, by which time Isabelle had gone and Caroline was taking a siesta.

'Come in,' Lambert called as Kip and Lara whispered in the hall, and so together they sidled into the room and stood uncomfortably against a wall.

'So, how are you?' Lambert asked him.

Kip paused as if giving the question real thought. 'I'm very well.'

'I haven't seen her for rather a long time. But how's your mother?'

Kip gazed at his shoes, which were worn and scuffed, but still managed to look expensive. 'She's all right,' he said.

'When you see her,' Lambert smiled, 'do send my regards.'

Kip nodded slowly. 'OK. But I'd better not say I saw you here.'

Lambert raised his eyebrows.

'She's not meant to know.' He looked behind him. 'About this place.'

'I see,' Lambert said, and then he and Kip looked at each other and, man to man, they smiled.

Lara tapped her foot. She wanted, more than anything, to be gone.

'So.' Lambert was still looking at him as he lounged against the wall. 'What next? You've finished school, I hear?'

'He's going to Kenya,' Lara interjected. She had to show she knew about his plans. That he was hers.

Lambert widened his eyes. I see, he seemed to say, I see, and Lara swore not to say another word.

'Yes. I'm going to work somewhere, with horses, on a farm.'

Lambert was nodding, as if weighing up whether or not he approved. 'Why not?' he said eventually. 'Are you interested in farming?'

'No.' Kip frowned.

'In horses?'

'Not really.' Their eyes met again and they both smiled.

'I like him,' Kip said once they were outside, and Lara took his hand. The feel of it was warm and smooth and – it made her heart skip to realise it – already familiar.

'Do you know him?' It was only really occurring to her now. 'I mean, my father. Have you seen him much before?'

Kip thought. 'Yes. Well, I used to see him when I was much younger. He used to visit before I went away to school.'

'When was that?'

'Seven.'

Lara turned to him and caught him before he had time to smile. 'That's so young,' she said, imagining herself at seven still pressed against her mother's sleeping body, the cotton of her nightdress, the secret smell of her hair.

'Yes, but if you don't go to prep school, then you can't get into Eton.'

'And you have to get into Eton?'

'So it seems.'

'What a horrible, disgusting rule.'

'It wasn't that bad. Well, not after the first term of crying yourself to sleep.'

'No!'

'Of course not. Only a few hopeless bed-wetters were still crying by Christmas.'

Lara looked at the drive. 'Where's the car?' but he led her towards the road.

'I walked.' He pulled her with him. 'Along the sexy path.' And she had to run to catch up.

'Is that the path with all the . . . statues?'

'No!' Kip said. 'That's perverted. 'That's Papa's creepy idea of a joke. This path is actually . . .' He was laughing now. 'It actually is sexy.'

As soon as they were in the secret overgrown thicket of the wood, Kip grabbed her and pushed her up against a tree. 'See!'

Bark scraped through the material of her dress and a stray shoot of a twig spiked her in the calf. 'Ouch,' she screamed. 'Christ. Get off!'

'I'm sorry.' He let her go and stood, his hand over his mouth, watching as she rubbed her sore skin. 'Are you all right?' he asked then and she softened at the sight of his embarrassment.

'I'm fine.' She put her hand out to him and pulled him back against the tree, the twig nothing but a nuisance now, and held him tight against her as they kissed. Their kissing was official now, their eyes open, their hands free to explore.

'I always wanted something to happen in this wood.'

'So nothing to do with me?' Lara ran a hand up under his shirt.

'Well,' he laughed. 'I have to admit it does help that you're here.'

Lara pressed against him, feeling his stiffness quiver against her, the sweet kernel of heat rising inside, the hunger and the longing and the safety of this public path.

'Will you stay tonight?' he whispered breathless in her ear.

'I can't,' she whispered back. It was what Caroline wanted – for her to come home the next morning, her clothes bedraggled, her mascara running down her cheeks.

'No,' she said. 'I can't. I really can't.'

'Go on.' Kip nuzzled her ear. 'Please.'

'I can't.' She could see the porch light burning itself out. 'Maybe . . . tomorrow?'

'Tomorrow we're going to the waterfall. With everyone. Even Papa, even Pamela. But you could come over later.'

'Yes.'

Promise?' He looked into her eyes and when she said yes he squashed her almost breathless.

This, she thought, is the happiest day of my life, and she felt her whole body burning up with longing. I promise. She was promising herself, and they walked on, arm in arm, turning sideways to avoid having to separate when the path became too narrow. They squeezed under low branches, scraped past brambles and then sidestepped through the field of soft-leafed maize.

'Look.' Kip climbed on to a low wall and when she scrambled up she could see the field beyond, full of sunflowers, their faces, every one of them, turned their way.

They stood there for a while looking across the fields and up at the wooded hills on either side. Beyond them a jet of water was spraying out of a pump and as they watched it caught the sun and turned into a kaleidoscope of colours. They walked on until the house came into view. The red of its roofs clustered together, the old grey stone of its steps and streets, and above it, on the hill beyond, glinting white, the little chapel with its bell that tolled the hour.

'We should climb up there,' Lara said, remembering the statue that she'd never reached.

But Kip ran his fingers through his hair and yawned. 'Too lazy,' he said, and, giving her one last quick kiss, he moved away before she could return it.

At supper Andrew Willoughby was talking about the Queen. 'She's not entirely unattractive,' he told the young end of the table, 'and actually quite funny.' He'd been presented to her at a parliamentary function and had floundered around for something to say.

'Can I seek your advice, ma'am,' he said. 'I've been asked to a Right Honourables lunch and I don't know how to refuse.'

'You can't refuse,' she said. 'It's not an invitation, it's a command.'

'So how can I get out of it?' Andrew had lowered his voice.

'Feverish cold in the morning.' She spoke very quickly and moved on to greet another guest.

Antonia told a story about a party at an embassy. The Queen and Prince Charles were expected and, when they arrived, the guests all had to line up on either side of the room.

'We got the Queen's side, and when she reached Papa he said, "Antonia, do you know the Queen?"

' "No," I said, "I don't think I do," and then I couldn't help it, I just got the most terrible fit of the giggles. "I don't think I do." ' She said it again, and the whole table laughed uproariously.

Lara, not having any kind of royal story in her repertoire, kept as quiet as she could.

Lara woke from a dream where someone had placed a square of chocolate inside her – had set it delicately into the hollow entrance of her womb where it had sat undisturbed for many weeks. You said you weren't a virgin, Kip had accused her, and she realised she'd forgotten to meet and greet her Iris. Had forgotten she had one at all.

'Yes,' she woke herself with shouting, and she realised someone was knocking on the door. 'Come in.' She sat up in bed and she remembered with a flood of relief that she had switched off the porch light.

'Good morning.' It was Lambert. 'You'd better get up. They're coming for us at ten.'

'OK.' She pushed back the covers and it was only when he'd gone she realised she had no idea what he meant.

'The Willoughbys,' Lambert explained once she was downstairs. 'They've invited us out to the waterfall. The Love Falls. Everyone's going. I thought you'd like to.'

'Yes.' She looked at him, the bright-blue Speedo trunks flying up into her mind. 'But you don't have to come, if you don't . . .'

He withdrew very slightly from her. 'I thought I would,' he said, and silently he poured them both a cup of pale tea.

*　　*　　*

153

Andrew's car was the first to arrive at half-past ten. Andrew at the wheel, Pamela beside him, and the twins' mother, Elizabeth Butler, arrived from London, in an orange hat and matching amber beads, resplendent in the back. Lara hovered by the door.

'Hup hup,' Andrew called to her. 'Jump in. We have to catch up with the others,' and obeying orders she slid in beside Elizabeth's oiled and scented body moments before the car sped off.

Lambert was on the other side, just visible behind the wide brim of the orange hat, and when she got a chance, Lara leant forward and smiled at him, grateful that he had come after all, and as if he understood, he smiled back.

Andrew Willoughby drove fast, as fast as Roland, but without the overt desire to shock or kill. Lara leant against the window, her face into the wind, and let the rush of air and sunshine stream over her, dancing patterns of light across her skin, filling her nose and mouth and ears.

The others were already there when they arrived, a small kingdom marked out with towels and blankets, bottles of water, bowls of fruit, cigarettes, magazines and lighters. Groups had already formed, the twins hunched over on their towels, Tabitha, May and Piers laid out in a row, chatting, sharing a cigarette, and Antonia, her black swimsuit stretched over her strong body, challenging Roland and Kip to feats of wrestling, throwing first one and then the other into the pool. And there was Allegra, looking up through a cascade of hair, and a boy calling to her from the water. He was shouting and thrashing and then, as if riding the crest of a wave, he rose up out of the pool and was tossed aside and Lara saw that it was Hugh and Isabelle's son, Hamish, and he'd been sitting on his father's head.

'Hugh!' Andrew called. 'Good man,' and Lara felt her

father stiffen as Isabelle, in a white dress, looked up from her seat on the rock above.

'How very nice to see you.' He stepped up to her as she stepped down, and there was the faintest question mark in Lambert's smile.

Lara didn't meet Kip's eye. She spread out her towel on the rock and watched him fooling around, hurling himself into the water, diving, splashing and teasing, his head sleek as a seal. Self-conscious, she slipped out of her clothes, embarrassed to think he might be watching her, afraid that he might not, but when she looked up he was climbing the rock steps with his sister, her hand clutching his wrist.

'So how are you today?' Piers asked her as she tore her eyes away.

'I'm very well,' she said, and then forcing herself to be polite, 'And you?'

'Very good.'

There was a pause and so to stop herself from watching she turned her full attention on him. 'So . . . um . . .' What could she ask him? 'So . . . how did you and May meet?'

He looked at her as if he didn't quite see what she meant. 'Well . . . May . . . well, I don't know.' He thought for a while. No. He shook his head, irritated. 'She's always been around.'

Lara was stunned. How could he not remember the day they'd met? But then she saw what Piers was telling her – May was a member of his club. She'd always been around, just like Isabelle's daughter was around now. She looked up and caught Allegra gazing at the top pool, pushing back her hair just in time to smile as Kip came hurtling down.

Lara turned to Piers, but he had his back to her now and was leaning over May's shoulder looking at her magazine.

'She's had them done, you can tell.' Tabitha was staring at

the protruding breasts of a star. 'And that nose wasn't like that even last month, I swear.'

May flipped over the page but Piers caught her hand and turned it back. 'Hmm. Not bad.' He perused it – its button end, its perfect slope. 'But not as good as yours.'

'Shut up!' May ripped the page in her effort to turn it, and Tabitha glanced over and caught Lara's eye.

'She used to have a bit of a conk,' she mouthed dramatically. 'Poor girl, looked as if she were up for a part as Shylock.'

Instinctively Lara put her hand to her own nose, which had a small bump in the centre, just before it curved. 'You actually did?' was all she could say, reeling with how much it must have hurt. 'You had a nose job?' and she tried to imagine May without her perfect English rose face.

'She was very brave,' Piers said. 'It hurt like hell. Did you know they smash you in the face with a hammer?' and he put his arm round May, as if affronted that she should have had to go through such an ordeal.

For some time Lara lay face-down on her towel, feeling the sun scorch into her back. She could hear the voices of the various groups, the unmistakable tones of Andrew Willoughby, the raucous laugh of Elizabeth and Pamela's oddly mirthless chuckle. Occasionally Hugh would interrupt with a guffaw and even less often she heard her father's serious voice, but his utterances, usually so rapturously received, were dismissed or ignored completely, and Lara's heart ached in the silence after his last word.

Once when he was brutally interrupted by Andrew on the subject of Boswell and his many cases of gonorrhoea, Lara lifted herself on one elbow and glanced over. But Lambert didn't notice her. He was sitting on the edge of the blanket, a little behind the others, and he had his hand stretched out so that, as if by accident, it could brush against Isabelle's arm.

Isabelle looked uneasy, listening intently to all that was being said, and occasionally laughing her low laugh as if relieved to have something to do.

Slowly, much more slowly than the others, the older people were removing their clothes. Andrew was stripped to the waist, and Elizabeth had taken off her skirt and was rubbing oil down the long length of her shins. Pamela wore a raspberry one-piece with black piping and matching espadrilles, and Hugh had unbuttoned his shirt to show a ripple of warm flesh and an abundance of grey hair below his crumpled face. Only Lambert and Isabelle were still fully dressed. Isabelle looked cool in her white cotton shift, while Lambert was an island of formality, in shirt and trousers and black polished shoes. He even had his socks on, those fine ribbed silk-mix socks she'd woken to find rubbed up against her thigh on that long-ago train.

'Oh my God! Oh gruesome,' Tabitha gasped. 'This one's gone wrong!' And Lara rolled over to find her holding up a full-page picture of a woman, her eyes lifted in permanent surprise, her nose collapsed.

Eventually lunch was called and Kip, blue-veined with hours of cold, flung himself down beside her. Roland stood on her other side and shook himself, and every female around the tablecloth, including Lara, although she was appalled to have done so, squealed.

'Who is this man?' Andrew looked up.

'I'm your son-in-law.' Roland was rubbing at his hair, the muscles of his thighs straining, the sheer black briefs drying in a silhouette around the bulge of his crotch. 'The father of your about-to-be-born first grandson,' and he looked out from the soft white of his towel and flashed him a grin.

'I don't remember giving my permission,' Andrew muttered crossly, and he urged everyone to begin.

The food was sumptuous. Artichokes and broad beans, plates of prosciutto, asparagus with shavings of Parmesan, tomatoes chopped with mozzarella and basil, thick wedges of omelette baked with spinach, cheese and herbs. Lara heaped her plate, wondering how you could build up such an appetite lying, doing nothing, on a rock, and she glanced at Kip who was wolfing his down like a greyhound.

'So tell me.' Elizabeth was the first to speak. 'Is it fearfully dangerous, jumping down that waterfall?' Her question was really for anyone who'd done it, but her eyes swerved round to Roland.

'Not at all.' Roland had his mouth full and a slice of mozzarella squelched out from the side. 'It's the most wonderful fun. Why don't you try it?'

'I couldn't possibly,' she protested. 'I'm much too old and anyway . . .' She looked down at the orange halter-neck and the deep-tanned crevice of her cleavage. 'Everything would come flying out.'

'Pamela, my darling.' Roland creased his eyes. 'How about you?'

Pamela shook her head. 'I decline,' she said formally, but all the same it was clear she was glad to have been asked.

Hugh leant over and reached for a bottle of wine. 'We're all too old and cowardly,' he said, splashing red into a cup. 'You'd better leave us alone.'

Lara saw her father look up at the cliff. He shifted uneasily and she felt her stomach contract. 'I'll have a go.' His eyes were steely, and Lara had to stop herself from calling out.

There was a silence while everyone waited for Roland to dissuade him. 'You're on,' Roland grinned. 'But I'll bet you a fiver you won't go through with it.'

Lambert raised his eyebrows. 'We'll see,' he said, and he let his hand trail along the length of Isabelle's bare arm.

'For God's sake, man, let your lunch settle first.' Roland spiked a red curl of prosciutto, and he lay back to wait.

The remainder of lunch was subdued. Lara ate what she could and regretted having served herself so much. What would happen, she thought, if he got to the lip of the pool and then panicked and had to be helped back down? She glanced across at Isabelle, willing her to intervene, but Isabelle was busy urging Hamish to eat something, anything green, even offering to lick the salad dressing off a bean if he agreed to try.

All around them others were eating too. It was the Italian hour for lunch, and families and groups of young people sat like them, around a central feast of food. But unlike the Italian families who accepted that after lunch was a time of repose, Hamish, Allegra, Kip and Antonia threw themselves back into the water as soon as they'd had enough.

'Hamish!' Isabelle called. 'Wait five minutes at least,' but in the face of other influences she let her voice trail off.

Lara thought she caught disapproval in the murmuring of women in flowered pinnies and in the half-closed eyes of fathers already preparing for a snooze. Men with short legs and round taut stomachs, old men the same age as Lambert.

Lara looked over at her father and saw he had undressed. He was standing staring at the water wearing only his blue trunks. His legs looked narrow and pale, but his chest, his neck and arms were strong. Maybe he will do it, Lara allowed herself to hope, and she purposefully looked away from the vulnerable bald spot on the back of his head.

'Right!' Roland stood up and stretched, beating a quick tattoo on his full stomach. 'Ready when you are.'

Lambert was already walking away, climbing, navigating the shallow footholds in the rocks that rose steeply to the top.

Roland winked at the others. 'We have a champion in the making,' and he clambered after him.

There was silence as everybody watched. For God's sake, Lara wanted to shout, leave him alone, but it was impossible to take her eyes off Lambert as he climbed. Lara hardly noticed when Kip stood close beside her, couldn't feel the electricity that usually sparked between them.

And there he was, standing, silhouetted against the sky. A moment later Roland stood behind him, so stupid, Lara thought, her heart in her mouth, that he would actually be capable of pushing him off the edge.

'Old fool,' Andrew Willoughby muttered. 'Go on then!'

Lambert began to step out along the rushing stones of the waterfall, his arms outstretched for balance. He stopped in the middle, just as the others had done. And waited. Lara felt sure she could see him measuring with his eyes, and she thought she heard Roland shouting out instructions to him over the roar, but Lambert didn't look round.

'Here he goes,' Kip said, forgotten, beside her, and it was true Lambert was leaning forward, his body tensed, and he was falling, shooting out with the spray, his body braced against the torrent, and everyone, for all Lara knew, everyone in the valley, gave a cheer. But he wasn't falling like the others. Kip, Roland, even Antonia, had leapt out from the water, had jumped rather than been taken, and now she saw her father was falling too close to the cliff.

'Shit!' Antonia said, and just at that moment he hit the water and disappeared.

Like a streak Roland jumped from above. He hit the water, bobbed back under, and while the others were still paralysed on their rock, he rose to the surface pulling Lambert with him.

Lara ran down to the water. 'Dad,' she called. 'Dad?'

Roland had his arm around him.

'Bring him up here.' Isabelle was running with a towel.

'I'm perfectly all right.' Lambert was limping, and he tried shrugging Roland off, but as his foot touched down pain shot through him and he nearly fell. 'I felt it crack,' he said, and he turned away and retched. There was a white gash along the side of his foot, filling up with blood, and his little toe was hanging loosely. 'I'm fine,' he said again, recovering himself, and he waved away the glass of wine that Elizabeth offered. 'I just didn't . . .' He made a sort of measuring movement with one hand. 'I didn't quite clear it.'

'But almost . . .' Isabelle was beside him, dabbing at the blood with a napkin. 'It looked marvellous at first . . .'

Lambert leant into her encircling arm. 'Yes . . . it did feel marvellous. Rather like flying and swimming all at the same time.'

He sank down then on the towel and Lara, who was sitting by, saw his face was pale.

'Is he all right?' she whispered to Isabelle, as he closed his eyes. She wanted to touch him, to put her hand on his forehead, but that wasn't how it was. 'Dad,' she whispered instead. 'Can I get you anything?' But he only moved his lips in a little breath of no.

'He's shivering,' Pamela said, and relieved to have something to do the women shook the crumbs from a large soft rug and tucked it over him.

'Dad?' she whispered urgently, but he answered her only with a faint smile.

'He's tough as anything,' Andrew said irritably. 'It's the shock. Leave him alone. Let him rest.'

'There's no fool like an old fool, eh?' Hugh shook his head

and with a celebratory pop he pulled the cork from another bottle of wine.

Lambert sat back against a rock, his leg raised a little on a bed of towels. His foot was already starting to swell, puffing pale-purple around the toes, and every time he moved it Lara saw him swallow in a concerted effort to control the pain. What if he'd fallen differently? If he'd hit his head, broken his neck? Lara felt herself quake, and she thought each time she looked at him that he was paler. For the first time it occurred to her – and it seemed idiotic that it never had before – that she knew almost nothing about him. She'd accepted his reserve and refrained from asking even the most natural questions. Did you have brothers and sisters? What happened to your parents? Why did you never fall in love? She said it now in their silent conversation, but of course he didn't answer. Why had she been so obedient? Why had she stuck fast to his rules? She put out a hand and touched his shoulder but he only flinched.

'I think we should get him back,' Lara said, speaking only to Isabelle, and without waiting for the others she began to gather up their things.

'I'll drive you,' Isabelle agreed and, with Andrew's cold eyes resting on her, they hoisted him up, one on each side, and helped him towards her white car.

'How was it?' Caroline came out to them, eyes raised at the unexpected vehicle.

'Lambert's a little hurt,' Isabelle called to warn her.

'I'm fine,' he shouted, swinging open the door, and as if to prove it he began to limp, the blanket still draped round him, his foot and leg streaked with dried blood.

'One invalid not enough for this household? Is that it?' Caroline shook her head, and she went in to call the doctor.

'There's no need,' Lambert insisted, but Ginny came out, and seeing him hurt she literally began to squeak. 'Oh no, oh no,' she repeated in her high mouse voice, and she manoeuvred him into a chair.

'Whatever happened?' Caroline was back.

'Well. It was . . .' Lara wanted to blame Roland.

'It was just bad luck.' Her father cut her off. 'I was foolish.' He winced. 'I didn't jump out far enough. I felt it instantly. My toe. It just went snap. I'm so sorry.'

'My dear . . .' Caroline soothed. 'The doctor will be here soon.'

'I'm perfectly all right.' He looked up at her. 'It's only a toe.'

'Yes,' she agreed. 'Of course it is.'

'It's not as if I'm a footballer. Or a jockey. I'll still be able to write.'

'But do you think . . .' Caroline bent down to him. 'That you'll be recovered by next week, for the Palio?'

'Of course. I'm well enough already.' Lambert reached over for his paper. 'Which horse am I riding again?'

'Dad!' Lara laughed, and she wished that she was still allowed to touch his hand.

Isabelle waited until the doctor had examined him.

'I imagine,' Caroline said, 'they're all waiting to hear the news at Ceccomoro.'

'Yes.' Isabelle gathered up her things. 'I had better . . .'

'Yes.' Caroline held the door for her. 'And do give Hugh my regards, I expect he'll be wondering where you are.' She smiled at her coolly.

The doctor had suggested Lambert keep his foot raised for several weeks and then to be as careful as possible not to knock it. 'A toe will never really heal,' Caroline had translated. 'If you nudge it against anything it can just break again.'

'The Italians.' Lambert had dismissed this. 'They always were a melodramatic lot. Several weeks.' He shook his head. 'I'll be better by tomorrow.'

They ate supper in the sitting room with napkins on their knees while Ginny rushed in and out checking all was well.

'There's someone outside,' she said as she came in, a bowl of berries on a tray, and a jug of hot white chocolate sauce. 'No one's knocked, but I can see a shadow . . . hovering.'

Just then Kip put his head round the door. 'I just wanted to say . . . I hope Mr Gold is feeling better.'

'Thank you.' Lambert looked at him. 'That's very kind.'

'Will you have a drink?' Caroline offered, and so Kip sat down with them, and they all watched him, his wide mouth and deep-blue eyes, his self-consciousness and confidence and odd, unlikely ease. He stayed and had another drink, and then another while Lambert eyed him as if he were an animal, examining him with such scrutiny that Lara could watch him too without being observed.

And then Caroline yawned. 'How will you get back?' she asked, and Kip, well trained, stood up.

'I'll walk. It's fine. The only thing is . . .' He looked directly at Lara. 'Lara promised to come up and stay at Ceccomoro tonight. It's been arranged.'

Lara was so taken aback she could hardly breathe.

'Well.' Caroline smiled to show that nothing Kip wanted would ever be refused. 'Lara. You'd better go up and get your things.'

Lara looked at her father. 'I'm not sure . . .' But her heart was thumping and nothing could have made her stay. She would have leapt from a window if she'd had to, or slid like Rapunzel down a rope of her own hair.

Lambert put his head on one side. 'If it's been arranged.'

Lara took her nightdress from under her pillow, her toothbrush, hairbrush and a change of clothes and, even though she knew it would not be opened, her book. She pushed them into a bag and ran back down.

'She'll be back tomorrow,' Kip promised, and they stood at the door, innocent as two potholers on a hike.

'Bye then.' Lara ran back to her father and leaning down over him she pressed her lips against his cheek. Are you sure, she asked him with her eyes, and she could have sworn that he said yes.

As soon as they were outside Kip began to laugh dementedly. 'I didn't think I could do it!' and reaching for her hand he ran with her along the road. ' "Well." ' He mimicked Caroline's clipped voice. ' "You'd better go up and get your things," ' and Lara had the horrible sensation that the whole thing had been a dare.

Once they were inside the sexy wood Kip pressed her to him. 'I missed you today,' and she realised that today, for the first time since they'd met, she hadn't thought of him.

'I missed you too,' she said, because she wished she had, and she leant back against what had already become their tree and gave in to their kissing.

They were getting good at it. Their mouths were unafraid, their tongues singing. They kissed until their kiss was the entire world. But Kip's hands were urgent too. They ran over her body, cupping her breasts, fumbling and unfastening her clothes. She could feel his belt buckle somehow come loose, the heat of the metal digging into her side.

'We haven't got . . . I haven't . . .' She tried to stall him, but he was pressing so hard against her, his face pushed into her neck. 'It's not safe,' she said.

He stopped and looked at her. 'Even if we had a baby,' he said, 'I wouldn't mind.'

Lara felt herself reeling. I don't believe you. She knew it was a lie, but all the same it was thrilling. If they had a baby she would be linked to him for ever. To him and all this too. Ceccomoro, the rose gardens and statues, and to some huge cold house somewhere in Yorkshire, with its estate, its cattle grids and farms.

'It's all right.' He was tugging at her underwear, pushing the cotton of her knickers over to one side.

She stood on tiptoe, helping him, flattening her back, drawing up one leg. They were breathing hard, frowning in concentration. We'll never do it. Her legs were trembling. But just then, as if it was meant to be, he was inside her. Lara opened her eyes, and for a moment they stood quite still and looked at each other. They'd done it, and they stayed like that, moving gently, their mouths a little open, weaving snake patterns up against the tree.

'Are you ready?' he breathed, and not knowing what he meant, she nodded just as he began to thrust against her so hard and furiously that she lost all sense of him, and of herself, could only feel his heat and desperation while she clung to him, following the thin thread of her desire, like coloured silk, until she felt him grow inside her, swell, and with one great shudder he was still.

Lara smoothed down her dress and was amazed to remember she still had her knickers half on. Kip turned away and buckled up his belt, buttoning his flies, leaving his shirt loose. That was the second time, it occurred to Lara, and she still hadn't seen a real-life penis. Would she ever see one, or would she go through her whole life with her eyes closed tight?

'Are you all right?' Kip looked carefree and a little embarrassed.

'Yes,' she said, but there was a sticky wetness coating each thigh that stung when she walked. 'Do you have . . .?' She was going to ask for a tissue, and then she remembered her overnight bag.

'Are you always so well prepared?' he asked her, and she picked up a handful of dry leaves and threw them at him.

They walked on, hand in hand. It was very dark and every rustle, now they weren't so distracted, reminded them there were wild boar living in these woods.

'What is that?' She stopped. She could hear the gypsy music high in the hills above them. 'Listen.' She tugged at his hand.

'It's the communists.' The music floated down to them in bursts. 'They must be celebrating something. Another kidnap maybe.' He squeezed her hand.

'But do they really kidnap people?'

'Sure.' Kip sounded nonchalant. 'Only a few years ago they got the former Prime Minister, Aldo Moro, held him for fifty-five days and then murdered him. He was found in the boot of a car.'

'Really?' Every nerve in Lara's body jangled. It won't last, she thought, it can't last, but even so her heart soared.

'Actually,' Kip went on, 'they might have found him before. They had a tip-off about his whereabouts, it came from someone in the government, but guess where they said it actually came from?'

Lara opened her eyes wide to show she had no idea.

'A Ouija board!' he whispered, and they both began to run.

*   *   *

There were people still sitting outside at the long table when they arrived at Ceccomoro, lit up by candles and lamps, lounging on benches and chairs. Andrew, Antonia, Roland, and as they drew closer Lara made out the half-slumped figure of Hugh and, as far away as it was possible to get from him, Isabelle petting a small dog.

No one saw them approach, and Lara hoped they might slip by, but as they neared the table Roland snapped round and caught them. 'Come and have a drink.' He reached out and grabbed her hand, and so, followed by Kip, she slid on to the cool slats of a wooden chair and accepted a tumbler of wine.

'The kind of woman I find most attractive, and I'm not proud to admit this . . .' Andrew Willoughby was holding forth. 'Is the kind of woman that is most likely to make my friends jealous. Someone really, very obviously, good-looking. Really stunning. Like Pamela, obviously.' He looked around and noticed that, if she'd ever been there, she was gone. 'Hmm.' He seemed dumbfounded as if he'd wasted a compliment on thin air. 'A little firecracker.' He was staring down the table at Isabelle now, who, with her plain hair and rough hands, glanced up, aloof.

'It's the subtle ones I like.' Roland stretched his arm around Lara and squeezed her right breast.

Her hiss of protest was drowned out by Hugh. 'Rubbish.' He was having trouble focusing. 'There's nothing subtle about Tabitha. She's the most beautiful of all the beautiful girls I know.'

'I wasn't thinking of her,' Roland said, but Andrew bowed his head as if the compliment was his. 'Thank you. She is lovely. It's true.'

Kip stayed quiet.

'I'll tell you the kind of person I find really attractive.'

Antonia took a slug of wine. 'The ones that no one else fancies, that only I have discovered.'

'The old dogs,' Roland said and Antonia pouted. 'Mmmm, yes please.'

'But you never introduce me to these dogs. Hmm. Why is that?' Andrew demanded.

Antonia turned away.

Lara wished the evening would end. She wanted to sleep. With or without Kip. To lie flat in cool sheets and end this day. She slipped her hand along the bench and pressed it against Kip. He moved his body very slightly to acknowledge her, but he didn't look round.

'The thing is . . .' Hugh said, his words slurring, his eyes droopy as a dog, 'so much beauty is in the eye of the beholder and so much of the zebolder . . .' He was tangling himself up now. 'Confidence!' He tried to rescue his theory. 'That's what gets us through.' Defeated, he laid his head on the table, and although everyone laughed he left it there and soon his snoring testified to the fact he was asleep.

The conversation went on without him. Roland and Antonia sparring across the table, while Andrew crept through the shadowy dark towards Isabelle, bending down beside her to nuzzle the dog.

'You can't drive back.' His voice was low. 'It's unthinkable.'

Lara stood up. She took Kip's arm. 'Where shall I sleep?'

'I'll show you,' and they walked round the side of the house, past the swimming pool, around the edge of the garden, past an overhanging roof from which a hammock was strung, and up a flight of stone steps. Kip pushed open a heavy wooden door, led her across a tiled hall, up another staircase, a wooden one, where finally he opened a door into a small, plain whitewashed room. There was a bed with a bleached-white cotton cover and one window, the shutters thrown open, a view on to the starry night.

'You can sleep in here,' he said, and hearing steps below them he kissed her quickly on the mouth. 'I'll be back later. The bathroom's along the hall.' She heard him clatter, whistling, down the stairs.

Lara pulled on her nightdress, and wandered out into the corridor. There were several doors. She tried one, and found another bedroom, empty, and then another with nothing in it but a chest of books. The third door she tried she found the bathroom, a room so full of moonlight she didn't bother flicking on the switch. She filled her hands with water and pressed them against her face. She felt ashen with tiredness, parched and empty, but when she looked up into the mirror all she saw were the bright-brown freckles of her tan. She brushed her teeth, rinsed and spat, and was just turning when she heard a voice. She stopped, her hand on the door.

'I think you're being absurd.' It was Isabelle, and she was laughing.

Whoever was with her was not charmed. 'I'm never wrong. Don't take me for a fool,' the man said.

'Andrew. I wouldn't. I don't.'

With one toe Lara pushed the door closed.

'You were with him. You were with him that time in London, and last week when I called.'

'No.' Lara could almost feel Isabelle shaking her head through the wall.

'And I know why he's doing it,' Andrew persisted.

'Why?'

'So you admit it?'

'No. I'm just curious, that's all.'

'Are you saying you don't know?' Andrew Willoughby gave a dry laugh. 'I spent bloody years. A decade of fruitless fucking. Getting nothing but girls. And then some cunt whisks in and suddenly my wife is giving birth to a son.'

'You can't mean . . .?'

'Isn't it obvious?'

'No.'

Lara looked down into the bath. There was a yellow stain where the water must have dripped, the enamel eaten away, green and brown in layers.

'So.' Isabelle was wary. 'Is that why you're after me? Revenge?'

'Not at all.' She could hear the rasp of his breathing. 'I'm after you because I can't resist you. Because you're gorgeous. Because your husband is asleep, and he will never know. And anyway.' His voice was sly. 'You said you were never with him.'

'So there you go. I never was,' Isabelle soothed, and she could hear them falling against walls as they staggered away along the corridor. There was the creak of a door opening, a low chuckle, and then quiet.

Lara trod as silently as she could along the hall and slipped into her room. She climbed into the bed, which was high and narrow, and pressing her face into the pillow she tried to sleep. Where was he? She wanted Kip beside her. Wanted him to press his body against hers. 'A decade of fruitless fucking.' She felt a rush of sadness. A great well of it, oozing through her veins, and she remembered her mother saying that Lambert had never intended to have children. That's why, she'd told her, you're so special. 'You showed him what he didn't know.' Her mother had cried a few soft tears when Lara told her about the invitation to Italy. 'You see,' she said. 'He's grateful to have you now.'

Lara shifted in the bed. Kip? She sat up, but it was only the shutters creaking. She lay back down and pushed her fingers in between her legs. She was still wet, a filmy wet like glue. Could it be useful, she wondered, for sticking envelopes or smoothing eyebrows flat? She brought her fingers up into the moonlight to examine them.

Just then there were footsteps on the stairs. Hurriedly she wiped herself dry with her nightdress, and pulling it down she closed her eyes. Her heart was beating and she forced herself to slow her breath. The steps approached, hesitated and then she heard the handle turn. She wanted to jump up, to throw herself into Kip's arms, but of course she wasn't meant to care. Instead she lay still, pretending to sleep.

For a moment there was silence, and then feet were slipping out of shoes, the clunk of a belt buckle falling as trousers hit the floor. And he was leaning over her. Her heart was beating crazily, her mouth flickering on the edges of a smile, and she felt a chill of air that sent her skin to goose bumps as the cover was lifted and he slid in.

'Hello.' His voice was hoarse, and oddly changed, and then a heavy arm draped down around her. It smelt of aftershave and suntan oil, and there was a thick metal watch chain that nipped her skin.

Lara opened her eyes. She felt her stomach flip and rise into her throat. 'What are you doing here?' She didn't turn. She didn't want his face so close to hers. 'Roland. I'm telling you. Get out!'

'Aren't you pleased to see me?' His voice was low. 'Lover boy passed out. Not man enough to take his drink. And I thought – poor Comrade Lara, all alone, waiting and waiting . . .' He began to walk his fingers, incy wincy spider, over her skin.

'I was asleep.' She struggled to sit up. 'Go away.'

'You wouldn't be so mean.' He was stroking her now, running his hand along her leg. She kicked to shake him off.

'I'm telling you!' And then she remembered that Andrew and Isabelle were somewhere on this floor. If they heard her, they'd know that she'd heard them.

'I think you're a little bit of a tease . . .' Roland murmured, sliding up the bed beside her, and when she protested, 'I'm not a tease,' he threw his head back and laughed. 'I said I think you're a bit tense, that's all. Here.' His hands were on her again. 'Let me give you a massage.'

Lara's eyes were on the door. 'No thanks.' She could make a run for it. Race down the stairs, try and find Kip's room, or even May's. But what if she rushed into Tabitha's room, or Hugh's, then how would she explain?

'Just a little rub. I'll do your shoulders,' Roland persisted, and so she turned away from him and offered up her back.

Roland's hands were oddly ineffectual. They rubbed and slipped against the cotton of her nightdress. 'Can't you take this off?' he said. 'It's hopeless.'

Tears pricked against her eyes. 'Please,' she said, 'just go away.'

In sympathy he put his arms around her and kissed the side of her face. 'I'm not that bad,' he said. 'You'll like it.' He stroked her hair. 'Many others have.'

'I won't,' she said. 'I don't want to.'

She wished she'd learnt judo or karate so that she could leap up now and, keeping her balance, floor him silently with one kick. But he was holding her, crooning, singing a little song. He was stroking her hair, fondling her ears, and for the moment anyway she felt safe.

'OK, let's just go to sleep,' he said, sliding with her down into the bed.

They lay spooned together, their breathing slow, Lara, her every sense alert in case he should move the arm that lay sprawled across her, moments from her breasts. She felt like a clam, curled into herself, but the more she curled the more vulnerable she was behind, and she was right, his hand was slipping across her drawn-up knees, edging over the ruck of her nightdress, sliding up the exposed skin of her thigh.

She moved her own hand fast and caught him. 'No.' She pulled his arm back around her and placed it on the sheet where she could see it. 'For God's sake,' she said, and her voice, irritable as a schoolmistress, made him laugh.

'Very stern,' he said, and for a moment she thought he was going to seize her and spin her round, but he stayed still.

He stayed still for so long that very gradually she started to relax. He had one leg over hers. A leg as heavy as a log, and his groin, she could feel it, encased in hot tight cotton, was pressed into her side. And then, as if in his sleep, he began to move his hand, so slowly she could hardly accuse him, the palm kneading her leg. It was nice. Soothing. If only it was Kip. And then his hand dropped down against her stomach. She held her breath. Could he be asleep?

For a while he was still and then slowly he began to move again, in lazy circles. She felt like a kitten or a baby being stroked, but revolted too, if she allowed herself to think. Soon, she repeated. Soon he'll be asleep and I can slip away, but just then his hand, the flat of it, rose higher and brushed against her nipple. Inspite of herself she felt a streak of fire run through her. She swallowed and moved, squashing both breasts into the mattress, but he moved with her so that his knee was between her legs and she was pinned. Lara kept her breathing even, her mind numb. *I'll* pretend to sleep, she thought, and then when he's not expecting it I'll throw him off. She tested her leg against his but it was made of stone.

'Mmm,' he drooled in response. 'This feels nice. And if you're worrying about my wife – solidarity with women and all that – she won't mind. She'd be relieved. Get me off her back for once.' He began to laugh and Lara felt the wetness of his dribble on her neck.

'I won't tell her,' Lara promised. 'Just go back to your room,' and again she tried to shift his weight.

'There's nothing to tell.' He stretched his arm over and caught her wrist. 'Come on, just give me a kiss.'

'No!'

'Go on.' He was sliding over her, the rough stubble of his cheek scraping her face, and she remembered hearing that prostitutes were prepared to do anything – anything! – but kiss. He was on top of her now and she freed her other arm, but as soon as she did he caught it. 'What will you do now, little Bolshevik?' He was crouching above her and the only way she could get up was to thrust herself backwards and into his lap.

'You're pathetic,' she said, and she tried to rip one arm free, but his grip was iron. 'Ow.'

The skin was stinging, and she tugged again and with no warning he pushed her hard against the bedhead and forced himself against her. He must have used his free hand to release himself because his cock, that was the right word for it, was hard and dry and forcing itself against her. Roughly he pushed her legs wider and with a grunt he was inside, tearing, gasping, sighing, forcing her up against the wall.

Lara closed her eyes. She wanted to be sick. She wanted to turn her head and bite him, and she realised she'd thought, right until that minute, that it was all some kind of joke. But she wouldn't call out. She couldn't. She didn't ever want anyone to know. Instead she stayed as still as she could and waited for it to be over. His body was hot and convulsing and draped over hers and she felt him straining and rigid in every nerve. She closed her mind off too, so that she saw nothing

175

but a long bright streak of colour, a sunset along a muddy river. And it was over. He was still. Head bent against her neck. Releasing her hands.

She heard him swallow. 'Sorry,' he muttered.

She didn't look round. If she could manage it, she'd never look at him again. Lara slipped down into the bed, her face turned to the window, and pulled the sheet as high as it would go.

'That wasn't so bad, was it?' Roland reached down to his jeans and pulled out a pack of cigarettes. 'May I?' he asked, but she didn't answer.

There was a pause while he lit up and exhaled.

'You weren't a virgin?' There was a tremor of uncertainty in his voice.

'No.' She was relieved to be able to answer with the truth.

'So what was all the fuss? Unless . . .' He laughed. 'You find me repellent? No,' he continued after three slow smoke rings. 'Unless you're saving yourself for Kip.'

Tears welled up and filled her eyes.

'You really like him?' Roland leant over and peered into her face. 'You really like the little sod.' He shook his head as if at her stupidity. 'You and the world. I'd better warn him.' But instead of getting up to do so he pushed himself down further into the bed and resting one arm on the mound of her hip he continued to smoke.

Lara stared out of the window. Already the sky was not as dark as it had been, the first dawn light was turning it to grey. She lay still – there was nothing else to do – and pulled her nightdress close. The stars were gone now and birdsong twittered up from the garden below. I'll never sleep, she thought, her eyes gritty, her body seared through with heat and shame. But slowly she began to relax, and reassured by the rhythm of Roland's snores, and too tired to keep her muscles tensed a moment longer, she allowed herself to sink against the bulwark of his body.

Lara woke to find herself alone. She lay still, hoping to convince herself the night had been a dream, but she could tell from the ache in her arms, the sting between her legs, and the one sharp scratch across her wrist, that it was real.

As quietly as she could she dressed. What time was it? The house felt silent, the garden empty below, but the sun was already high above her and the room was warm.

She opened the door and looked along the hall. There was no one. Nothing, and so she ran, not glancing at the row of white wooden doors, all closed. 'Hello?' she warned as she turned the handle of the bathroom, but there was no one there. For a long minute she stared at herself in the mirror, amazed once again to see no sign of change, and then she splashed her face with water, over and over, until the smell of Roland was gone.

'Thank God you're back.' Ginny greeted her at the door, and lowering her voice she told her, 'Your father's had a fever. He's been calling for you. At least we think it's you.' She turned towards the sitting room, a glass of water in her hand, and Lara followed.

Lambert looked strangely small. He lay on the sofa, draped in a blanket, his face pale, his hair spiky with sweat.

'Oh there you are.' He put out a hand.

'Dad.' Lara sank to her knees beside him. 'Are you all right?'

'Not too bad.' He smiled and she felt a stab of pain to think she mattered to him. 'I won't go anywhere again,' she told him. 'I'll stay here with you.'

'No.' He tried to sit up. 'I'm perfectly all right.'

'Shhh.' She put her hand on his shoulder and he lay back.

She saw his foot then. It was swollen, black and green, the bruise having spread in a river of colour up towards his ankle. Who would have thought such a tiny bone could set up such a protest?

'The doctor is coming again,' Ginny said. She set a bowl of steaming water down on the floor in which rosemary and lavender leaves floated. 'If you could soak your foot in this,' she said, 'it would be very healing.' Lambert didn't move. Ginny dipped a flannel and wrapped it round his foot, brushing against his toe just momentarily and causing him to wince.

Lara sat by his side on a low chair. What could she say to distract him? Unable to think of anything, she pulled her book out from her overnight bag and began to read to him from *The Grapes of Wrath*.

'You're back, I see.' Caroline came down from her afternoon sleep, and just for a moment she eyed Lara with real interest. 'Isn't it the most wretched luck' – she smiled down at Lambert – 'but hopefully in a day or two . . .'

Caroline was swathed in layers of organza, cream, pale-yellow and lilac with the finest matching silk ribbon in her hat. Her wrists and ankles were so narrow that the bones protruded, giving her a newborn-animal look.

'You smell marvellous,' Lambert murmured as she bent over to brush his cheek with a kiss.

'Well, I'm off to Siena. Today is the day they bring the earth to the Campo. They bring it from the countryside and lay it down to make the track. In fact Antonio always used to say to me if I was ill, or low, "Don't worry, soon they will bring the *terra* – the earth – to the Piazza. It is a sign that the

Palio is really very near." ' Once more she leant down over Lambert and as if it were quite natural began to stroke his hair. 'Don't worry,' she whispered in a soft Italian accent, 'soon they will bring the earth to the Piazza.'

Lara shot a quick look at her father to see if he thought Caroline was mad. It was as if she were drunk. Drunk, or Italian.

'I shall go and touch the earth,' she said, beaming at them, and ignoring their bemused faces she left the room.

Lambert closed his eyes. 'Is it time for my medication?' he asked, trying to sound casual, but beads of sweat were standing out on his forehead.

'Your painkillers?' Ginny was already there. 'You should ideally . . . no, I think it is time,' and she tipped two large capsules into her hand and passed him the glass of water.

As soon as the pills began to work his face relaxed, his fists softened and he turned to Lara, his eyes half closed. 'Did you have a nice evening,' he asked, as if he'd only just noticed she was back, 'at Ceccomoro?' and she nodded, very fast.

Soon Lambert was asleep. Lara sat beside him a little longer. It didn't seem right to watch someone without their permission but even so, while Ginny was out of the room, she allowed herself to stare. His ears were small – she'd never noticed that before – tight against his head. No lobes. That means something, she thought, at least to the Chinese, but whatever it was she couldn't remember. His skin, in the bare patches between stubble, was fine and powdery smooth. He had a web of lines across his forehead, a groove down each side of his mouth. His eyes were deep-set, his lashes pale with age, but his eyebrows were raised as if even in sleep he was intrigued. His nose was large, much larger than it ever looked when he was animated, and it had the same kink and curve to it, although magnified, twice the size of hers. She brushed her hand against his and although his eyelids flickered he didn't stir.

'It's OK,' she said, and she thought of their ritual of the Perrier water and the way they'd shared the last flat sips. 'Shh,' she said, although he was silent, and when she could think of no other reason to keep sitting there she wandered up to her room.

'Lara?' Ginny's whisper followed her up the stairs. 'Lara!' but she didn't trust herself not to cry in front of Ginny so she stepped into the bathroom and quickly turned the handle of the shower, drowning out her voice.

Lara stood for a long time under the running water. She washed herself, hard and businesslike, as if it were not her body but an old chair she was rubbing down. She lathered shampoo into her hair, kneading her scalp, scratching at it, twisting the water out with a last yank, feeling the violence in her fingertips, knowing they were meant for Roland. Just thinking his name made her want to scratch herself, draw blood, and in some kind of hopeless retribution she peed right there in the shower, seeing the yellow stream mix and wash away between her feet. She couldn't imagine why, but it made her feel better, and she got out and wrapped herself in a towel. No, she said silently to the mirror where she usually stopped to admire herself, and she climbed into bed.

She woke to the sound of Ginny's high voice. 'She's still sleeping. She's been sleeping all morning.' There was a mumble and then Ginny again. 'Mr Gold? He's sleeping too. He's not at all well. But come in and wait.' Lara held her breath. 'Oh do come in. I could make you a cold drink. Lara's bound to be up soon.'

Ginny's voice was louder than usual, echoing up, she imagined, for the benefit of her own ears, but not long after there was the crunch of gravel, and crawling to the window she saw Kip slouching away. He was wearing dark jeans and a purple-and-white-striped shirt and even from there she could see that his shoulders were hunched. Lara knelt on the floor, her eyes above the sill, and watched him go. It made her heart ache, but she couldn't call, not till she was sure she could contain her secret, force it down so deep it didn't show.

Lara crawled back to her bed. She wanted to sleep again, lose herself in dreams, but hard as she tried she couldn't manage it. Reluctantly she got dressed. She put on old shorts and a faded T-shirt and went downstairs. She took her college books with her and looking in on her father, who lay stretched out on the sofa, she tiptoed out on to the terrace, avoiding Ginny who was busy rolling pastry at the table, and went down to the pool. She piled her books up in the shade under a lounger and with a frown to prove to herself she was serious she opened the first one on a chapter about Britain at the time of the French Revolution, and marking and underlining words and passages, she read a letter written to the Earl of Dartmouth in 1791:

All Birmingham is in an uproar. The meeting of the Revolutionists to celebrate the infamous Revolution in France has given occasion to the most dreadful proceedings. Someone had written in large characters on the Church 'To Be Let', or 'This barn to be let or pulled down', for the report of the writing is various. So great was the offence taken at this writing that the mob assembled and destroyed all the windows of the hotel where the Revolutionists met. They then burnt down the new meeting house, the old meeting house, and Dr Priestley's house at Fair Hill with everything therein contained. The Doctor had escaped into Shropshire, or he would certainly have made his last exit. The mob solemnly cut off his head in effigy.

Cut off his head. Lara thought and she knew she would have to do something violent. She swiped at an oleander, stamped to scare a salamander, which darted away, and still seething she took off her clothes and not bothering to go back up to the house for her bikini she jumped naked into the pool. The water sliced up between her legs, cut in under her armpits, stung the roof of her mouth. She forced herself to the bottom, opened her eyes to see the other world of it, the tiny bubbles of her breathing, the leaf points of her hands. She felt swift and strong. She kicked and spun, keeping herself under, her head reeling until finally she was sucked upwards where, her lungs tearing, she burst into the air. There was no one around. She cut through the water in backstroke, baring herself to the sky, kicking against the side and turning until every sinew in her body felt strong.

'Lara?' It was Ginny, calling from the terrace. 'Lunch,' and Lara felt so grateful to her that she almost skidded as she ran naked to the lounger for her clothes.

Caroline was out all the next day too, watching over her horse, the one she hoped would race in the Palio, and Lambert continued to sleep.

'It's the painkillers,' Ginny said, more confident with every day. 'And the shock. It's good for him to rest.'

Lara took her book and went and sat beside him, but really she was watching. The more she watched him, the more she noticed. The veins on his hands, the clean-cut whiteness of his nails, the sprout of hair protruding from the unbuttoned top of his pyjamas. He slept with his head turned to the side, and she realised that this was the part of him that was most familiar. This view of his jaw, half turned away, as if she'd been watching him like that her whole life. All afternoon she sat with him. The kitchen was silent, the house quiet and the only noise apart from her father's slow breathing was the hectic rustling of crickets.

Eventually Ginny came in to prepare supper, and Lara sat on a high stool and watched her instead. She made it look so simple, slicing pears, dipping down to lift the core, sliding them into a dish of melting butter, sprinkling them with sugar. She dropped in a vanilla pod and placed them in a low oven, and rolling up her sleeves still further she began making gnocchi. She mashed already cooked potatoes into a purée, kneading in flour, butter, salt, pepper and eggs. She rolled it under her hands until she had a long thin worm and then with a knife cut it, brutally, into many smaller worms. She dented each one with her finger so that they curled into a crescent, elegant again, and set them aside while she made a sauce.

When I get home, Lara thought, I'll amaze my mother with this dish, and she thought disparagingly of the watery tomato sauce they made for their spaghetti, the onions and mushrooms still visible amid the tinned lumps of the pulp.

'You have to let it reduce,' Ginny taught her as they watched her sauce turn thick and treacly with simmering, but the truth was that she and Cathy were always in too much of a hurry, too ravenous to leave anything to simmer.

And in Finsbury Park there was very little to remind them of Italy. The shops were almost all West Indian. Yams and sweet potatoes spilling out on to the street. Melons and papayas and a multitude of roots and bulbs and knobbly, prickly, star-shaped fruit for which she didn't have a name. There were Cypriot shops too which sold white loaves of bread sprinkled with sesame, tubs of humous and taramasalata, white packets of feta and black vinegary olives on which they feasted when they couldn't be bothered to cook. The bread was moulded into sections, making it easy to tear apart, and as she watched Ginny so artfully blending her ingredients she had a sudden pang for these instant picnic meals.

If Kip visits tomorrow, Lara told herself then, I'll see him. I'll pretend nothing is wrong. And comforted by this promise she spent the evening listening to Caroline, who had returned home flushed with hope for her horse, talking of people and places, of jokes and journeys, of animals and elderly aunts, none of whom she'd ever heard of.

'Yes,' Lambert said when prompted. 'I do remember,' and he kept a fond smile on his face.

The next day Kip didn't come. Lara sat by the pool, read her father's day-old paper, read some more of her own textbooks, even dipped distractedly into her novel. Maybe *she* should visit Kip? Officially it was her turn. But she couldn't do it. Several times she walked around to the front of the house, peered along the road, and then terrified she would bump into him, breathless from his race along the sexy path, she ran back inside and arranged herself, nonchalant, under a shade.

Only Ginny noticed anything was wrong. 'Fallen out with your friends?' she asked, and taken back by the vehemence with which Lara denied this she didn't mention it again.

Lambert was still marooned on the sofa. 'Could you . . .?' He was attempting to get up.

'Of course.'

She stooped down and he held on to her shoulder, limping very slowly towards the bathroom. Just once he let his foot knock against a metal standard lamp and he let out a howl of pain. Sweat broke out over his forehead and he had to steady himself. Lara waited outside, humming loudly to block out any intimate noise, and then when he came out she helped him to the sofa where he sat down.

'*Porca Madonna*,' he said, but she could see it was an effort for him to smile.

Later she heard him talking on the phone.

'No really, I don't need visitors. Not at all.' He was dismissive. 'It has nothing to do with you. Don't be ridiculous – I'd just rather recover on my own.' There was a pause, and then a little more irritably, 'Oh for goodness sake, really, if I have to explain . . . Thank you,' he said eventually. 'I'm glad you understand. That's very good of you.' And he put down the phone.

The little toe on Lambert's foot had turned completely black, the bruise spreading over the misshapen hump of it, to purple, green, then fading out to yellow on the other side. 'But I do feel better,' he said, and to prove it he ate several crostini and a plate of salad. 'I've been having the oddest dreams lying on this sofa all day,' he began, and then as if remembering that dreams are only interesting to you and no one else, he bit his lip.

'Like what?' Lara encouraged him. 'What kind of dreams?'

But just then Caroline came in from visiting her horse, and Lambert looked up at her. 'Did you get my paper?' he asked, all else forgotten, and Caroline brought it out from behind her back.

Caroline and Lambert sat together and looked at the obituaries. 'The Earl of Donoughmore has died aged seventy-two. Is that respectable?'

Lambert shrugged. 'I used to think so but now I'm not so sure.'

The Earl of Donoughmore, Caroline read, *who died in the Republic of Ireland, was in the public eye seven years ago when he and his wife, the Countess of Donoughmore, were kidnapped from their home in Clonmel, Co Tipperary . . .*

'Oh yes,' Lambert nodded. 'I remember now. Wasn't that odd? Go on.'

The kidnappers were thought to have been seeking influential hostages in the cause of the Price sisters who were on hunger strike, Lord Donoughmore having been Conservative MP for Peterborough thirty years before. But after he was freed – the hunger strikers having given up – he remarked that he had no influence with the British Government and did not think that the Government 'cared a damn' about his or his wife's life.

Lambert laughed. 'I'm sure he was right.'

'Two sons, one daughter . . .' Caroline put the paper down. 'The usual sort of thing.'

It was a beautiful night. They sat with the doors open on to the terrace, talking very little, listening to music – old records full of sliding rhyming refrains. Caroline smoked, giving it her full attention, and Lambert, unable to resist, picked up the paper again and read every word of every page as if he were licking clean a bowl. Lara looked out at the night. What would Kip be doing? she dared herself to think, and she had to press her hand flat against her chest to calm herself.

'Early tomorrow' – Caroline stretched – 'the horses will run trials in the square. There are twenty of them, and ten will be chosen.' Lara thought she saw her shiver. 'But I have a good feeling about this year, about this horse, a good feeling that we'll be chosen.' She looked at Lara as she stood up. 'I'm leaving first thing. If you're interested you'd be welcome to come.'

'No,' Lara said much too fast. 'I mean, I promised.' She looked at her father. 'I just really think I should stay with Dad, that's all.'

Caroline nodded. 'Well, wish me luck,' she said. 'It's not even the best ten horses they're looking for, it's the ten most evenly matched.'

'Good luck,' they said together, and with a light step Caroline skipped from the room.

Lara woke in the middle of the night. She lay completely still, her blood racing, her mouth dry. Had she heard something? A pebble thrown up at the window? A shout? Please let it be Kip. She felt sick with longing, and she climbed out of bed. But there was no one there. Just the gravel drive and the two cars, the shadows of the bushes, the dark leaves of the trees beyond.

She went to the other window, open to the moon, and leant out. There was the light, flickering in the hills, and then a snatch of music floating down. How long would it take, she wondered, to get up there, to find the path that led to that all-night party where people passionate with politics danced under the stars.

And then she heard the noise that had woken her. It was the scrape of furniture and it was coming from downstairs. Very quietly Lara stepped out on to the landing. There was silence now but as she reached the first step she heard it again, the dragging sound of a chair. Lara ran downstairs, peered into the hall, and there, sitting at the kitchen table, was her father, his work spread out before him, his foot propped up at an angle on a chair. Lara stood in the doorway and watched him. He had his head resting in one hand, a pen in the other, and he was staring at nothing at all. How long would he stay like that, she wondered, but unable to bear the suspense she coughed a little and moved towards him.

Lambert looked up. 'Can you not sleep?' he asked her, and having lost her line, she sat down.

'What are you doing?'

'Oh, I thought I'd better get on.' He gave a weak smile and then, as if catching sight of a word or a phrase that displeased him, his face fell again. 'The thing is . . .' He didn't look at her. 'I've spent my life trying to isolate myself, push everyone away so I could work . . . and now' – he hesitated – 'I feel . . . I've just realised. I've done it. I'm completely on my own.'

Lara wanted to touch him but she didn't dare. I know, she could say, but she didn't know. Instead she nodded. 'How is your work?'

He brightened a little. 'It's getting on.'

Lara went to the fridge. She poured two glasses of peach juice and brought them back to the table. 'Thank you,' Lambert nodded and together they sat at the table, sipping the thick juice, eyeing each other occasionally while Lambert wrote and Lara stared out at the black night.

After half an hour or so she yawned. 'Will you work all night?' she asked him, and he laid down his pen and stretched.

'No, I'll get some sleep.' Without reaching for her arm he limped back into the sitting room and sank on to the couch.

'Night then,' she said and he turned his face to the wall.

*   *   *

188

Lara was still in her nightdress the next morning when Caroline burst through the door. 'We've been chosen. Our horse. Chosen to run!' She was wearing her immaculate chiffon, the creases lying perfectly flat, but her face was flushed, her cheeks hectic with red.

'That's marvellous.' Ginny was chopping lettuce for lunch, letting it spring up behind the knife in long unfurling curls.

'Who will ride it?' Lara asked. 'Which *contrada*?'

'Il Nicchio. The Shell. Once the horses are chosen they are given numbers and then each number is allocated a *contrada*. It's one of the few things that can't be fixed.'

'Il Nicchio,' Lara said. 'Can we bet?'

'There is no betting. Well, not officially,' and Caroline explained that it was more complicated than that. 'It is the jockeys who pledge the money, and then only at the start of the race, when the horses have been lined up, although of course everyone in every *contrada* is bribing everyone else to allow them to win, to trip up their enemies, to go easy on their friends. It is vastly complicated and hard to ever get to the bottom of because officially, and to many Sienese, it isn't even happening.' Caroline turned, peering towards the sitting room. 'And Lambert?'

'I'm here,' he called faintly. 'I'm just going through my investments. Wondering how much I'd have to transfer into the coffers of Il Nicchio to make your day.'

'Lambertie,' she said, and she went through to him. 'My dearest one. You've brought me luck.'

Caroline left them again early the following day to watch the trials. Now that the horses had been chosen they had to get used to being ridden round the square. The sound of the starting cannon, the roaring of the crowd. There were six trials, morning and evening, over the next four days and Caroline intended watching as many of them as she could.

'I feel so much better,' she laughed. 'I don't know what's wrong with me. I feel well.' And with a wave of her hand she was off.

By late afternoon Lara was so bored she reneged on her promise never to leave Lambert, and set off for a walk. 'I won't be long,' she said but she couldn't tell whether he heard her or not.

She walked up the hill, away from Ceccomoro. It was just beginning to grow cooler, and she felt the release of freedom as she strode on. She passed a field of olive trees and another of sunflowers, stopping to admire their heavy heads, dark-brown with seeds amid the bunting of their petals.

Unexpectedly a cyclist toiled by, dressed in clinging shorts and a T-shirt spiked with holes. He crunched over the rough road, sweat running from his body. '*Buona sera*,' he panted and she wished him a good evening too. Evening already. Another day. She'd done it, pushed another day between herself and Roland. If she could just keep walking, or waiting, or whatever it took to make a space, then one day she'd be all right, and she watched the cyclist – the sinews in his legs like wire – as he forced himself along.

When he was out of sight she turned in a slow circle and looked at the wooded hills around her. She'd never imagined that Italy would be so full of trees, and she remembered a story that Ginny had told her about a fire, started deliberately, which had scorched away an entire Tuscan hill. The sky had filled with smoke, the heat was overwhelming, and to make it worse the fire department had emptied the contents of the pool where Ginny worked, sucking it up to pour on to the fire. But that must have been years ago because the trees had all grown again now. Lara looked back along the road towards the house. The sun was sinking behind the mound of a hill, throwing long layers of shadows across the slopes below. She'd better go back, she decided, and she started down the road.

As soon as she turned into the drive she saw the jeep. Her stomach lurched. The jeep meant Kip. Meant Roland. For a moment she turned her back on it, but knowing this wasn't a choice, she forced herself in through the front door. She could see them on the terrace, milling and lounging and lighting cigarettes. May and Piers and Roland, Nettle, Willow, Kip. Lara's whole body was quaking, her stomach turning, her blood quivering in her veins. She moved into the gap behind the stairs and put her hand to her mouth to steady herself. 'Hello,' she mouthed, to remind herself how to do it, and without giving herself more time she walked out through the glass doors.

'Lara!' May was the first to greet her and when she looked up she saw real warmth in her eyes. 'Where have you been?'

'Nowhere,' and then before she lost courage she turned to Kip. She caught him looking at her and quickly they both glanced away.

'Comrade.' Roland lifted his glass as if it were vodka, and although it was actually a large goblet of wine he drained it in one.

Lara backed away, taking a glass herself, and while the others were distracted, listening to Caroline describe the events of that day, she moved as far from Roland as she could get, brushing past Kip, close enough to let her shoulder rustle against his. He grabbed her hand as she moved off, catching her little finger.

'So are you coming?' She'd forgotten to listen and it was May talking to her. 'We're going into Siena.'

Lara could still feel the heat of Kip's hand, but she held

tight to her promise. 'I'd better stay here.' She babbled. 'You know . . . my dad . . .' and it was only when they all began to troop out that she realised she'd been hoping for a reprieve – hoping that Lambert would realise her sacrifice, or that Caroline, who'd just arrived back, would intervene.

She followed them to the door and watched as Roland swung himself into the front with Piers. May and the twins climbed in over the metal lip and Kip pulled himself in after them. Kip looked round briefly but just as she was about to wave his attention was caught by somebody inside. The engine started, the wheels spun and with a blast of white dust the car was gone. Lara sat on the doorstep as if she'd been wounded. God, she hissed, and she punched herself on the arm to redistribute the pain.

That night Caroline was in almost feverish high spirits. She talked about the morning's trial and what it had revealed. There was another trial now, maybe even at this very moment, and two more tomorrow, but she was under doctor's orders to rest. If Il Nicchio wins – she tapped her fingers – it will be the first win in twelve years for the Shell. If Il Nicchio wins – she could hardly sit still – my horse will be a hero. Will go down in the history books. Will never be forgotten. 'But there is La Selva,' she mused, 'La Selva, the Woodland, has a good horse, and of course poor Il Bruco, the Caterpillar, hasn't won since 1955, so they are, as ever, hopeful. Can you imagine?' Caroline continued, 'There are grown men and women of Il Bruco who have never known their *contrada* to win. How would that feel?' she pondered, and she looked from Lambert to Lara as if neither of them could imagine so much loss.

'Which *contrada* did your husband come from?' Lara asked, but Caroline shook her head. 'You have to be born within the city walls to come from a *contrada*. Antonio was originally from Rome but as a young man he fell in love with the Palio. He brought me to it for the first time, actually, to cheer me up after my last divorce, and I was smitten too.'

'Who won that year?' Lara asked and, without hesitation, Caroline answered, 'La Giraffa.'

'You know,' she said a little later, 'married couples from different *contrade* usually go home to their own families the night before the Palio. It's not a law, but feelings run too high for them to stay away. People take to the streets, singing, chanting, waving flags. The night before the Palio is one of my favourite nights. It is the biggest trial, the dress rehearsal really. I do hope you'll come?'

'I think I should save my strength for the big night,' Lambert frowned.

'And I . . .' Lara looked towards her father.

'Do go,' he said. 'I think you should.'

'It'll be a long evening,' Caroline warned, and Lara wondered how that could be the case when the race only lasted ninety seconds.

'It'll be the most intense ninety seconds of your life,' Caroline promised. 'It's incredible.' She danced her hands. 'It's like an orgasm.' And Lara tried not to blush.

Lara lay in bed and read *The Grapes of Wrath*. Occasionally she tiptoed to the window, hoping she might find Kip standing below with a red rose or a half-drunk bottle of champagne, returned from Siena, and unable to bear another night without her. But there was no one there. Even the revolutionaries on the hill were quiet, no sign of firelight, not a flicker of a song. At one in the morning, still unable to sleep, she tiptoed downstairs, hoping to find her father bent over his desk, but even Lambert was asleep, his damaged foot uncovered, the toes still black.

Lara put out her light and tried to sleep. She counted sheep, tried to remember the names of every person in her English class, even the ones who sat silent at the back, and when that failed she got up again and as quietly as she could she practised the moves of her Indian dancing, stretching out her arms, lengthening her neck. Only her eyes must move. Her eyes, her head and her shoulders. This was the simplest dance, but within it, as with every dance, there was a message. It was in the shape of the hands, the ring finger bent back, and in the bells that strapped around your ankles and tinkled when you danced. Once she'd mastered this she allowed her feet to slap gently on the floor, back and forth, heel and then flat, and she remembered how she'd longed to progress, not so much for the skill involved in the dance itself but in order to be allowed to wear the clothes.

White was the colour of the apprentice, a white cotton tunic with bangles and bells. The more experienced dancers dressed in silk. Peacock-blue, green and pink. Slap, went her feet, slap slap, and swift as a salamander she turned her head from side to side. The longer she danced the more clearly India came back to her, and with a shock that she could ever have forgotten him, she thought of Thubten Dawa.

He'd come to see them where they lived in Bangalore, introduced himself and asked if there was anything they needed. They were living in the back room of an Indian widow and her daughter, and although there was nothing they needed, Thubten Dawa stayed to talk. He was studying economics in Bangalore, having until last year lived with his family at the refugee camp at Bylakuppe. Thubten was wiry and dark-skinned. He was kind and calm and very handsome, and soon he was visiting them most afternoons, sitting on the wall outside the widow's house, chatting, gossiping and laughing.

By the end of the first week Lara had forgotten that she'd ever been in love with Sam. Had ever thought she'd not recover when they'd said goodbye to him in Delhi. Her lessons flew by in anticipation of seeing him each afternoon. Thubten Dawa. She still had his message to her in her diary. 'My greatest wish for you,' he'd written, 'is that you become enlightened.' Lara pressed the palms of her hands together over her head and stepped forward, heels first like a camel.

Dawa, she remembered, Dawa means the moon, and she thought how once they'd taken a bus to the sea. They'd gone to visit the temple at Mamallapuram where the original Indian dancing had been danced, and finding it deserted, Lara had performed, wearing her bikini, for no one but her mother, two lepers and Thubten Dawa. It had been Lara's idea to ask Thubten if he'd like to come. He would like to, he said, very much.

As soon as they arrived they'd gone to the beach. There were very few people there, several men in shirts and trousers, and women in saris, a small party of them wading fully dressed into the waves, but Cathy and Lara wrapped themselves in their dhotis and changed into costumes. Thubten Dawa, very serious, took off his shirt and rolled up his trousers, and together the three of them stepped into the water. The sea was warm. Warm compared to the ice chill of their Scottish lake, but Thubten was not so sure. He walked in carefully, slowly, and then an unexpected wave hit him in the face.

He stepped back, fell, and a moment later he leapt up. 'Salt,' he gasped. 'It tastes of salt!' And as if chased by black magic he ran to the safety of the sand.

Lara and Cathy stood in the shallows and laughed. They laughed and laughed. They couldn't stop. It tastes of salt, they said to each other and Lara thought how strange it would be if it tasted of anything else.

The next day, as soon as she woke, Lara knew Kip wouldn't come. She lay by the pool without sun cream until her skin smelt scorched, and later when she was getting dressed she allowed herself to stand naked in front of the mirror for the first time since that night. That night, the words were like a punch, and she said them again, spitting them out, that night, that night. But repetition didn't soften them. Her face looked pale, even through the mask of brown, pale and spiteful and hard. 'That night,' she said more softly, and she thought of Kip and their kissing. The way they'd leant against their tree and intertwined themselves like branches. They'd kissed until their kissing was like talking and their tongues had formed whole libraries of words.

Lara stood in a sea of abandoned clothes.

'Are you ready?' Caroline called up the stairs. She'd already told her she wanted to leave for the trial at four o'clock.

'Yes,' Lara called down and she pulled on her jeans and a shirt, slipped on her sandals and ran down.

Caroline stood by the door, her bag in her hand, quivering to be gone.

'One minute,' Lara begged, and she ran out to the terrace where her father was reading, his foot propped up and draped with a poultice of Ginny's remedy of herbs. 'See you later.' Lara leant down over him, and as she did so he started and the book dropped from his hands.

'Yes,' he said, and when he looked up his eyes were bleary and the lines on his forehead had deepened into grooves.

'I'm sorry, did I wake you?' she asked, but even as he

shook his head there was a loud impatient hoot from Caroline outside.

They drove in silence along the road towards Siena, only murmuring occasionally to acknowledge the traffic, which grew heavier as they reached the outskirts of the city. Caroline sped up a side road, roared along a narrow terraced street, made a steep turn that gave them a view of the city walls. She waved cheerfully at a policewoman who was beckoning frantically for people to drive past a car that had caught fire, and as they went Lara turned and watched the flames fly higher, the black clouds of smoke billowing out.

Caroline wove skilfully through back streets until they arrived at the post-office square at the top of the town, where she pulled into the entrance of a building. A man appeared at the car window, Lara assumed to reprimand her, but instead he greeted her with an eager flow of Italian, and held the door for her to get out. As benevolent as a Queen, Caroline rewarded him with a smile and a few perfect phrases before handing him her keys and walking away.

Lara ran to catch up. There were people everywhere, all flowing down towards the Campo, some wearing scarves emblazoned with the colours of their *contrada*, others holding flags, almost all eating ice creams. Lara had never seen so many grown people eating ice creams. In Britain ice creams were for children, something they were expected to grow out of, but here it was a national pastime, to sit and lick at enormous melting cones.

'This is my favourite *gelateria*,' Caroline said, as if she'd been reading her thoughts, and they crowded into a glass emporium and craned to get a glimpse of the flavours on show. 'You should try the *crema*,' Caroline said. 'It tastes like custard. Or the meringue, which isn't like anything you'll ever get at home,' and taking Lara's smile as acceptance she ordered her a double cone, and one for herself too.

The ice creams were huge and in danger of sliding off, so they stood in the shop and ate them. Caroline ate hungrily and so did she. The ice cream was delicious, frothy and light, and it occurred to Lara that it was the first food she'd really tasted since that night. Stop it, she cursed at herself and she bit into the cone.

'We could have one more?' Caroline's eyes were straining in the direction of the counter. 'The chocolate shouldn't be missed.'

Lara gave an involuntarily laugh of surprise, and regretted it instantly, because instead of ordering two more doubles Caroline wiped her fingers carefully on a tissue, patted her bag tight against her shoulder, and suggested they walk on.

'Today is the day when all the *contrade* parade their horses through the streets,' she said. 'They sing their own song, shake their fists at their enemies, and later, after the *prova* – the trial – they have a celebration dinner. Each *contrada* attends a feast to celebrate the fact they might be about to win, even Il Bruco, even though they haven't actually won for twenty-six years.'

They walked past a square where long tables, more of them than she could count, were laid with white cloths, set with plates and bowls and glasses. It's so clever, she thought, to celebrate when everyone is still a possible winner. To celebrate the night before the race.

At the bottom of the street as it led into the Campo there was a barrier where they showed their tickets, and there was the Piazza, transformed. A ring of earth had been laid around its edge and banks of seats had been set up against the walls of every building. Already the centre of the square was full of people, who, Caroline told her, had been waiting there all day. They looked like a scattering of confetti, the thousands of multicoloured T-shirts all squashed together.

'It's best to see the procession from a side street,' Caroline said, and she almost ran along the earth track to the first street on the left.

They crowded into a doorway where behind them people bulged and pushed, squeezing in and out of the tiny café with slices of pizza and bottles of water. They hadn't waited long when they heard the singing. It started with a swell, a sudden warrior-like singing, and then the marchers were upon them.

In the lead was a wild-eyed horse, and right behind, four, five, six deep, was the *contrada* of the Goose. They were all men, their chests thrust forward, their heads back, roaring out the song, shaking their fists, bursting with oaths and pride. They were followed by the women, short and fierce – fighting people – and then a troupe of children, singing at the high tops of their voices.

'My God.' Lara had caught some of Caroline's thrill. 'What are they singing?' And Caroline, her face flushed, told her.

'We are the best, the rest are shit! Our *contrada* is the most beautiful in the world!'

'Really?' Lara strained for the next *contrada* to appear.

She was pushing forward herself now, and with a burst of the same song, the *contrada* of the Eagle in its gold, black and blue stormed by. The horse looked frisky, its head held high, and everyone stepped back from it, the crowd almost collapsing into the doorway of the shop as it pranced to the side.

'But they're singing the same song.'

'Yes,' Caroline told her, but with different words. '*We* are the best, the *rest* are shit, *Our contrada* is the most beautiful in the world.'

Contrada after *contrada* rushed by, each one singing their own fierce song. The melody made the hairs stand up on Lara's arms, made her heart swell with fierce yearning.

'Here comes Il Nicchio. This is our horse!' Caroline pushed herself forward as the grey mare was paraded past.

The *contrada* of the Shell marched behind in a blaze of white and pale-blue, a rank of big-nosed, balding men, warrior chests stuck out in front.

When the last *contrada* had passed, its song echoing away into the square, Caroline took her arm. 'Now, we need to make a rush for the square.'

They fell in behind a stream of people, all going the same way, all pushing and running towards their seats.

'Over here.' Caroline was nimble as a goat and Lara followed her along the cordoned-off fence of the track to a bank of seats behind the starting line.

An official opened a little gate for them and Lara clambered up the steps. The seats were halfway up the stands and Lara put out her hand to help Caroline climb. To her surprise she accepted it.

'Done,' she said, breathless, as she slipped into her place, and together they leaned forward to watch as men appeared with long brooms and began sweeping their footsteps from the track.

Not long after a rope was brought out, coiled around a stick and carried by two men. It was stretched across the track just below them, attached to a weight, and once it was in place a hush fell over the crowd. It wouldn't be long now. Soon the horses would be released on to the track. They were waiting, Caroline said, inside the huge hall of the Palazzo at the bottom of the Campo.

And here they were, trotting up the hill of the square, the riders making unfamiliar shapes with no saddles or stirrups, their legs simply hanging down. Lara peered closer to identify each jockey in their colours, the patterns of each *contrada* layered over their hats. Ahead of them, on the far side of the course, was a hazardous corner where horses were most likely to crash, riders fly off, bones shatter.

The ten horses stopped several paces from the starting line, twisting and turning, jostling and waiting, while the crowd whispered and chatted and craned to see. And then there was a crackle of the loudspeaker and a series of sharp shushes to anyone who dared speak. Lara felt the tension all around her as every single person in the square, as many as a hundred thousand, held their breath. And then a voice rang out, and amid a splatter of applause La Civetta – the Owl – pranced forward, and skittering, side-stepping and attempting to walk him backwards his jockey shifted him into first place alongside the central fence. Il Bruco – the Caterpillar – was the next to be called out and Caroline shook her head. 'No luck.'

Quickly, and with growing excitement, all ten horses were called out, Il Nicchio at eighth place, beside him, at nine, Il Drago, the Dragon, and the tenth horse L'Aquila, the Eagle. L'Aquila stayed back.

'Why doesn't he come forward?' Lara asked, almost un-able to bear the tension as she watched Il Drago shift and shove against Il Nicchio's flanks, squeezing the horse right out of the race, forcing its head to turn so that if the race did start it would be facing the wrong way.

'The tenth horse is the King Maker,' Caroline explained. 'He is only allowed to start when each horse is lined up in order,' and just at that moment every horse seemed magically to be still.

Now, now. Lara craned forward and the crowd hissed and jeered as still L'Aquila didn't start. The longer he waited the more unruly the horses became.

'Once it took so long to start,' Caroline told her, 'that the horses had to go inside again to be calmed down.'

'Once,' she remembered a little later when the crowd was almost spitting with frustration at the sly and wily jockey that rode for L'Aquila, who sat on his horse shooting out glances at the starting line where the horses stamped and snorted in a kind of stew, pausing every so often in perfect order, but always when L'Aquila was facing the wrong way.

'Once the Palio took so long to start that some of the horses had to be re-shoed.'

'My God.' Lara covered her mouth to stop hysteria rising.

'Once . . .' Caroline's eyes were dancing, 'it got so late that everyone had to go home and come back again the next day!'

Lara imagined she would be there for ever, her nerves singing, her eyes pinned on the tenth horse, but just at that moment L'Aquila swept round and with the other nine horses burst through the rope. It happened so fast Lara couldn't see how anyone had known, but an explosion went off at the exact moment L'Aquila started and the air echoed with the thud of the blast. Everyone leant forward, some palely silent, others shouting, shaking their fists. She tried to pick out Il Nicchio in the mass of colours, but the horses were already on the far side of the square, galloping up the hill, clustered together.

There was no commentary, no explanation, and then they were streaming by again. One pulled out in front, the legs of the jockey so limp and hanging he looked like a child on a seesaw, while yet another reined his horse in so he was running leisurely and alone, behind. Come on, come on. People were standing. But of course it was only the trial, the dress rehearsal, and the jockeys weren't racing their horses fast. No one careered into the dangerous corner at San Martino where the square sloped down, and no one whipped or tripped their enemies.

Lara felt relieved and disappointed all at once. Caroline stood up as the horses passed again. They were streaming round the last lap now, three bunched up together on the slope, and then there was one, a clear head before the others. L'Oca. It was L'Oca. It was the Goose and it was winning. It was going to win. Had won. Geese everywhere waved fistfuls of green scarf and sang their warrior song, but no one was fooled. It was the trial and it didn't matter.

Slowly and carefully Lara and Caroline climbed down on to the earthen track. Lara shivered and when she looked up she saw the sky was unusually dark. Thick clouds bunched and overlapped, and while she stood there wondering at the unfamiliar sight, drops as fat as tears began to fall.

'I didn't notice it grow colder.' Caroline seemed perplexed, but they both knew the weather could have turned any time in the last three hours and they'd never have known.

With the rain came gusts of cold air that drove in sideways. It flattened the soft material of Caroline's blouse. She clutched her arms across her chest and Lara saw how thin they were without the padding of her carefully cut layers.

'We'd better go.' Caroline's teeth were chattering, and all around them men, women and children were disappearing into side streets, melting away from the square

Silently they walked uphill. They passed the ice-cream shops and the kiosks, already filling up again, and when they reached the post-office square, they waited while their car was retrieved for them from the underground vault of the building into which it had been stowed.

Caroline sat in the driver's seat for a moment as if she were in a trance. Raindrops had collected in her hair, glittering like pearls. They clung to her porcelain skin and ran like lotion down her neck. She looked as beautiful as a mermaid. Her face and neck and arms, her fingers even, shimmering. But she was shivering, fumbling with the knobs to find the heater switch, letting out a blast of dusty air that blew into their eyes. Lara glanced into the back, hoping to find a shawl or a blanket to offer her, but there was nothing.

'Right.' Caroline took a deep breath and, holding herself straight, she steered the car for home.

Lara wanted to talk. She wanted to ask a million questions. Why did L'Aquila miss so many opportunities to start the race? Was it allowed? Would he be punished? And did the fact that L'Oca came in first mean anything for the next day? Had Il Nicchio run well? She couldn't remember now where Il Nicchio had finished. She couldn't remember Il Nicchio at all. How do they choose the jockeys? Are they from the *contrade*? And then she remembered her father telling her that the jockeys were mostly from Sardinia. They were famous jockeys, with no particular allegiances. Chosen only for their skill. But once chosen they were guarded night and day. Guarded even as they slept, as were the horses, from any member of another *contrada* who might wish to ensure they didn't win.

'Caroline.' She turned to her, and although it was dry in the car, and the heating had begun to work, Caroline's face still shimmered with wet. It stood out from her skin, collecting in a haze over her forehead. 'Are you all right?'

'Tell me,' Caroline cut in first, 'did you enjoy the *prova* – the dress rehearsal?'

'Oh yes.' Lara could hardly find words. 'Thank you for taking me. I'm so glad we stayed to see this.'

'It was my pleasure,' Caroline said softly, and she looked at Lara as if she were seeing her for the first time. 'Don't be too hard on him,' she added.

Lara waited. 'On who?'

'On your father. It hasn't been easy . . . He's . . .' She sighed. 'You must try and understand.'

There was silence. Just the wipers, wiping.

'I do, I think.' Or did she? 'I will,' she agreed, and Caroline turned the car on to the rough road.

The porch light was on when they arrived back. And not just for me, Lara thought, but suddenly she felt sad.

Lambert was lying on the sofa, his leg propped up with cushions.

'It still looks ghastly.' Caroline bent over it, and it was true. Purple and puffy and swollen halfway to the knee.

Lara tried to imagine him hobbling through the narrow streets of Siena. Navigating the steps into the Campo. Hauling himself up into the almost vertical tier of seats. And what if the race took hours to start? What if it took days?

'How was it?' Lambert was looking up at her.

'It was amazing. The Goose won.'

'It was the trial.' Caroline was leaning against the door, defying anyone to mention her pallor. 'I'm off to bed. I want to be up early . . .' She raised an eyebrow warningly at anyone who might dissuade her. 'I want to see the last trial. The Provaccia. It's the only race in existence where each jockey is trying his hardest not to win.' She laughed. 'Goodnight then.' She kept one hand on the wall as if for support. 'Sleep well.'

'Goodnight.' They both watched her go, and for a few minutes neither of them spoke.

Ginny had left out a cold supper. Soup, pale-green in a cool bowl, salad and a plate of salami. Lara made herself a sandwich – salami, it could hardly count as meat, and luxuriating in this rare chance to eat a casual snack rather than a formal three-course meal, she sat beside Lambert with her plate. For a while they listened to the rain.

'Dad,' she asked him, imagining the race track turned into a sea of mud, 'does the Palio ever get cancelled?'

'Well.' Lambert put down his book, and closing his eyes for a moment as if better to draw out the appropriate facts he told her how in 1798, due to a recent earthquake, the July Palio was cancelled. 'In 1800,' he went on, 'both the July and August Palio were prohibited by the French Occupation forces, and five years later a Palio was cancelled due to an outbreak of cholera. The August Palio of 1900 was not held because of official mourning for the assassination of Umberto I of Monza, and of course no Palios were held during the two world wars. Usually,' he went on, 'the Sienese try not to let political or national issues interfere with the Palio, but sometimes it is inevitable. It's not that the Sienese don't care about politics, they just care more about the Palio.'

'Oh.' Lara was glad she hadn't mentioned her worries about the rain. 'But Dad,' she said, looking quickly at his leg. 'Will you be terribly disappointed if you have to miss it?'

'Not as disappointed as I'll be if we have to miss our train.'

Lara started. Our train? She'd forgotten that they were going home the day after the Palio. The day after tomorrow! 'But will we actually?' She felt her panic rising. 'Will you be well enough, I mean?'

'Even if I have to ride Caroline's race horse all the way to Calais with my leg in plaster and a suitcase on my head.' He smiled as if to help the joke along, but she saw from the set of his jaw how desperate he was to be gone.

Lara stood on the doorstep and stared out into the night. It was still raining, the drops flashing white in the arc of the porch light, sleeting splintery and black beyond it. Should she run and find Kip, she thought, her heart beating, fear pumping through her body. Should she run along the sexy path, creep up on the house, slide in through the front door, along the stone corridor and into Kip's room? She could slip into his bed, lie against his body, feel the sinews of his legs and arms, the silk skin at the nape of his neck, the warm ridge of his ribs. I'm sorry, she'd whisper. And he would roll towards her and wrap her in his arms. She'd keep her eyes open while they made love, watching his mouth, his eyes, the way his hair fell over his forehead, too busy smiling to think about anything else. To think about Roland. And anyway, she'd forgotten about him. She'd proved she could do it that evening at the trial. For three hours she hadn't thought of him. For three hours he'd been nothing to her. Gone. The nip of his watch chain, the smell of aftershave, the weight of his fingers and his thigh.

'I am the best,' she spat in imitation of the most ferocious of the *contrade*. 'You are shit!' and she wished she knew the words in Italian so that she could march across the valley, into the woods and over the hills, beating her chest, shouting and singing. Declaring war. 'Nothing.' She said it again. 'Nobody at all.' She threw his name out into the rain. Trampled it into the gravel. Spat at it. A roll of thunder rumbled in the distance. She raised her fist to it. Answering back. So there!

'Lara?' Lambert was behind her. 'Are you all right?'

'Oh. Yes.' Lara felt herself blushing. 'I was just thinking . . . thinking about how the race would be affected . . . you know, by the rain.' A streak of lightning broke open the sky and she stepped back.

'You're getting wet.' He put a hand on her arm, and limping forward, he gently closed the front door. 'I think

I'll try and go up tonight,' he said, peering towards the dark staircase. 'I'm starting to feel rather squalid, living in my bed-sitting room.' And so painfully, slowly, his arm around her shoulder, they shuffled up the stairs. 'Thank you,' he smiled on the landing outside their rooms, a foreign gentleman of the most unknowable kind.

'Goodnight,' and she watched him limp forward, supporting himself against walls and doors, his shoulders hunched, his hair greyer, the lines across his forehead deep as an old man's.

'Goodnight,' she whispered, and she went and sat on her bed. Almost immediately another crack of lightning whitened the room. It made her jump, the shock jolting through her body, forcing unexpected tears into her eyes. She brushed them aside, but instantly there were more. She shook her head bitterly. 'Fuck off,' she told her sobbing self. It was as if another haughtier, more disapproving self was sitting beside her. 'Stop it.' But it was too late. She couldn't stop. She sat, not even covering her face, and let her tears pour out. They were hot and slippery, and she gulped as they kept on coming until she began to wonder if they'd ever stop.

She lay down on the bed and pressed her face into the pillow, and still she cried, her sobs rolling through her, filling her mouth and nose, shaking her ribs until her face was boiling and her head was cracking right across the skull. Eventually, half blind, she fumbled her way to the bathroom and splashed water against the lids of her eyes. She looked into the mirror and finally she saw it – she *had* changed. A last cracked sob flew out of her. She bent her head again and splashed until her face, her arms, her neck, her whole body was numb.

By the time she arrived back in her room she felt calm. Hollow. Holy even, as if there was nothing inside her but light. She went to the window and looked out and even the rain was falling less densely. She opened the window and breathed in. The air smelt delicious. The mulch of pine, the lavender and rosemary from Caroline's borders stretching for a drink. She stayed there so long, leaning on the window ledge, that her head began to droop until reluctantly she climbed into her bed and turning her face to the wall she closed her eyes.

It may have been the doctor's car that woke her. Lara didn't know. But when she looked out it was already there. She rushed across the landing to her father's room. The bed was empty, and filled with alarm she pulled on a cardigan and ran downstairs. Ginny was in the sitting room, watching while the doctor used the phone.

'*Pronto*,' he barked in an impatient staccato. '*Pronto. Si.*'

'What's happened?' Lara gripped her arm.

A tear dripped from Ginny's face. 'She said she needed to be up early. So I went to wake her with a cup of tea. I thought to myself, before I have my swim . . .'

Lara felt her eyes grow rounder in her head. 'Caroline? Is she . . .?'

'I don't know how long she'd been like that.' Ginny took a big gulp like a fish. 'I was frightened to try too hard to wake her. I mean . . . she looks so fragile, doesn't she? Like a little bird. I didn't want to shake her. I thought it might be dangerous and the doctor said that was right. That was the right thing to do. Not to move her. He came ever so quickly. Said he'd been expecting this call all summer. Said it was a miracle how long she'd lasted.'

'But is she?' Lara felt her stomach knotting. 'Is she . . .' She couldn't say it, and then the doctor turned and told them that the ambulance was on its way.

'No.' Lambert was standing in the door, as straight and tall as was possible while balancing on one leg. 'I must insist on it,' he said. 'She must not be moved.'

The doctor looked at him, bemused.

'I know her.' Lambert was trembling. 'I've known her all . . . almost all my life. She wouldn't want it.'

The doctor looked at the ground. 'The ambulance. It will be here soon.'

'But what are you saying? That she'll recover? That if they take her to hospital she'll be her old self again?'

The doctor heaved his shoulders. 'They may be able to revive her.'

'So she can die in hospital, without any of the things she loves?' He was holding on to the table for support.

'There may be people who wish to say goodbye. Friends. Family. It will give them the time they need to reach her. That's important. No?'

Lambert was silenced. He hung his head, and then a beeper went off somewhere on the doctor's body and he turned away.

By the time the ambulance arrived Ginny was making bread, pounding and beating the dough. Throwing it down like a fat white wrestler on to the slab of stone. Lara stood to one side as the ambulance men brought Caroline down. They had wrapped her carefully in an emergency blanket, tucking it in under her chin, and Lara saw that even in unconsciousness she managed to exude an air of glamour.

They stopped in the hall and Lara gazed down at her face. She didn't look like the woman who'd eaten ice cream in the streets of Siena the night before. Who'd shaken her fist at the enemy. Who'd held her hand and run, quick as a cat, up the steep steps. She was still and pale, but her skin, she'd be pleased to know it, was as white and dense as cream.

Lambert limped out into the drive and watched as they manoeuvred her into the back of the ambulance. And then to Lara's surprise he heaved himself in after her, dragging his sore foot, wincing as he knocked it against the step.

'I'll be back later,' he called to Lara, and she saw that he had a book and a silk scarf of Caroline's in his hand.

'Call if you need me to come.' Ginny wiped her hands on her apron. 'Just call, I won't go anywhere.' She waited until they'd clanked shut the ambulance doors, and with a quick dab at her eyes she rushed back into the house to check on the bread which was under a tea towel rising.

Lara felt ashamed. Had everyone else known, not that Caroline was ill, but that she was actually dying? and she listened while Ginny dialled numbers from a list on Caroline's desk. She had two sisters, it transpired, and an uncle. A best friend, and two ex-husbands who were still alive. Ginny spoke tenderly and low. Promising each one that she would call back as soon as there was news. One of the sisters, or maybe both, were making plans to fly. To arrive today, if at all possible. And Ginny intimated that there was little time to lose.

Lara sat in the house. It seemed wrong to go outside and loll by the blue pool. Instead she fingered through a stack of Caroline's records, Edith Piaf, Billie Holiday, Nina Simone and an album of Brahms' Violin Concerto, which seemed safe enough to play. She walked through the wall of crashing rolling music to the kitchen to gauge Ginny's reaction but Ginny was busy separating eggs, collecting the whites in a large bowl, the yolks in a smaller, cracking the shells with a neat sharp knock. 'Who is all this food for?' Lara wanted to ask, but she didn't dare.

Ginny reminded her of the Bangalore widow. They'd paid a few rupees a week to sleep in her back room, to share her and her daughter's food three times a day. And the food they ate was delicious. Curry for breakfast, lunch and supper, but so light and fine and full of delicate flavour – cardamom and fennel – that you were always ready for more. But it shocked Lara to see what went into the preparation of these meals. Every waking moment, from dawn to dusk, the mother and the daughter worked. Grinding spices. Making parathas. Shopping for okra, potatoes, beans and coriander. Chopping and de-seeding. Washing out pans. Filling them with food again.

Until then they hadn't met many Indians, mixing mostly with Tibetans, friends of friends of people they knew from Samye Ling. The Tibetans felt familiar, with their shrines and their pujas, their gossip and their jokes, but the Indians were foreign. When I'm reincarnated, Lara had prayed, I hope I don't come back as a daughter or a wife. I'd prefer to be a dung beetle or an elephant. Anything other than that endless chopping and mixing, cleaning and scouring. Anything other than that life of chores. But Ginny would have been in heaven.

She was whipping the egg whites into peaks, sifting in a shower of icing sugar, whipping and whipping until each peak stood alone. She lined a tray with greaseproof paper, oiled the paper, spooned on a froth of white.

'There,' she said, in satisfaction. 'Now we have meringues,' and she put them in a low oven to bake. But her happiness was short-lived. 'What,' she wailed above the violin surge of Brahms, 'will I do with all these yolks?' and to calm her Lara suggested they have breakfast.

They sat down together at the table on the terrace, their plates piled high with golden scrambled egg, the cloth spread with toast, honey, fruit and tea.

'Thank you,' Ginny said, as if it were Lara herself who had

been cooking since dawn, and for the first time that morning she sat quite still.

Lara wanted to tell her about the Tibetan monks and how once, during a death puja, one of them had put a whoopee cushion under the orange-robed bottom of another monk. There was a gurgle, a squelch, and then a low loud fart. The monk threw his hands up in the air and then rocking, his eyes crinkled, he began to laugh. Everyone laughed. Monks and lay people, men, women and children, and she could still see their warm, round faces, laughing and laughing as they prepared to make a puja to death. But Lara couldn't tell Ginny about this in case she mentioned that unmentionable word – death. Even her mother, who still meditated at her shrine, filled the seven little bowls with water, for the eyes, the hands, for lights, for incense, for music, food and flowers, who still sat her blue-painted, long-eared Buddha on a crochet table mat that Lara had made one winter when there was nothing else to do, even her mother avoided the word.

Would you want to go to hospital, if you were . . .' Lara swallowed. 'If you were dying?' She'd said it, and she watched as Ginny blanched.

'No.' She took a moment. 'Not really.' And then warming to the idea, 'I'd like to die in my conservatory with my face full in the sun and that sweet stalky smell of tomatoes just tickling in my nose.'

'I'd like to die' – Lara had never thought about it for herself – 'just drift away as I slept on the top bunk of a train in an Indian ladies' carriage.' She could feel the soothing rattle of the wheels as field after field swished by.

'I'd like someone there.' Ginny pondered. 'Or would I?'

'Yes.' Lara closed her eyes, imagining Kip, weeping, clinging to her hand. 'Well, maybe not in a ladies' carriage. Maybe first class.' She could see herself covered with a pink-and-green water-lily quilt. 'Actually . . . no.' Life seemed so precious suddenly. 'On second thoughts. You know what? I don't think I will die.'

'Of course you won't,' Ginny said kindly and she began clearing away plates.

All morning the telephone rang and Lara sat on the terrace listening to the low hushed tones of Ginny, giving information, soothing with kind words. Twice she called the hospital but she was only told that Caroline was stable, and each time, although Lara stood beside her, signing and whispering for news of Lambert, Ginny always put down the phone without having asked. 'He's not a patient. You can't ask them to track down visitors.'

But eventually some time after lunch Lambert called. He sounded tired and worn down and he told Lara that against much opposition he'd agreed to let the hospital take the nerve out of his toe. 'They can do the operation tomorrow,' he said. 'Otherwise for the rest of my life I'll keep breaking it, over and over. In fact I will still keep breaking it. But once the nerve's removed I'll never know.'

And the Palio? Lara thought. But instead she asked about their train.

'I know.' Lambert sounded pained. 'We'll go the next day. As soon as I can escape. Will you ask Ginny to bring me in some of my things, my books and papers, and if she can find a newspaper?'

'And what about Caroline?'

There was a silence and Lambert took a deep breath. 'She's not come round.'

'Shall I visit?'

'No.' He was adamant. He almost shouted. 'Please don't.

Come and get me when I'm leaving.' He hesitated, and then in a quieter voice, 'Or did you mean visit Caroline?'

'I don't mind. Whatever would be useful.' She wished she'd never mentioned visiting at all.

Ginny, who was hovering, seized the phone and pressed it importantly to her ear. Lara stood beside her and let her fingers trail over Caroline's desk, idling over the list of names, the neat stacks of papers, the headed notepaper, the jar of pens. There was a tray with change, some paper-clips, a comb, and then slipped in beside a brochure for a hotel were three square oblong tickets with *Palio* in large black letters across them. Lara inched her hand forward, and while Ginny was scribbling down the contents of Lambert's list, she drew them towards her and slipped them into the pocket of her shorts. A shiver ran through her, tightening her scalp, and she shook her head and walked out into the sun. She sat on the top step of the terrace and fingered the tickets. So precious. So valuable. It made her heart beat. What would happen to their seats now?

'I'm off then,' Ginny called from the house.

Lara stuffed the tickets back into her pocket. 'OK.'

Ginny had a basket filled with food, a bag of books and folded clothes. 'I'll be back later. There's soup and bread and meringues for supper. If the sisters don't arrive I may even sit up with Caroline tonight.' Ginny was beaming. She'd come into her own. 'Will you be all right?'

'Of course.' Lara followed her to the door to wave her off. 'Bye then,' she said. 'Send my love.'

'Do you want me to call you later? If I can't get back?

'No! Really. Don't call. I'll be fine.'

But she already felt like crying. Why couldn't she go too. She almost stamped her bare brown foot. It was only when the car was gone and she turned into the empty house that her spirits rose. She stretched out her arms and whirled around, and although she knew it was disrespectful it was impossible not to relish the freedom of having the house to herself. She ran from room to room. She ran across the garden, down the steps, past the pool and tried the door to Ginny's room. It was unlocked and she opened it a fraction, just to see. But it was just a room. Simply furnished. A voluminous dress draped over a chair. The boulder-like contours of a discarded bra beside it. She shut the door quickly.

Feeling wicked, she ran back to the house, up the stairs, along the corridor and turned the handle to Caroline's door. Her heart was pounding. She shouldn't be doing this but she needed to see everything. She couldn't be alone in the house until she had. Caroline's room was full of Caroline. There were flowers on the dressing table, cushions plumped where they'd fallen from the bed. Her wardrobe door was open and there, reflected in the dressing-table mirror, were silky hanging dresses in shades of ivory and beige. There was her sun hat sitting on a chair and another more elegant hat with a sheer scarf tied round it on a shelf.

Lara took a step forward. Caroline's rings were on her dressing table in a china bowl. And her watch with its thin gold strap was laid beside it. Lara pulled out the chair and sat down. She picked up one of Caroline's brushes and dusted powder over her face. It gave her a soft, out-of-focus look and so she swept on a little eye shadow and patted her cheeks with rouge. Very carefully she lifted Caroline's hat from its shelf and tried it on and then whirling round she felt the silk scarf tickle her bare arms.

She ran to the cupboard. There were crocheted tops, pleated skirts, elegant strapped sandals all in muted colours. Lara ran her fingers through them, relishing their softness and their rustle. She pulled one down, a dusty pink, a dress she'd never seen, and held it up against her. It felt cool and slippery against her skin and although she knew she shouldn't she slipped it on over her shorts and T-shirt. The bust was fitted, lined with satin, ruffled in fine layers of silk, the neck was wide, just capping her shoulders, and as she slid the zip it held her waist willowy and firm.

She turned from the mirror and looked over her shoulder. Her dark hair just reached the low back. 'Ohh,' she sighed with longing, and just then, as if it were an echo, she heard a noise. She spun round and stared into the mirror. It had sounded like the soft thud of a door. She stared at herself. She looked ridiculous. Her face, half made-up, the hat, preposterous, with its scarf floating out. She took it off and slid it back on to its shelf.

And then she heard it again. The snap of a cupboard closing. She tiptoed to the top of the stairs. 'Hello?' she called, but no one answered. She ran into her room and pressed her face to the front window. There was no car in the drive. There was no one to be seen from the back window either. No one at the pool, or on the steps that ran down from the terrace. 'Hello?' she called, a little less friendly, and she crept downstairs.

There was no one there. The terrace door had closed, that was all, and the force of it had slammed shut a cupboard. But now she was scared and she couldn't shake it off. She walked round the house. Opening and closing doors. Attempting to take charge of it again. But even when she went outside and sat on a lounger she couldn't get rid of the feeling that she was not alone. She was on a hilltop in Italy, with everyone who should be here ill or dying or gone.

And then from inside the house she heard a gush of water. Her heart knocked against her ribs, her blood seared through her and, without waiting to find out more, she scooped up her plimsolls and ran round the side of the house and out into the drive. Where could she go? She was on the road now and a car screamed past. A man in sunglasses hooting as he sped by, two others leering at her from the open windows, making obscene gestures with their hands and tongues.

She ran the other way, and then finding herself beside the woods she plunged into the lane and sped along the sexy path to Ceccomoro, too frightened of whatever ghosts might be pursuing her even to think of communists or wild boar. She didn't stop until she was in the field. It was baking hot. It must be four o'clock, at least, and there was no sign of the rain that had lashed down the night before.

She rushed on through the maze, scratching her bare arms, catching at the fine material of her bunched-up skirt, only slowing when she was almost at the house. It seemed so long ago that she was here. But she shook this thought away.

There were no shouts from the pool. No murmur from the garden. And so very quietly she stepped on to the terrace. She smoothed her hair down as she went. Wet her fingertips to erase the white scratches on her skin, shook out the pink skirt, and still seeing no one she pulled open the door of the main house.

It was cool and silent. She stopped to listen. But there was nothing. Not a sound. Of course. They were all gone. They had gone to the Palio. Quickly she opened the door into the television room. It was dark. With no disgruntled shadow. No Kip in his jacket waiting for rain. She walked on, peering into a bedroom. Clothes strewn everywhere. The curled line of a roll-top bath through an open door beyond. Lara walked back along a corridor, out of a side door and into the main square. She ran up the street and stepped into the kitchen. All neat and cleared away as if no one would ever be needing supper again. My God! she thought. They've packed up. They've gone back to England.

And then she heard the hoot of a car. 'Get a move on!' It was Roland. Bellowing. 'Come on!' and this was followed by another long impatient beep.

Lara ran to a window and looked out. There was Andrew Willoughby's dark car, smoothly reversing out, and beside it the jeep, spilling out with stragglers, the engine revving, black smoke puffing out. Roland had his head through the driver's window and almost as if he were looking straight at her he opened his mouth and yelled, 'KIIIP!'

Lara raced back along the corridor, skidding over the stone floors until she reached the front door. The door was half open, sunshine falling through like scattered straw. She felt her heart crash. She'd missed him. By moments, she'd missed him. She leant against a wall, and just then Kip appeared from a side room holding a shoe. He opened his eyes wide when he saw her and instinctively she put her finger to her lips.

'KIP.' The shout came again and they held each other's stare.

'Wait here,' Kip whispered and he dropped his shoe and hopped outside. 'Go without me. Go on. I can't be bothered.' She could almost see him shrug his shoulders. 'Anyway I've lost my shoe.' And without a word of argument the jeep screeched out of the drive and roared away.

Kip stood in the doorway. 'Hello,' he said and Lara felt a sudden fizz like sherbet prickling inside her nose. Don't cry, she told herself. Don't cry.

'Bloody hell,' he said. 'What have you got on?' Lara looked down and saw she was still wearing the dress.

'It's Caroline's.' A scalding tear rolled down her face. 'She's dying. And Dad's in hospital with a broken toe.'

The sob that was rising spluttered into a laugh. 'I mean . . .' She covered her face.

'It's all right.' Kip was beside her. He traced a scratch along her neck. 'It's just a shame it's today, on the one day of the whole summer when something actually happens.' He slid an arm behind her and began to walk with her along the hall, shuffling his bare foot under her plimsolled one so that they were dancing, round and back and along in a lopsided waltz.

'You mean the Palio?'

Lara slipped out of his embrace, and hitching up the dress, felt for the pocket of her shorts. Did she still have those tickets? Or had she put them down when she was fooling around in Caroline's room? 'Look.' She was easing out the crumpled paper, bringing it up to show him. 'Is this what we need?' and as if the music had ended they came to a trembling halt.

Kip took the tickets and examined them. 'My God. What else have you got under there?'

'Nothing.' She wriggled round to undo the zip and let the dress fall to the floor revealing her shorts and T-shirt. 'They were . . . It was Caroline . . . she . . . left them on . . .'

'That's fucking brilliant!'

Kip reached up to take a pinstriped jacket down from a row of pegs. 'You'll be cold later.' He threw it to her, and he took an identical one for himself. 'Come on. Let's go.'

There was only one car left. A small white Fiat with the keys in the ignition. 'Pamela won't mind,' he said, and he swung open the door.

'Can you drive?' Lara asked.

Kip frowned. 'Of course.' But the gears jumped and screamed as he tried to find reverse and then, once he found it, he stalled. 'I'll be all right once we get going,' and he spun the car round so fast it nearly smashed into the wall. 'Right,' he said, when they were facing the open gates, and very carefully he nosed the car into the drive. But instead of taking the white road that wound down through the valley, he turned left on to an unmade track. 'Just till I get used to this car,' he said. 'It'll give me a chance to practise.' At first they bumped along slowly, jolting between craters and rocks, but as Kip became more confident he drove faster and faster. 'The thing is,' he said, as if quoting from a lesson, 'is not to brake, just to hit the rocks and let the wheels glance off them.' Lara was silent. She was concentrating too hard to speak. 'If you touch the brake,' he said happily, 'you've had it.'

Lara closed her eyes. It seemed dangerous, but the alternative was worse. Eventually they reached the tarmac of the made-up road and, although the smooth feel of it was a relief, now there was the added danger of other cars. They hooted and overtook while Kip swore and laughed and stuck his fingers up as he careered over crossings and screeched to a halt at red lights. But soon the traffic got so thick that it was impossible to go fast, and after several wrong turns, U-turns and reverses, they arrived at the post-office square where he pulled up at the same building that Caroline had stopped at the afternoon before. The same man appeared. But instead of friendly exclamations he shook his head. Scoot, the man seemed to be saying. Scoot.

'Signor.' Kip put out his hand to him, and ignoring the man's orders for them to be gone, he introduced himself, using his full title and the name of Ceccomoro, and having engaged him in a fluid and passionate conversation, Kip handed him the keys and strode away.

'I didn't know you spoke Italian.' Lara hurried to keep up.

Kip just shrugged his shoulders. 'Not really. Not much. Don't tell the others or God knows what they'll make me do.'

There were streams of people walking towards the square. The same ice-cream shops were open, crammed with grown-ups, and as if it were compulsory Kip stopped and bought them both a double-scoop ice cream. They stood in the corner just as she and Caroline had done and ate the soft melting ice.

'I came into Siena last night,' she told him. 'To see the trials. With Caroline.' And then it occurred to her that this ice cream, this meringue and crema, may be the last thing that Caroline would ever eat.

'Yes, I came in too.' Kip leant forward and took a bite of her ice cream. She'd forgotten about it and it was dripping down on to her hand. 'I was with Roland. We were right in the middle of the Campo. With sixty thousand other lunatics. Couldn't see a thing.' Lara looked round for a bin. 'Or twenty thousand. I can never re-member.' He took the ice cream from her and demolished it in two huge bites. 'All I'm saying is . . .' He leant forward and whispered. 'Unlike you. I didn't have a ticket. But don't worry. I won't call the *carabinieri* to find out where you really got these tickets. I'll just use my infor-mation in other ways. Remember' – his hair was tickling her face – 'from now on you are in my power.'

Lara laughed. She wanted to feel happy but the thought of Caroline had unsettled her. Where was she anyway? Were she and Lambert in a hospital in Siena? They might be anywhere. They might be just around a corner, listening to the crowds making their way to the square. She should have asked. Should have insisted that she visit.

'Come on,' Kip said. 'Let's go and watch the procession.'

'What if we see the others?'

'The others are squeezed on to a balcony with some rich toff Italians. We might see them. But they'll never see us.'

They walked out into the street and Kip took hold of her hand. His palm felt warm and sure and silky smooth from sun. He hadn't asked her why she'd stayed away, and if he hadn't asked by now there was a chance he never would. She felt a surge of gratitude and leant against his arm. It was like being a child again, this licence to hold someone else's hand, and she realised how much she'd missed being able to sit curled into her mother's lap, to share her bed, her bath, her body as if it were her own. It hadn't seemed possible these last few years. Since they'd returned from India. Since her body had begun to change. Maybe after a year of travelling, of sleeping side by side, of sitting week after week on the Budget Bus in the tented compartment of their seats, maybe after that they'd both needed to retreat. But now she felt so hungry for Kip's closeness that it hurt. She squeezed his arm and smiled, and when he looked round she tried not to let it show – the certainty that she'd never ever have enough.

'We've got one spare ticket,' Kip remembered as they neared the barrier.

'Keep it,' Lara told him. 'Just in case,' and she had a vision of Caroline rising up out of unconsciousness at the sound of Il Nicchio's name.

'The moment of truth,' Kip said, and he showed their tickets, and they were through.

The Campo was a multicoloured mass of people. The centre, a dense storm of colour, the seats around without a single space. Lara resisted looking up to where each window and balcony was hung with red tapestries, spectators leaning out over the edge. The procession had already started, the Palazzo bell was tolling, and they were ushered along the track of earth until they came to the starting point opposite the little starting cannon. And there were their seats. In the best possible position. A gate was opened for them and they climbed up to the second row and sat behind a family all wearing dark-red T-shirts from the *contrada* of the Tower.

'Who do you want to win?' Lara whispered, and he said he was hoping that it would be Dragon because Dragon was the winner the year he was born.

'Dragon won the year after, too, the year you were born,' he said. 'We can both be honorary Dragons.'

He knows when I was born! she thought. 'Caroline has a horse running for Il Nicchio,' she told him. 'She wanted . . . wants him to win so badly.'

'Oh God. Don't let Il Nicchio win. For some reason my father has pledged a fortune if Il Nicchio wins. He says if it does he'll be ruined.'

The procession was moving now. The drums were rolling, and men in medieval costume were walking along before their horse. There was a drummer, two men holding banners, a man in full gleaming armour and several others holding swords and flags. They were all dressed in bright yellow and green and the two horses that followed were draped in the same colours. 'Il Bruco,' Kip hissed, and Lara remembered that it was the Caterpillar that never had any luck.

Il Bruco stopped directly in front of them. God, they must be hot, Lara thought, as she craned forward to see their costumes, the tights and capes and heavy hats. The jerkins and belts, the double velvet sleeves. And then the banner wavers began to dance. They threw up their banners, caught them, tossed them to each other, stepped over them, leapt and danced and twirled. Their banners matched their costumes, a dazzle of green and gold, with a caterpillar crawling on a twig, a gold crown above it, a red rose by its side. The drum rolled, the banner wavers leapt, one over the other, and the crowd applauded. And then the little group moved on.

Next came Il Drago. Kip clapped wildly and looked around to see if there were any other Dragons in their stand. Dragons wore red with a trim of fur along the bottom of their capes and one black and one red leg disappearing into knee-high boots. Their banner was edged in gold with a gold dragon at its centre, and when they knelt and twirled and threw their banners the sky looked as if it were on fire. Kip and Lara were surrounded by Towers, Porcupines, Eagles and Shells but not it seemed a single Dragon.

The Woodland were next, in orange velvet hats, creamy damask capes and jerkins and soft suede boots. After each display the little troupe, followed by two horses, one that would run, and another, saddled up and ridden by the jockey, moved on. The drums rolled, the brass band played and another *contrada* appeared at the far corner of the square.

'There's Il Nicchio,' Kip pointed.

Il Nicchio's flag was blue with a large shell in its centre. Its banner wavers wore fur-lined capes, with white gloves, red tunics and tights with zigzags of red and gold. They stopped a little further along and Lara had to crane sideways to see their display. But it was just the same. Twirling, flinging, leaping and catching. The flags unfurling and fluttering as they flew into the air. Lara imagined them practising and practising all year long, their hearts pounding as they threw the banners high, never relaxing for a moment till they'd caught hold of them again.

And now the procession was marching. The big bell on the Palazzo tower was tolling, the drums were beating, the brass band playing. A group of children in white with leaves of laurel marched behind Dolphin, the last of the ten competing *contrade*, and then after them, one by one, came the seven who were not racing. These seven threw their banners with equal flourishes, passed and stepped and danced to the roll of their drums. Their supporters sang to them, and shook their fists at their enemies, just as heartily as if they had been running too.

After the seven came a strange and sinister procession. Six men on horses in velvet skirts with veils of chain mail, the men with solid metal visors with nothing but a slit through which to see out.

'Who are they?' Lara asked and Kip told her they were the ghosts of the *contrade*.

'The *contrade* that are no more.'

Out of each of the men's helmets rose an emblem. A serpent – its mouth open and spitting – a fist, its fingers clasped around a knife. There was a cockerel too, a lion, a wreath and a bear.

'But what happened to those *contrade*?' Lara asked.

Kip shrugged. 'Died out, I suppose. Got taken over.'

After the ghosts on their veiled horses came a cart pulled by four white oxen. A cheer rocked the crowd, and everyone who had a flag began to wave it.

'That's the Palio,' Kip told her. 'That painted cloth. Whichever *contrada* wins the race – that Palio is theirs.'

Lara saw it, billowing tall as a sail. It was painted with a horse's head, a sickle moon, the head and shoulders of a woman. The cart was surrounded by men in armour, and on either side were buglers blowing into the sky.

Each ox was led by a man in an earth-coloured jerkin and, as it passed below them, Kip leant close in to her ear.

'You see those oxen?'

Lara nodded.

'The jockeys' whips are made from the dried skin of their . . .'

'What?'

'Their . . . you know . . . their . . .' He was gazing at them as if by staring she would see what he meant.

And then she did see. 'No!' How could she have missed them? The great leathery penises as dark as bulrushes against the white of their coats. 'That's horrible.' She put a hand to her mouth, and then to cover her reaction, she added, 'I mean, horrible, horrible that they use whips.'

'They don't just use the whips on the horses,' Kip said. 'They whip each other.'

'Is that allowed?'

'What do you want them to do? Whisper sweet words of encouragement as they overtake?'

'Why not?' She thought of the race that Caroline had missed. The final trial where each horse tried hard not to win.

Kip slid his hand around her waist. 'And then the winning jockey has to eat the ox's bollocks in this evening's feast.'

'No!'

'No.' Kip couldn't stop laughing. 'You're hopeless. Of course they don't.'

They sat together, holding hands, laughing and spluttering, until with a roll of drums the collected banner throwers, one from each *contrada*, lined up in front of the Palazzo, and hurled their flags as high as they would go into the sky. Seventeen flags flew high against the Palazzo tower, the colours dancing like a fountain, and then down they plummeted again. The trumpeters trumpeted, the people cheered and a group of men in smart grey suits strolled along the track, exuding wealth and power, their faces smooth, their mouths drawn down at the seriousness of what was to come.

'Your friends from the Mafia.' Kip nudged her.

The track was emptying. The white-clad boys with their laurel leaves swished by, and then the sweepers appeared and, brushing away the footsteps and the hoof marks, they

227

smoothed the earth. But a scuffle had broken out from the central area, somewhere near the balustrades. There was shouting and movement, and two ambulance men were rushing across the track.

'Someone's fainted,' Kip said. 'It happens all the time,' and a body was lifted up and passed over the fence. It was thrown on to a stretcher and unceremoniously whisked away.

The sweepers appeared and swished away their steps and a moment later everything was quiet. Even the bell had stopped. The silence was unnerving. That bell must have been tolling for hours. Lara could feel the echo of it pulsing in the air.

'Look at the pigeons trying to get a drink,' Kip whispered, and it was true, a flock of birds was circling over the square, swooping down hopefully and then rising up again when they found their way to the fountain was blocked. There were people sitting on it, clinging to the masonry, getting a high view for free.

And then the air was split with the roar of an explosion. Lara jumped. The people cheered. It meant the horses were in the Campo! They were trotting out through the vast doors of the Palazzo and now there they were, climbing the hill at the far corner. Everyone craned to see. They were coming round the bend, the jockeys in their coloured hats, their whips in their hands, trotting towards them, and just like the night before, they assembled a little way from the starting rope which had been weighted and stretched across the track.

'Is this . . .' Lara turned to Kip, but a woman from the Tower, blonde and with immaculate make-up, turned and shushed them savagely.

And there was silence. Silence in a crowd of 60,000. No one would dare faint now, she thought, and just then a name was called. Il Drago. Il Drago reared up and then sped down to the line, where it proceeded to turn round and round as if outraged by its position against the fence. Another name was called, and another. Some greeted by cheers, others by boos, until nine horses were in place.

Lara craned forward. 'Which is the tenth horse?' she whispered, one eye on the woman from the Tower.

L'Istrice, the Porcupine,' Kip hissed back, and they watched as L'Istrice pranced and reeled, the jockey's eyes never leaving the line-up for a moment. 'Last-minute dealings,' Kip murmured. They could almost see the deals being done out of the corners of the men's mouths. But Il Drago was rearing again and had to be ridden back and forwards several times before it would calm down. Finally once it was in place Il Nicchio startled. It nudged the others sideways and had to be turned around and settled too. And then for a miraculous moment each horse was still. Each one ready in the order in which it had been called. Even L'Istrice was facing the right way. Start. Lara urged. Start. But the King Maker didn't make a move. There was a bulge in the centre of the line as several animals started to back up, squeezing the last two against the fence. Il Drago was growing agitated, and the crowd that was pressed against that part of the fence started back as he reared round.

'You know they give them drugs,' Kip murmured.

'To calm them down?' Lara asked.

'No, to liven them up.'

A shout rang out. One lone shout of frustration above all the others, and Lara took her eyes off the horses and looked around her. She had to. She couldn't breathe with the suspense, and then without meaning to she glanced up at the overflowing balcony of the Caffè del Campo. And there they were. Piers and May. Roland, Tabitha and Pamela. They were leaning over the red-draped edge, peering down into the crowd. Lara looked away as fast as she could, but even as she did so she caught sight of Lulu, her honey-coloured hair swept back, her dress plunging down to reveal the deep gold of her neck. Lara felt a prickle of unease. Was that why Kip hadn't mentioned that she'd stayed away? Maybe he hadn't noticed. Maybe he'd been too distracted by Lulu's return to mind.

She pulled on the pinstriped jacket, tugging it over her thighs, letting the sleeves engulf her. She stared hard at L'Istrice. It was circling and throwing its head, the jockey's legs clasped to its side with nothing but his reins to hold him on. The line-up at the rope was still in disarray. Horses skittered backwards, others spun round, the eighth was nudging and pushing until the ninth was standing right across the start. Each time a horse was shunted out it did its best to get back into line, but the others made it as difficult as possible for it to regain its place.

They must all be standing beside their enemies, Lara thought, but she couldn't remember which *contrade* were aligned. Hisses filled the air. Shouts and boos and whistles. Words of advice.

'Now!' Lara couldn't help whispering every time even some of the horses were still. 'Now!' But L'Istrice was not allowed to start.

'He's collecting up more bribes,' Kip whispered, and once again Lara allowed her eyes to roam over the crowd.

She let them rest on the thousands in the centre, examined those behind the mattresses at the San Martino corner, draped in scarves, hanging from their seats, imagining them to be more bloodthirsty than the rest. And then she looked up, just for a second, at the balcony. Andrew Willoughby was there too, and beside him, Lara couldn't believe it, was Isabelle, with Hugh leaning up against the wall behind.

Shouldn't she be visiting Lambert! And then she remembered that he didn't want anyone to see him until he was discharged. She turned away. She wouldn't look again, but almost immediately, she couldn't resist it, she glanced up one last time. Roland was staring straight at her. His eyes locking into hers. She snapped her head away, pulled the jacket tighter, but even so a shiver ran through her so violently that her shoulders shook.

'I think this is it!' Kip gripped her hand. 'Yes. Yes.'

The horses were in line. The crowd was straining. She could feel them, in agony, holding their breath. But no. They erupted in outrage. L'Istrice's jockey had turned his horse around. It's unbearable. Lara hung her head. She wanted to scream. It'll never ever happen. But just then L'Istrice, with no warning, wheeled round and sprang ahead. The square exploded with the starting cannon. The rope was down. The horses were running. And everyone was up on their feet.

She could still see the tenth horse, flashing ahead, but the others were gaining on him, had reached him, were squashed together in a heap. They were heading for San Martino where the track turned sharply and dropped downhill. They hurled themselves around – thank God for the mattresses – but no one fell. On they went, Il Nicchio in the lead now, and then for a moment they were out of sight, until, comical almost, like toy soldiers, they came cantering up the hill on the other side. They were streaking past, the colours of their *contrada* on their hats, and everyone was screaming, shouting, as L'Onda in the inside lane began to gain, began to push past La Selva who was struggling to overtake Il Nicchio for the lead. And then L'Onda fell. Il Nicchio flew on. La Selva – the Woodland – following and then Il Drago tangled with another horse and they both came crashing down.

'NO,' Kip shouted.

'NO,' Lara echoed.

But there was no time to mourn. Il Nicchio was safely in the lead. Il Nicchio. Caroline's horse. 'NICCHIO,' they both screamed with everything they had.

A riderless horse was streaking along in third place now. A riderless horse could win the Palio. That was another of its rules. 'NICCHIO!' The crowd was screaming too, swaying, weeping, singing, beating their chests.

'NICCHIO,' Lara screamed. 'Go on. Go on.' She felt as if she were floating. 'NICCHIO!' Her life depended on it. Caroline's life too.

Il Nicchio was streaming past them again. Once more he braved the turn at San Martino and in a flash he was forcing on up the last hill, frothing and straining, was racing round the last corner, with the riderless horse no nearer than his rump, and yes, he could hardly fail to win.

'NICCHIO.' Lara was screaming with her whole body. Screaming so hard she was lost. 'NICCHIO!'

It seemed the whole world was screaming as he galloped that last stretch, and before the horses had even reached the rope Il Nicchio's supporters were hurling themselves on to the track. One man crashed down from the seat behind her, using her shoulder as a step, and there they were, the men and women of the Shell, crying, shouting, kissing each other, stretching their arms up to the sky, to the Madonna, to God.

Lara watched open-mouthed. Never in her life had she seen so many people so overwhelmed with joy. They surrounded the jockey, lifting him off his horse, kissing and embracing him as they swooped him up above their shoulders and rushed him along.

'Quick.' Kip took her hand. 'Let's go. Let's get there first.' He pulled her with him as he jumped down from his seat, keeping hold of her hand as they nudged and squeezed their way through the mass of people.

'Where?' she asked, as they ran up the steps away from the Campo, along the curving street of shops, down and up and into other identical curved streets.

'Quick,' he said, and breathless they came out into the square before the Duomo.

They were not the first. Thousands of people were already there, and many more were pushing themselves inside. Lara and Kip squeezed in through the door and found themselves pushed forward on the wave of the crowd. All around them people were singing. That same painful blood-curdling song of the previous day's procession. Lara stopped, gulping in the thick hot air, damp with stone and overpowering sweat. A woman pushed her from behind, and a line of small children snaked under her outstretched arm.

Kip reeled her in towards him and then a shout rang out, the singing burst up louder, and everyone swarmed forward. It was the jockey, shirtless, being carried high into the church. The song swelled, rose into the vaulted ceiling, reached the painted stars.

'Sometimes they bring the horse in too,' Kip told her.

She strained to see, standing on tiptoe, staring round, while behind her more and still more people pushed into the cathedral. The singing rose and fell, the air was stifling, and Lara couldn't imagine there was room anywhere in that whole cathedral for a horse.

'I remember now,' Kip said as if he'd heard her. 'They bring the horses in before the race. Each one is taken to its local church to be blessed.' But still they waited, her pin-striped shoulder pressed against Kip's own, the whole huge cathedral full of heat and singing, sighing, happiness and hope.

'Shall we be Nicchios from now on, instead of Dragos?' she whispered, and he turned to her and beamed.

'Fickle,' he said, 'but why not?'

Eventually they sidled their way out. It was easier navigating their way against the stream of people, ducking past women's shoulders, pushing through knots of weeping men. Finally they burst out through the door. They unclasped hands, and feeling almost shy they stood in silence on the top step and looked out into the grainy night. People were still streaming up from the Campo, but more slowly now, more calmly, embracing each other only sporadically, crying only a few tears. Lara and Kip began to walk. The moon was out and the stone walkways and closed-up shop fronts, the sudden views and windows hung with washing, the flags and coats of arms all flickered in its light.

They arrived back in the square to find that many of the seats had already been taken down, the cafés at the top of the Campo had re-opened and long tables spread with white cotton cloths were being laid.

Kip pulled out the tickets. 'Dinner included.' He pointed to the lines of small print, and disbelievingly she sat opposite him at the end of a long table that stretched almost to the edge of the track.

Soon the other places were taken by Italian men and women, some deflated, others arguing, but none quite clearly from the victorious *contrada* of the Shell. Wine was poured and they were served the first course – a cold spinach pâté, the second a plate of tortelloni stuffed with cheese. There was no menu and no choosing. They all ate and drank together, she and Kip, the smart middle-aged Italians, the diners at tables on either side. As they ate the square filled up again. People streamed by, some sucking giant dummies, others beating drums.

Three men serenaded Kip and Lara, another tried selling Kip a rose. Lara remembered Kip's aversion to anything romantic, and to disassociate herself from the lilting music she rolled her eyes. But really she loved it, the accordion and the fiddle and the strums of the guitar, and she wondered if it was these men she'd been listening to all summer, practising love songs in the hills, and not after all a group of communists planning who to kidnap and which town to bomb.

'Why the dummies?' she asked Kip, when the trio, unrewarded, had moved on, and a man seated beside her replied in perfect English.

'When the Palio is run, Siena is re-born.'

Waiters moved among them, filling their glasses, while more courses were brought, a bowl of salad and after a plate of blood-red meat.

'It's the ox,' Kip told her, and she squinted to see if he was teasing. 'No it is. Well, not the ox we saw just now, obviously, but it's a local speciality. Go on, try it, it's good,' and he cut into a slice.

Lara looked down at her plate. Nothing could entice her. 'I think I'll leave it,' and although it pleased her to think she'd been true to her vegetarian beliefs, in reality she was too squeamish to eat anything that lay in a sauce of its own blood.

The waiter frowned when he removed her plate as if the animal had been killed especially for her ungrateful self, and to please him, although he showed no sign of noticing, she finished the ice cream that followed, every last scrap of it, and drained her glass of wine. By the time they got up to go her head was reeling.

'What shall we do now?' Kip stretched, and not able to decide, they linked arms and walked anti-clockwise around the track, looking at the people sitting outside other

235

restaurants, standing chatting and drinking at the long, glossy, caramel-coloured bars inside.

They plunged into the unlit area that formed the base of the square and peered into the courtyard of the Palazzo where the horses had been held. They walked on, examined the sharp corner at San Martino where the seats had been collapsed, the fences gone, the mattresses and injured horses carted away.

'Quick!' Kip said. 'Winner takes all,' and without warning he began to run, his jacket flying, his bare heels lifting out of his shoes.

'Wait!' Lara sped after him, her head pounding. 'Wait!' she called. 'The Palio's been run,' but he had disappeared.

Lara ran as fast as she could, pushing past the teenagers with their linked arms, the men and women with small children, bright-eyed and perfectly dressed. Where had he gone? She stopped and looked around, and then from her right she heard a whistle. There, instead of Kip, was a whole table of Willoughbys. Andrew Willoughby at the head, Lulu beside him, Roland not far away and Isabelle too.

'It's our little revolutionary.' Andrew's eyes were swimming behind his glasses, and to avoid Roland she looked straight at him.

'Yes.' What else could she say, and for a moment it seemed the whole table was staring at her.

Lulu leant forward. 'I thought you'd gone.'

'Oh yes, well.' Lara felt as if an apology was called for. 'My father hurt his foot . . . and . . .'

'Is he . . .?' Isabelle looked up through a strand of falling hair. 'Is he here?' And Lara remembered he was ill. That he was in hospital. That Caroline was there too. She put a hand to her mouth. It was hours since she'd left the house, probably without even remembering to shut the door. And the porch light? Had she left it on? Or off?

'Yes,' she stammered. 'I'd better find him,' but Andrew reached out and caught hold of her arm.

'I ask you.' He was looking back at Isabelle. 'Don't honestly tell me you don't see what I mean. They look like bloody twins.'

Isabelle sat up straighter. 'I don't see,' she said. 'Leave the girl alone.'

'Honestly, darling.' Pamela leant forward. 'It's just that she's wearing Kip's jacket, that's all. That's all it is. Don't be such a bore.'

'Where is that boy anyway?' Andrew had taken up his glass and still holding her arm with one hand he raised it to his lips. 'Where's the little runt!'

'He didn't come. Don't you remember?' Lulu frowned. 'He lost his shoe.'

'Well, I want to talk to Herr Professor Goldstein.' Andrew said it as if it were a joke – a name made up from Cluedo. 'Wolfgang . . . Lambert. Whatever he's called.' He looked coldly at Lara and lowered his voice. 'I used to know him, you see. Knew him in the old days. He can't fool me with that idiotic change of name.' He let go of Lara to tip more wine into his glass, and she glanced behind her, praying that Kip hadn't come back looking for her. But the bottle was empty. 'Waiter,' he waved. 'More vino. Thinks he can make a fool of me. Now. After all this time. Bringing that girl here for one reason, and one reason only . . .'

'Oh honestly,' said Pamela. 'Of course he's yours. Anyone can see it. Stop making such a fuss. And anyway,' she added ill-advisedly, 'even if he isn't, what difference does it make?'

Lara swallowed. 'I'd better go.'

She looked along the table, saw only averted eyes, even Roland seemed for once to be paying attention to his wife. Only May smiled sadly at her as she backed away.

'Don't forget,' Andrew called. 'Send him over. Sore toe or not. Tell him I want a word.' But Lara had begun to run.

She ran as fast as she could along the track, forgetting even to look for Kip, wanting to get as far away as possible, until with a thud she bumped into him walking the other way.

'Talk about the tortoise!' He laughed, grabbing hold of her, and for the first time that night he moved towards her for a kiss.

Lara pulled away. 'I saw them!' she said. 'Your family. At the Caffè del Campo.'

'Yes,' he said, grinning. 'Why do you think I told you to run? No one should have to see Papa the night he parts with money.'

Lara sank against him. She closed her eyes and breathed in the lavender and soap smell of his shirt. 'Let's go,' she said. 'I should really be getting back.'

Slowly they walked uphill towards the car. They stood in the square while the man retrieved it for them and then with only a few false starts Kip pulled away. They drove in silence through the quiet streets and on into the darker night. What did Andrew Willoughby say? She didn't want to remember, but she couldn't keep his voice from snaking in around her ears. Twins, he'd said. 'They look like bloody twins,' and then she remembered his voice in the upstairs corridor at Ceccomoro. 'A decade of fruitless fucking . . . and then that cunt whisks in and my wife is giving birth to a son.' What was Andrew saying? That Kip was Lambert's son? That she and Kip were sister and brother? And just then something dark and crazed and scurrying charged across the road.

'My God!' Kip slammed on the brake so hard they skidded. 'I think that actually was a wild boar.'

'A wild boar,' Lara repeated, and she thought of the game they'd played by the river. Her father was well then. And Kip had never been in love. She glanced at him, her heart swollen, so tender it felt like a bruise.

'It's gone.' Kip peered into the darkness, and more slowly he drove on.

Lara watched him surreptitiously. It's not true, she told herself. Andrew was drunk, that's all. No one else believed him. 'Of course he's yours,' Pamela had said. 'And anyway . . . even if he's not . . .' Lara kept on looking at him as if that might dispel her doubts. But there was something about Kip that was familiar. She'd always sensed it. So familiar she felt as if she'd been longing for him all her life. I'll have to tell him, she thought, her body quaking. At least I'll have to tell him he can't stay the night. But then what would she do? She couldn't go back to Ceccomoro, and if Ginny wasn't back from the hospital, she didn't dare spend the night alone in Caroline's house.

'Kip?' She put a hand on his arm. 'Would you come back and stay at mine?' and she gripped the seat with her free hand to stop herself from trembling.

'Seeing as you're begging me.' Kip grinned and he accelerated so that the little car rattled up the hill.

The house was dark when they arrived and there was no car in the drive. Lara got out and Kip switched off the engine.

'There's no one here,' she whispered, and Kip whispered back, 'So why are we whispering?'

They walked round to the back of the house where they stood on the terrace and looked down at the pool. It glowed indigo in the moonlight but the trees beyond were silhouettes of black. For a moment a flare flashed up in the hills and Lara strained her whole body for a catch of music, but there was none. I'll think about it tomorrow, she promised herself. There's nothing I can do tonight, and she led the way down the steps to the pool.

It wasn't warm. There was a bite to the air and the water when she dipped her foot in it sent a shiver up her spine. But Kip was kicking off his jeans, pulling his shirt, half buttoned, over his head. He turned away and stepped out of his boxer shorts.

Now was her chance, she thought, finally to see a man naked, even if he was her brother, but before she could look he had hurled himself into the pool.

'Ahhhhh!' He came up shrieking and Lara glanced anxiously at the house. But no light flicked on, anywhere, and nothing changed.

She moved into the shadow and began as slowly as she could to undress. What should she do? The more she thought about it the less sure she became.

'Coward!' Kip taunted and she turned towards him and pulled her T-shirt over her head.

There was no escaping his watching eyes, just hovering above the water as she approached the pool. Her skin, for all her sunbathing, shone white, the stripes of her bikini line fluorescent. She put a foot in, then another, and unable to bear being watched she threw herself in. She swam fast for a few moments, ducking her head down, and then when she came up she was warm.

'The difference between you and Lulu' – Kip was close beside her – 'is that she knows she's beautiful, and you haven't realised it yet.'

'You're mad.' Her smile was wide as the moon, but all the time she was thinking, He doesn't know why he likes me. I'm familiar; he can't help himself, that's all. She concentrated on treading water. 'What I don't understand . . .' she said breathlessly to distract herself, 'about you and Lulu, I mean, is . . . why aren't you more . . .' She wanted to say grateful, or amazed, but instead she said, 'More interested?'

'I don't know.' Kip's breath was close against her face and she could feel him treading water too. 'I suppose she's not my type, that's all.'

Lara laughed, but fear shot through her, draining her face so that it ached. To hide herself she put her arms around Kip's neck and kissed him.

'It's not as if' – he kissed her back – 'your eyes are especially beautiful, or your mouth, or your nose.'

'No?' Lara swallowed a mouthful of water as she began to sink.

'But altogether . . .' He was sinking too. 'It all looks perfect. To me.'

'You're mad.' She kissed him again, but inside her kiss, she promised: This is the last time. This is the last time I'll ever do this. I swear.

Kip didn't notice. His hands were on her naked body. Tracing the curves and bone, the plains and edges of her, waterlogged, but somehow light as air. His body felt different too. Cool and contracted. His stomach flat and hard, his back a board. He twined his legs around hers, and she gave in as they rolled and kissed, splashing and kicking to stay up, not wanting to spoil the difficulty of it by moving down to the shallow end. Eventually they paddled further in and leant against the side where they kissed until their mouths were scorched.

'It's very underrated, kissing.' Kip pressed himself against her, but she knew he meant there must be more.

'OK,' she agreed, holding hard on to her promise, and then, impossible as it seemed, they rolled and pressed and almost sank until finally he was inside her, escaping the hardness of the water to a place where everything was soft. They clung together, the chilled edges of their toes and ears forgotten while they began to move. It was like a dance, with

241

the ballet bar behind them, the moon above, and Lara closed her eyes. Ripples of pleasure pulsed through her, filling her up, and then just as easily receding, so that she was left with the cold hard thrust of him, insistent as he pushed her back against the bar. She closed her eyes tighter. Told herself that it was him. It was Kip. Whoever he was, he wasn't Roland.

And then in desperation she remembered the pipe-cleaner dolls that she and Sorrel had pressed together one summer holiday in Scotland. They'd taken the man doll and pressed him up against the doll woman's body, entwining their legs and arms so that their bodies crunched. Lara had felt a flash of something hot inside her. It was the first time she'd felt it – a fizzing of desire, and she'd blushed as Sorrel sent the dolls into the doll's house to bed. It kept her smiling, this memory, kept other thoughts at bay, but when it was over she was so exhausted she thought she might sink. She closed her eyes and let herself drift under, just for a minute, just to see how it would feel, but her body forced itself back up, and when she looked, Kip was scrambling out.

'It's bloody freezing,' he said, and there it was, his penis. It was still hard, why was that? And curving out in front of him, bouncing as he walked. Lara covered her mouth. But she couldn't hide her laughter.

'What?' Kip looked at her. But she kept on laughing.

'It's just so funny,' she said, her shoulders shaking, and she felt overwhelmed with relief.

Lara and Kip ran up to the house, naked, clutching their clothes, watching out for tiny lizards skittering away from them on the stones. The terrace door was open and they ran through the sitting room, over the white rug, and up the stairs. They ran into Lara's room and too cold for anything else they threw themselves under the covers of her single bed.

'Where is everybody anyway?' Kip asked, his teeth chattering, and just at that moment Lara thought she heard the phone.

'Shhhh.' She put up her hand. But either it had stopped, or it was nothing. 'They're at the hospital.'

'Oh yes.'

They lay there in silence, slowly warming up. A hundred thoughts and questions flitted through her mind. Have you ever . . .? What . . .? Would . . .? But when she glanced behind her at Kip, his eyelids closed, his mouth a little open, it seemed nothing at all needed to be said. It's not true anyway, she told herself, tears oozing up into her eyes, but all the same she twisted round again and stared at him to check for signs.

'What?' Kip frowned. He could feel her watching him, and so she slipped back into the curve of his body and tried not to think of anything at all.

Lara had been in Bangalore for a month when the girls she was training with were asked to perform at a hotel. There was great excitement, extra practice and much time spent standing patiently while swathes of material were fitted and folded and pinned on to their bodies. But none of this included Lara. Lara wasn't ready to perform, would need to practise for at least another thousand hours before she could be dressed in peacock colours and stand on a stage. Instead she and Cathy sat cross-legged on the floor of the hotel dining room, while small groups of girls took their turn to dance.

The teacher sat with the musicians, wielding a cymbal, watching. She watched their eyes, their hands, their shoulders and their feet, her body so alert it was as if she were dancing herself. The children danced the dance of Krishna as a baby. Krishna was a naughty and delightful baby – stealing yoghurt and honey whenever he got a chance. And then later, the older girls danced the story of him grown-up, being tempted by the Gopis who were some sort of milkmaid or cowgirl, but lovely all the same. They fled, they flirted, they called him with their eyes. Come hither, they seemed to be saying.

The teacher dictated the rhythm, clacking with her cymbals, high as a pin. Below the cymbal the violin wailed, and below that the drums scattered and thumped. The girls' hard feet stamped, their bells tinkling, and Lara, determined to practise harder, to put in her thousand hours, and soon, turned to beam at Cathy. It was everything she had promised her. And more. But to her surprise Cathy looked unhappy. She was watching the dancers, true, but she was half turned towards the audience. Fat and white and perspiring. Lara saw them through her mother's eyes, and when she looked back at the young dancers she noticed how their eyes were painted – made enormous with lids of blue, that there were jewels hovering at the tips of their partings, and exposed across their ribs was a stretch of smooth bare skin.

'It should be more than entertainment,' Cathy muttered later. 'The messages are for the gods not the ex-pats.' But she didn't put Lara off when she rose at dawn the next morning to practise before school, holding out her arms, folding back her third finger, circling her wrists until they stung.

When Lara woke she couldn't think where she was, couldn't imagine whose arms were draped around her, whose hot head was squashed against hers on the pillow. And then she remembered. She lay still, hardly daring to move in case Kip woke too, jumped up and rushed away. She closed her eyes again, tried to sink back into the heat of his body, but she could tell it was already late – there was strong sun in slices at the edges of the curtains, and the crickets were shrieking in the grass.

Very carefully Lara extricated herself from the cage of Kip's arms, sliding out from under him, seeing his cheek, which had been resting against her head, fall into the hollow of the pillow.

She pulled on a shirt and crossed the landing to peer into her father's room. Lambert's bed was still empty, his clothes folded out of sight. Books and papers were piled on top of a low cupboard and beside his lamp was a tower of hardback books. Could he still be at the hospital? Had something gone wrong? And anxiety spread out from a knot, already there, at the centre of her chest.

Lara ran downstairs. She glanced into the deserted kitchen, the sitting room with its sofa cushions still perfectly plumped. She stared at the telephone and then, checking, she put it to her ear. The line was purring, optimistic, as if someone might be waiting to tell her what was going on.

'Hello?' she tried hopefully. '*Pronto*?' But of course there was no one there.

Back in the kitchen she opened the fridge. There was milk, fruit, glass bottles of peach and apricot juice. There was mozzarella and pancetta in folded paper packets and black olives in a tin. Lara stood indecisive. Where was the cereal? And the bowls? It made her flush to think how entirely she'd come to rely on Ginny's bustling self.

Instead of looking, she pulled out the loaf of home-baked bread and tearing off a corner dipped it into a jar of blueberry jam. She was starving. She dipped the bread again, but this time the crust broke off, leaving the jam thick with crumbs, ruined possibly in Caroline's fastidious eyes. Quickly she began to spoon it out, and then, with no alternative but to eat it, she cut two slices of bread and heaped them high. She poured two glasses of juice, opened every cupboard till she found a tray, and delighted with herself for inadvertently providing breakfast she carried it upstairs.

'Kip,' she whispered, 'Kip . . .'

One corner of his mouth lifted, but he didn't stir. Lara set the tray on the floor, and squeezing into the narrow space beside him she wriggled until Kip shifted over on to his side. She leant down for a slice of bread, and cupping her hand to protect the sheet from falling berries, she took an enormous bite. Happiness flooded through her. Pure, unadulterated joy. She took another bite, and another, all the time looking down on Kip's sleeping face, half turned away from her, the line of his jaw, the hair over his forehead, his ear so neat against his head, the lobe hardly a lobe at all . . .

She stopped chewing. She'd remembered her promise. What had she told herself the night before? That everything between them would be finished. She took a gulp of juice and lay against Kip's back. But he doesn't know, she allowed herself to argue, and if he never knows, I can forget too. And she *could* forget. She could forget anything. Hadn't she forgotten Roland? The weight of his leg, the tear in her wrist as she tried to pull away. And anyway, what was she supposed to do: throw Kip out? She slipped an arm around him, and fearful, she pressed her hand over his sleeping heart.

When she woke again Kip was leaning over her, lifting the second slice of bread, scattering berries across the sheet.

'Careful,' she warned as a splash of jam fell on to the pillow, but Kip crammed as much as he could into his mouth.

'Any more?' he asked when he could speak, but she was too busy picking berries off the linen, licking her finger and attempting to blot the stains with spit. 'Leave it' – he stretched – 'it doesn't matter. Someone will wash it.'

'But what if it's ruined?' The more she rubbed, the worse the marks became.

'So what?' Kip was looking at her.

'It seems disrespectful, that's all.'

Kip whipped the sheet away and hurled it into a corner. 'It's gone,' he said, 'but if you want me to I'll bury it. We'll hold a service. Is that respectful enough for you?'

Naked, and now sheetless, he rolled on top of her and begun to nuzzle her with his nose, making small snuffling noises, her hands in his, his erection smooth and tickling her belly, until she gave in and began to laugh.

They made love, Kip, slow and tender, his eyes on her, Lara, so busy forgetting she could hardly look up. Forgetting Roland, forgetting Andrew Willoughby with his slurring words, forgetting Lulu: 'I thought you'd be gone by now.' Forgetting May. She remembered and then forgot Caroline on her stretcher, and her father hobbling towards the door, climbing up into the ambulance with only a book and a silk scarf. But Kip was kissing her, turning her and stroking her with such insistence that eventually she lost the battle to forget. Her thoughts turned to waves – thick waves of colour – and the marrow in her bones to streams of syrup, so that she hardly knew where she ended and he began, and she felt so full of sweetness that she thought she might forget everything, for ever, as long as he promised not to stop. And then she did remember.

'We should be careful, though.' She gripped him, but Kip's back was bathed in sweat.

'Oh.' They held each other. It was too late. 'Next time,' he whispered. 'I've even got some Durex somewhere,' and they lay together, exhausted, laughing nervously, their bodies slippery and wet, too lazy to get up, drifting in and out of sleep.

'My God, I'm starving.' Kip was sitting up in bed, and Lara felt it too, a gnawing ache at the pit of her stomach, a dizzy lightness in her head.

They pulled on their clothes, and ran downstairs.

'There's soup.' She lifted the lid off last night's supper, 'and meringues.'

But Kip was staring into the fridge. 'I could make scrambled eggs,' he told her, 'at least I think I can,' and he began breaking eggs, a whole box of them, into a bowl, dropping one and stepping round it as he reached for the bacon.

'There's a cloth in here, I think.' Lara opened a cupboard.

Kip was chopping like a maniac.

'Move.' Lara nudged him to get at the curtained space under the sink.

Kip looked down at her. 'What are you doing?' The egg lay smashed and seeping, the yolk miraculously unbroken, the white spearing out over the floor.

'Cleaning it up,' she said. 'Unless you want to?'

'Oh leave it. Someone will do that,' he winced, and Lara felt her whole body flush with indignation.

'Ginny, you mean?'

As she searched among the cleaning fluids and jars of polish she had a vision of her mother mopping the classroom floor after school in Eskdalemuir. It was a job she was lucky to get. School cleaner. And happy to do. Lara had helped her. Wiping down the desks, unsticking the chewing gum, sweeping dust and hair and rolled-up wrappers from the corners of the room.

'It's ready.' Kip served the food on to two plates and carried it out to the terrace. But Lara was still struggling with the broken egg. It slipped away from her as she tried to catch it and even when she'd managed to slide it into the bin it left a glossy sheen on the floor that refused to vanish.

'I told you to leave it to the experts,' Kip yawned, once she finally sat down, and Lara saw that now the egg was something else she'd have to forget.

'What time is it anyway?' Their plates were empty and Kip was leaning back in his chair. 'It must be at least four.'

'Really?' Lara ran into the sitting room where she knew there was a clock. 'My God. It's almost five!' and convinced suddenly that her father, or at least Ginny, must have been trying to call her, she picked up the phone. But there was nothing. No one there. She stared down at the desk. Where was that number? 'What's the name of the hospital, do you know?' and she started searching through Caroline's scattered papers for a clue.

'Which hospital?'

'Where they took Caroline. In the ambulance.'

'I don't know.'

'But if we went into Siena . . . surely we'd just find it?'

Kip laughed. 'How do you mean? Walk?'

'We could drive there, couldn't we? I mean we've still got Pamela's car.'

Kip opened his eyes wide. He looked so startled his scalp seemed to lift away from his head. 'Fuck.' He went to the front door and opened it. 'You're right. She'll kill me. Come on, we'd better go.'

'Where?'

'We have to take it back.'

Lara looked out at the drive. She couldn't go to Ceccomoro. Her legs felt weak just at the thought of it. 'Couldn't you just take me into Siena, and then I'll make my way to the hospital from there.'

'Lara.' Kip was frowning. 'They're waiting, you know that, don't you, they're waiting for Caroline to die.'

Lara sat down on the step. Was that it? Were they just waiting, privately, the three of them, without her?

Kip took her arm and tried to pull her up. 'Come on,' he said. 'We've got to get the car back.'

'It's all right. You go. I'll stay here.'

'Really?' Kip looked round him. At the silent house. The hills, the valley thick with trees. 'I'll tell you what' – he crouched down beside her – 'we'll take the car, dump it in the yard and then walk back along the sexy path. We'll only be gone for half an hour.'

Lara didn't answer.

'Or I suppose you could stay here and wait . . .' He sounded unsure.

'What?'

'Nothing. You'll be fine.'

Kip moved towards the car. What was he so nervous about. Kidnappers? The ghost of Sid Vicious? Wild boar? He opened the door and slid himself in, and with the door still open, he turned the ignition. 'Bye then,' he called, reversing round. 'See you later,' and he began to pull away.

Lara watched him, her pulse racing, so unsure what to do her thoughts crashed in her ears. 'Wait!' she screamed, and she ran after him. 'I'm coming too.'

There was no one to be seen at Ceccomoro, although the yard was full of cars. The jeep, Andrew's sleek Mercedes, and two other identical hire cars. Kip squeezed the Fiat over by the wall.

'I won't be a minute,' he said. 'I need to get something,' and before she could protest he had disappeared round the side of a building.

She waited, listening to the distant sounds of the kitchen, the clatter of a sink, the whizz of machinery, the faint murmur of the staff already preparing the evening meal. Opposite her stood a dilapidated building, rough with uneven stones, and beside it was the olive press which was now a room for storing tennis racquets and balls. May had taken her in there once, shown her where the donkey used to walk in circles over the stone floor, turning the handle of the giant press until all the olives were squashed. Poor little donkey, she'd thought, its grey nose to the floor, but May had handed her a racquet, refusing to believe her when she protested that she'd never played.

'Listen,' May had said. 'If you and Kip are still . . . you know . . . next year, I'll invite you to the wedding.'

'OK.' Lara was too flustered to protest, but she could still feel the heat of her blush.

'Now that's enough complaining.' Elizabeth Butler, in her orange hat and shades, was stepping into the yard, followed by her daughters. Lara sank down against the wall so that her body was shielded by the Fiat. 'You'll love it, you'll see.' She turned sharply on Nettle who'd murmured something moaning or defiant. 'Rubbish! I won't hear another word about it.' And she flipped open the boot of their car. The girls' mouths dropped and their shoulders sagged. 'Bye, and thanks again.' Elizabeth waved as Andrew Willoughby appeared on the steps.

'Bye, my dear ones,' he said, and he and Elizabeth kissed airily at least three times.

Lara sank down further.

'Terrible bores,' Andrew declared before they'd even pulled out of the yard. 'Why do we have to invite them every year?' and Lara squinted over the bonnet of the car to see who he was talking to now.

Lulu had her back to her, but Lara still knew it was her. The golden shoulder blades, the rolls of honey-coloured hair. 'Poor Andrew,' Lulu cooed, 'such a bother. Next year I'll invite everyone I know in Hollywood. Then you'll be amused.'

Andrew gave a dry laugh. 'That's what worries me. But as long as you still come,' and Lara heard him, he gave her a loud smack on the bum.

'You horrible man!' she protested, and then she screamed louder. 'Kip!'

Kip stood in the stone doorway. Lara saw him glance round fleetingly and when he didn't see her he shrugged.

'Where have you been?' Lulu had her arms around him. 'Just because I brought Todd back with me, it doesn't mean you have to run away.'

'And Kip,' Andrew added, 'I can't remember what it's all about, but Pamela's bloody furious about something and I think I heard her mention your name.'

Kip rolled his eyes and attempted to untangle himself from Lulu's embrace. 'Where is Todd anyway?'

'Oh, he's being ridiculous. He's decided to stay on LA time while he's here. Says there's no point adjusting. He should be up in an hour.'

'Idiotic man,' Andrew mumbled and he disappeared through the wall.

Lulu had her arms round Kip's neck, her body pressed against his. 'Todd thinks the whole set-up here is hysterical. Real life lords and ladies – he's going round calling everyone by their full title, although he keeps calling Andrew My Lord and curtsying when he sees Pamela, although I've told him you're the real Lord and Mummy's just the girlfriend. Your sisters are pissed off as hell.'

'Lulu.' Kip stumbled a little, so that they were leaning back against the wall. 'Listen . . .' and he lowered his voice so that Lara, even though she craned to hear, could only make out Lulu's soft interjections – sighing, laughing, cooing.

Lara felt sick. Should she make some noise? Alert Kip to the fact that she was there, watching? Instead she stayed quiet, her knees cracking, her arms scorched behind the metal bonnet of the car. But as she watched, their conversation seemed increasingly urgent, pulling them together – their two heads close, their foreheads touching, their knees entwined, and then Lulu was kissing him.

Lara looked away. She felt nauseous and sweat broke out, cold and clammy, across her skin. She tried to cough, to clear her throat, but her throat was dry. When she looked up again Lulu was beaming and Kip had pulled away.

'I've told you before, whenever you need to do a little research you know where I am . . .' and with a flounce of her whole long languid body she skipped away.

Kip wiped his mouth, fast, with the back of his hand, and looked around. His eyes darted past her, unseeing, and he turned and with his shoulders hunched he walked off in the direction of the sexy path.

Lara waited before following. The sun was low in the sky, slanting down across the fields, layering the terraces above in shadow. She walked through the corn field and pushed her way into the maize. Where was he? She wouldn't run, she wouldn't hurry, but all the same she looked round nervously as she stepped into the murky darkness of the sexy wood.

And then something snatched at her arm. She screamed and pulled away, but Kip was wrestling her, laughing like a madman, almost knocking her over as he trapped both her arms in his. 'Get off. GET OFF!' It took him a moment to realise she was serious, and a moment more to let her go. 'I don't want to! Leave me alone. I want to get back.' And shocked at herself, paling, she remembered that she really did want to get back. I'm sorry, she could have said, but she was too ashamed.

She hurried on. If it was so easy, she berated herself, then why hadn't she called out before? With Roland. Why hadn't she? The nausea that had subsided rose up again. But she knew that, before, she hadn't really believed the world was ugly. Even though in India she'd seen beggars and lepers, seen rats scampering over sleeping bodies and a man masturbating under a sack in the street. In Scotland she'd seen a builder with his fingers caught in a sash window, his face a pale-green, his lip bitten. But even so she hadn't imagined it could happen. Even when it was happening. When it was too late. If she'd screamed, or called out, or asked for help, she'd have made it real. For all time. For everyone to know. Lara started to run. At least this way it was a secret. No one would ever know, and she wouldn't be the girl connected to dirt and shame and slime.

'Bloody hell,' Kip huffed when he caught up with her on the road. 'What's got into you?' But all Lara knew was that, very badly, she wanted to be home.

'Still no one here.' Kip stopped in the drive. 'I told you . . .'

Lara ran into the house and up to the bathroom where she hung her head over the sink. If she could just be sick, then she'd feel better, but although she retched, three times, nothing came up but a thin trail of saliva. 'Oh,' she moaned. She wanted to be purged. To be clean and empty, and she stared down at the plughole and imagined herself spiralling down it. Spinning away. Smaller and smaller until she was washed and tiny as a shell. She brushed her hair and then her teeth, and taking a deep breath, remembering that, whatever else, she couldn't be in this house alone, she went downstairs.

Kip had put on a record. A tinkling melancholy album of Nina Simone. *Love me or leave me or let me be lonely, You won't believe me but I love you only, I'd rather be lonely than happy with somebody else* . . . Lara stood in the doorway and looked at him, lying on the white sofa, his shoes scuffing the cover of one arm. What would Caroline say, she thought, but Caroline wasn't here.

'More cheeps, more beer?' Kip smiled hopefully up at her, and shielded somehow by the music, she opened the fridge and examined what was left inside.

'I don't think Caroline is a beer sort of person,' she called back as if everything was normal, and she lifted out a bottle of wine. She carried it with two glasses and a corkscrew, the tin of olives, Ginny's plate of meringues, and sat beside Kip's sofa, on the floor.

'Who's Todd?' she asked, to show him that she knew.

'Oh Todd, he's Lulu's . . .' Kip flushed and took hold of the bottle of wine. 'I'm sorry.'

Lara handed him the corkscrew. 'Do you think this wine's all right? Or is it terribly expensive?'

'I hope so. Let's drink it all,' he grinned, and he began to twist out the cork.

They said nothing until they'd swallowed the first glass. It soothed Lara and gave her hope.

'Are you longing to get home?' Kip asked gently as he poured a second glass.

'No.' Lara was surprised.

'It's just, you'd be gone today, wouldn't you, if Caroline hadn't . . .'

'Oh yes.' Lara took a gulp. The day after the Palio. And she remembered how desperate her father was to be home. 'What about you? Will you be going back to London soon?'

Kip frowned. 'A few more weeks, and then . . . yes, I expect I'll go to my mother's for a while . . .'

Lara looked at him, and something about his doleful expression forced her up off the floor and on to the end of the sofa where she leant against his legs. 'And then you'll be going to Kenya?'

'But we could see each other in London,' he offered. 'Before?'

'Yes,' she agreed, although she knew they mustn't. 'Where does your mother live?'

Kip yawned. 'In Knightsbridge.'

'Knightsbridge.' Lara closed her eyes. She could get the Piccadilly line all the way down from Finsbury Park, past Holloway and Caledonian Road, stations bypassed so mercilessly by the Victoria line, into King's Cross, a maze of black and petrifying tunnels, a place to be avoided at all cost. But the train would take her on to Holborn with its air of panelled sitting rooms and cigars, through Covent Garden – impossible to dissociate from the long-gone barrows of fruit and vegetables that used to roll across the cobbles. And then there was Piccadilly Circus, friendly and festive, and Green Park, which, unlike Finsbury, was full of the word park. Hyde Park Corner, and you were at the edge of Buckingham Palace. Would Charles and Diana be back from their honeymoon by now? And then Knightsbridge. The home, not of knights, but of Harrods, and very occasionally the Victoria & Albert Museum.

'Knightsbridge,' she murmured to make it sound real.

'In one of those crescents behind Pont Street,' Kip prompted, as if that would help, and she thought of the wooden floorboards of her own terraced house, the back door into the garden, the bathroom with its flower-framed mirror and rag rug. When you pulled open the fridge there was never wine and olives. Some milk usually, a wilting lettuce, and a half-eaten tin of Berry's food.

The record was starting over again, the arm swinging automatically to the start. *Love me or leave me or let me be lonely, You won't believe me but I love you only . . .* Kip roused himself and flipped it over and poured out the last drops of the wine. Lara's head felt thick and her limbs were heavy. She was amazed to find that she was sleepy, when really it wasn't long since they'd got up.

She pushed her legs down further, tucking her toes behind Kip's back. 'Does she live on her own, your mother?' she asked, and Kip nodded.

'Well, apart from me.'

'But you're not really there.'

'Well, no. Sometimes. In the holidays. What about yours?'

'No. I mean yes. She just lives with me.'

'Never anyone else?'

'Not really.'

Lara had once asked Cathy why she and Lambert separated. She didn't know why she asked her. She didn't really want to know. Or at least she assumed she *did* know. They didn't love each other, that was all. But that wasn't actually the case.

'Your dad was away,' Cathy had told her. 'He was often away, doing research, but one time, you were about four . . .' Her face blanched at the memory. 'I *saw* him. On Kensington High Street, standing in the street with a woman. They were all dressed up. At least she was, and he was hailing a taxi, holding the door for her to get in.' Just remembering, Cathy had begun to shake.

'What did you do?' Lara asked, because she couldn't leave her standing there, suffering.

'Well.' Cathy sniffed, and in spite of herself, she started to laugh. 'I had an affair. With a friend of his. Someone who'd always liked me, and when your father eventually came back, from his research trip, he found the flat full of roses that this man, who was actually rather gorgeous, had sent round.' Cathy closed her eyes for a moment. 'But your dad . . . he couldn't accept it. He knocked over every vase and bottle, smashed most of them. Stamped on them. Hurled the roses out of the window. I promise you it was as if he'd lost his mind. "I can't trust you now," he said. "How do I even know if Lara is mine?" and he packed up everything that was his from the flat. "But you do it," I confronted him. I was terrified. "You have affairs," and you know what he said?' Cathy's face was blotched with grief. ' "It's different for me." '

Lara had taken hold of her hand. 'Was that when we moved to Scotland?'

'Not long after.' Cathy's tears were sliding down her neck. 'It helped.'

Later, when Lara went upstairs to say goodnight, she found her mother sitting cross-legged in front of her shrine, her eyes closed, her lips moving, her hands like lily flowers resting on the tops of her knees. He doesn't know, she thought, if I'm even his, and without waiting for her to finish, she went back down.

Lara looked over at Kip. His eyes were half closed but he was mouthing to the music. 'Have your parents been divorced for long?'

Kip looked surprised. 'Oh, they're not divorced. Papa's out here in Italy for financial reasons. Saving the family money. That's what Mummy thinks anyway. It sort of works, as long as everyone remembers never to mention Pamela.' Kip frowned. 'I mean he comes back, once or twice a year, and then he always stays at home, at least I think he does.'

'I mean doesn't . . . but?' Lara frowned too. 'What about . . .' but she saw it was pointless to go on.

Lara was woken by the telephone. She was up by the second ring, stumbling over Kip's sleeping body, scrambling towards the desk. 'Hello?' It was her father. She could tell by the way he cleared his throat, but for a moment he said nothing. 'Dad?' she ventured and he told her then.

'Caroline has died.'

'Oh.' She didn't know what to say. 'Oh no.'

'This morning. Not so long ago.' There was the tiniest of tremors and for a horrible moment she thought he might be going to cry. But instead he lowered his voice. 'Look I don't want to stay here. Ginny won't hear of leaving. But I need to get out. Get home.'

'To here?'

'No. To London.'

Lara felt her heart lurch. 'Today?' She looked over at Kip who was still on the sofa, wrapped in Caroline's mohair blanket, his hair sticking up wildly at the front.

'Ginny thinks we should sit with Caroline. She's sitting with her now. Listen. The train leaves some time around lunch. Can you pack up my things, and come and collect me and then we'll go on to the station.'

'But I . . .'

'Who could you ask to drive you?' His voice was almost unrecognisable with hurry.

'The man who cleans the pool? Or the gardener?' Lara had never seen either of these men. Did they come every day before she got up?

'No. Lara. Listen. If you could ring and ask for a taxi. Ask them to come to the hospital. I'll be waiting in the entrance. At twelve.'

'But I . . .' How would she find a taxi? Or if she did, could she speak enough Italian to give them the address? What was the address here anyway?

'Lara?'

'Yes?' Never before had he asked her to do anything for him. Well, he had once asked her to buy some sausage from the German Food Centre in London but when she arrived, flushed with success, it turned out he'd wanted a different kind of sausage. Smoked sausage in a jar. Not in a tin. The look of disappointment on his face had made her spirits plummet, and just thinking of it she felt them give way now.

'Thank you,' he said. It was as if she'd already done exactly what he'd asked. 'Goodbye,' and very gently he put down the phone.

Lara looked around her. All she could see were Caroline's things. Her magazines, her glasses, a packet of Silk Cut, a stray scarf curled over a chair. What would happen to them all? Would Caroline's family descend on the villa and take everything away? The hairbrushes and rings. The chiffon blouses. The hat boxes and shoes. Would they notice that her pink dress was missing? Until now she'd never known anyone to die. Had never actually believed that it was possible. Her mother's parents, her grandparents, were the only old people she knew. Apart from the Tibetan monks at Puruwala and the ones at Samye Ling. And they were timeless. Fearless. So prepared for death that they were joyful. Lara's grandparents were timeless too. Old since her first memory of them, but never getting older. She had visited them when she was small, and then again the summer after she came back from India, when the smell of the dog's meat boiling on the stove, the lights and liver, a pot big enough to feed a whole family of Tibetans, had disturbed her so much she'd gone out for a walk and walked so far and so distractedly that she'd got lost and had to be brought home by a farmer.

'Kip?' She knelt down on the floor. It was already twenty to eleven. 'We've got to collect my dad from the hospital. We have to get up. Can you help me?'

Kip turned over and buried his face in a cushion.

'Please.' She shook him. 'We have to catch the train.'

She left him and ran upstairs to Lambert's room. His blue dressing gown was lying on the bed, his books and papers in piles on every available surface.

'Kip,' she shouted. 'Please get up.' And then she remembered that he didn't know. She ran back downstairs and knelt beside him. She put her face close to his ear and as gently as she could she told him. 'Caroline is dead.'

Kip turned his face to hers and opened one blue eye. 'But Nicchio won. We kept her seat for her . . .'

'Kip,' she whispered, urgent. 'I need to get to the hospital and collect Lambert. And then we have to get to the train. I promised him. He's waiting. Can you help me find a taxi?'

'A taxi?' He stretched. 'Round here, I don't think there is such a thing.'

'Couldn't we call one?'

Kit shrugged. 'I don't know. Do you have a number?'

Lara shook her head. 'What if you went back to Ceccomoro and borrowed Pamela's car?'

'No way!' Kip shivered in mock terror.

'But I have to be there.' Lara felt her voice rising, out of her control. 'I have to. In an hour!'

'Bloody hell.' Kip recoiled. 'Calm down.'

Lara ran back up to Lambert's room. I'll carry the bags out on to the road myself, she thought. I'll hitch into Siena. Why not? Lambert's pyjamas were tucked under a pillow, his handkerchief folded into a triangle on the bedside table. Lara found his leather holdall, surprisingly worn for a man who never travelled, and began to pile his books and papers in. She opened the cupboard and as carefully as she could lifted down his suits. She folded them, and reached up for his trousers and his shirts. In a drawer she found his socks, dark-grey and black, and beside them several pairs of white cotton underwear. When she'd laid them in, she looked around for anything that might be left. His hairbrush, his empty glasses case, his wallet, and pulled the holdall on to the landing. In her own room she tipped the contents of her drawer straight into her bag, snatching at the rest of the clothes on hangers, throwing in her books. She seized her hairbrush and her toothbrush and zipping everything up she dragged both the bags downstairs.

Kip was standing at the fridge. 'I'm starving,' he said, and he pulled out a tall bottle of apricot juice and took a long thirsty slug.

'Kip . . .' she began in protest and then she remembered. Caroline had died.

Next Kip pulled out a plate of sliced ham and a soft waxed packet of cheese. 'Pass the bread,' he said, and he sliced into a round of mozzarella.

Lara seized the bread and held it high. 'Only if you help me.'

'You've got to see it from my point of view.' He reached out for the loaf. 'What's in it for me?'

Lara frowned. 'I . . .' But while she hesitated he snatched the bread.

'You're asking me to drive you to the hospital, collect your father, take you to the train . . . Why would I?' He drizzled a thick slice with olive oil and heaped it high with ham. 'Why would I?' He shrugged. 'When I don't want you to go.'

Lara stared at him. It was the most romantic thing anyone had ever said, but all the same she felt like crying. It was already eleven. She could see the clock out of the corner of her eye. 'I don't want to go either,' she pleaded. 'But my dad . . . it's hard to explain. He has to get home. And I . . . I have to go with him.'

Kip turned his back on her and bit into his sandwich.

'You'll be back soon, anyway,' she coaxed, 'and we can meet in London.' She rushed into the sitting room and taking up one of Caroline's sheets of writing paper she scrawled down her phone number and, just in case, her name. 'Here,' she said, and in response he held out the sandwich to her. 'No.' She was too desperate to eat. 'Just take me to the hospital, and I'll get a taxi from there. I'll do anything . . . please.'

'Anything?' Kip looked as if he were trying to decide. 'How about a blow job?'

Lara was stony-faced. I hate him, she thought coolly. I hate him. That's all there is to it.

'All right. All right.' Kip crammed the last of the food into his mouth. 'I'll go, but I want you to know. The big P's going to slaughter me.'

'Fine.' Lara took hold of both the bags, and without waiting for him to change his mind she pulled them to the porch. 'Or shall I come too?' she asked, imagining dragging the bags behind her along the sexy path. 'Will that be quicker?' But Kip was already running.

'Don't be an idiot,' he said and he was gone.

Lara stood in the drive and waited. What if he gets waylaid again? What if he forgets and never comes back? She counted to a hundred. Kicked gravel across the drive and picked the heads off lavender, pressing the flowers into the pulse of her wrist, mashing out the scented oil. Eventually, she walked round to the back of the house and stared down at the pool. It looked abandoned. Deserted even. With leaves and dead beetles flecked across its surface. Where was the pool man? Did he know he was no longer needed? And then she noticed her polka-dot bikini, strung out some days ago across the back of a lounger to dry. Lara sprinted down. She seized it, and consumed with the idea there might be other valuable things forgotten, she raced back into the house. But every-thing, everywhere, was Caroline's. Her writing paper and pens. Her bowls of potpourri, her scarves and magazines.

Upstairs Lara's room was empty. She looked under her bed and into the already emptied cupboard. She peered into her father's room, sweeping her hand over clear surfaces, open-ing and shutting drawers. But then, and it made her heart stop to think she might have missed it, there was his passport in a drawer beside his bed. She lifted it out, dark-blue, gold-crested, and as she did a photograph slipped from between the cardboard covers and fluttered to the floor.

Lara stooped to pick it up. What could it be? Her father wasn't the sort of man to carry photographs, and for one giddy moment she thought it might be an old picture of her. But it was much older. A sepia-brown photograph of a family – the parents dressed in their black-and-white best, and between them their children, a tall boy in a suit, and a girl of about twelve. Lara turned it over. Otto, Olga, Lissia and Wolfgang. Their names were written on the back in pencil with the same care with which the family were posed. Wolfgang . . . Lara stared into her father's face. His hair was thick, his face still soft, but his eyes had the same determined look as they did now. Lara opened the passport, she leafed through its pages, hoping to find something more, but there was only the one small official photograph of Lambert as he was now, greying and severe.

A car hooted in the drive. Lara jumped. She slid the photograph back into the passport, picked up the bikini and ran down. 'Kip,' she shouted, unable to believe that he was back, but there, standing in the doorway, was Roland.

'Both these going?' He stooped down to the bags, and beyond him she saw Kip swing open the door of the jeep. Lara held the passport tight against her chest and stared at him. 'Hey . . .' he said, holding her gaze. 'Don't be like that.'

'Like what?' Lara narrowed her eyes, and summoning up all the hatred she could find in her, kept staring.

'Well, you know . . . give a chap a chance . . .'

Lara said nothing, she kept on looking and eventually he turned away.

I should have hitched, Lara thought. I should have just run out on to the road, and she remembered her mother abandoning the Budget Bus and taking lifts all the way from Germany just to get them home.

Roland threw the bags into the back. 'Stroke of luck, eh?' he said, as if nothing had passed between them. 'I was just setting off for Siena anyway when lover boy came hurtling up.'

Very slowly Lara moved towards the car. Beep, beep, Roland hooted playfully, and without raising her eyes, she climbed over the metal ledge into the back.

They drove in silence, Lara watching the road roll out behind them, not daring to look round in case she caught the side of Roland's leer. 'So what do we think?' Roland said. 'Lulu's new boyfriend? Is he gay?'

Kip laughed. Impressed.

'Shame he has to go back. I was looking forward to seeing what he was going to wear to the funeral. The pink shorts. Or the apricot shorts. Or . . . just to really thrill us all, the pink *and* apricot shorts.'

'The funeral?' Kip asked for her. 'Caroline? Bloody hell. Is that arranged already?'

'Seems so. All set in place months ago. Andrew and Caroline have been planning it together. Every last detail. Scheming away. You know we had that tedious Ginny woman on the phone this morning, at the crack of dawn, in tears, offering her services. Saying if there was anything she could do to help.'

Kip glanced round at Lara as if only now he really believed that Caroline was dead.

'I mean, the impudence. She'd only known her five minutes.'

'When is it?' Lara had to ask.

'Ah ha!' Roland was triumphant. 'Our comrade finds her tongue. When is what? Our first date?'

'The funeral.' Her voice, intended to be cutting, came out huffy and cross.

'Woah, don't get your knickers in a twist. It's on Saturday. At three o'clock.'

On Saturday? Shouldn't they be staying? Wasn't it wrong to leave so soon? After all, Lambert was Caroline's very special friend. They'd known each other almost all their lives.

'So,' Roland asked, once they'd sped down the wooded hill road and were out on the junction where the signposts appeared. 'Which hospital is it anyway?'

Which hospital? 'I don't know.' Lara felt panic rising. 'Is there more than one?'

'Sure.' Roland waved an expansive arm. 'There's the Santa Maria della Scala and . . .' He paused. 'Kip, where was that place your papa went when he hit his head? Le Scotte. There may be others as well.'

'Just go to the Santa Maria.' She picked the first one. 'And if he's not there . . .' she trailed off.

The Santa Maria della Scala was in the square opposite the Duomo. Roland parked the car as close as he could get and Lara got out and ran. She felt almost out of control as she raced along the alleyways, down the steps and out into the square. She hardly glanced up at the Duomo, its gold-and-blue Madonna blazing in the sun, but pushed open the door into the hospital, her heart in her mouth, hoping, praying, promising to devote her life to God, if her father were just waiting there. But there was no one in the cool quiet hall of the hospital. Just a smart groomed woman behind a desk.

'*Si?*' She raised her head, but it was long past twelve now, and Lara turned and ran.

'It's definitely the Scotte.' She scrambled back into the car, and Roland winked at her. 'Lucky you've got me as your chauffeur, eh? It's not everyone you'll find is so very obliging.'

Lara put a hand up to her mouth and turned away.

It was twelve-forty-five by the time they reached the second hospital and there to her relief was Lambert standing outside, leaning against a wall, the sun beating down on his bare head. He was carrying a shoe, and a string bag of books, and his bad foot was white and bandaged, fat as a bread roll.

'I'm so sorry.' She rushed towards him.

'Thank God.'

'Kip brought me . . .'

They overlapped each other and clumsily they attempted to embrace. But Roland was hooting. There was someone behind him trying to get past.

'Quick,' she said, and she took his arm and led him towards the jeep.

Kip got out and helped him into the front. 'I was very sorry to hear about Caroline.'

'Yes,' Lambert swallowed. 'Thank you.'

'Do you think she knew?' He lowered his voice. 'About Il Nicchio . . . I mean before . . .'

Lambert turned and smiled, but his face was pale. 'I whispered it to her. I think she heard.'

Lara leant forward from the back. 'I packed your bag.' She hesitated. 'And I brought the tickets and your passport . . .' She waited for a sign. 'I put your books in, and your glasses case . . .' but Lambert only glanced distractedly at his watch.

'How long, do you think, before we're there?'

Roland shrugged. 'Not long.' He nosed dangerously into a faster lane and narrowly missed colliding with a car.

Lara sat in the back still clutching her bikini. Lambert's passport was in her shirt pocket, its edges stretching at the seams. And inside the passport, the photograph of his family. She could ask him about it, bring it out, point to his mother and his sister. Tell me about them. Olga and Lissia, and she ran the names together to make her own middle name. 'Your father chose it,' Cathy had told her, long ago. 'He liked it,' she said simply, but it occurred to her now that Cathy must have always known.

Kip sat opposite her, his knees turned away, with no danger of nudging against her own. 'Right, this is it,' he said, as if he were relieved, and Roland pulled into the station.

Kip leapt out of the back and swung open Lambert's door. 'It was very nice to see you again, Mr Gold.'

'It's been very nice seeing you again too, Kip.' Her father spoke slowly, and with exaggerated care, as if he'd only very recently learnt English. 'And don't forget, do give my regards to your mother.'

Lara stood on the sweltering tarmac and looked at their two profiles. It isn't true, she insisted, but all the same her stomach knotted. Lambert and Kip continued to face each other. It was as if there was something important that they both wanted to say.

'Mummy would love to see you, I'm sure.'

'Yes,' Lambert frowned. 'Tell her I'll call. I will.'

Lara pulled the bags out of the open back. 'We'd better go. We'd actually better hurry.' She had to move before Roland attempted some kind of goodbye. Lambert nodded, and with as much dignity as he could muster, he began to hop and shuffle towards the train.

'Bye then.' She smiled a thin smile at Kip, but as she moved away, dragging the bags behind her, she thought, I'll die if we part like this. I'll die. Wretched, she continued on, until, unable to stop herself, she turned, imagining he'd be gone, or laughing some horrid laugh with Roland, but he was still standing there, squinting into the sun.

'I'll call you,' he mouthed, and he raised the white slip of paper that she'd given him and pressed it to his lips.

A smile leapt across her face. She nodded, desperately, and put her hand to her heart and held it there for him to see.

In an instant Kip was by her side. He kissed her, fast and light on the lips, and just as quickly he sprang away again.

'Lara?' Lambert was turning towards her, leaning for support against a post. 'Is this our train, do you think?'

'Yes,' she said, 'this one,' and when she next turned the jeep was gone.

There were ten minutes left. Lara found two seats with a spare seat opposite on which Lambert could rest his leg, and dizzy with Kip's kiss she jumped down on to the platform.

'I won't be long,' she called, thinking all the time, I don't even care if he is my half-brother, I'll see him secretly. What can we do? We're in Love!

She careered along the platform and into the shop where

she bought biscuits, water, several bags of crisps and, finding nothing else, more biscuits. Moments later she was sitting in her seat.

'We did it,' she said, noticing for the first time that the carriage was full of backpackers, women, exhausted and dusty, with short cropped hair and noses that looked Dutch. But Lambert was leaning his head against the window, beads of sweat standing out on his brow.

'Are you all right?' She touched his arm, and unable to wait she tore open a packet of biscuits and crammed one into her mouth. Oh my God, she thought, as soon as she began to chew. Ginny! Does she even know we've gone? 'Dad?' she coaxed him. 'Does Ginny know?' But Lambert had his eyes closed.

Lara ate another biscuit. Drank some water. Ate a packet of oily crisps. We did it. She looked out of the window. We had a holiday, and now we're going home, and she had to remind herself it hadn't all been a success. They stopped at their first station, and Lambert flicked open his eyes.

'Binario,' she pointed. 'We're at Binario again.' But Lambert didn't smile.

They sat together in silence, gazing out of the window, watching the scorched countryside slide by, and the further away they travelled from Siena, the more impossible her plans for a secret future with Kip became. I just won't answer the phone, she promised herself, and then he'll be away in Kenya, and by the time he gets back . . . and unable to think beyond that she closed her eyes.

Lara must have slept because when she next looked up Lambert was crying. Long, silent tears were falling down his face, and his sleeve was wet where he'd attempted to mop them away.

'Oh Dad.' Lara was appalled. She caught the eye of the

woman opposite, who politely looked away. 'Dad, I'm sorry.' She couldn't think what else to say. 'Is it Caroline?'

'She was my friend,' he said simply. 'Right from the start. She was the only one who tried to help me.'

'Yes,' Lara said.

'And I let her down. Just like I let them all down.'

Lara put a hand on his arm. She could hardly bear to hear him say it. 'But you were there. This summer . . . last night . . . I'm sure she appreciated . . .' but Lambert shook his head.

'Caroline came to stay with us in Dorset,' he choked. 'Just before the war. And she did everything to help me.'

'To help with . . .?'

'My parents.' He looked at her strangely as if it was a puzzle to him that she didn't know. 'They needed money to get into Britain. So we wrote to everybody. All the well-connected people Caroline knew. We spent all day and half the night on letters, sitting upstairs in Lady Holt's study. And when we'd gone through everyone's address books, we wrote to other people, people of whom Caroline had only heard. But the replies came back. "Sorry." "It's impossible." "Out of the question." Then one man said he might be able to help. His own father was a haberdasher, although on rather a grander scale than mine. I wrote to my parents. Don't give up. I'll get the money. But the man withdrew his offer. His son, apparently, some idiot just out of public school, had run up the most appalling debts, gambling, and had crashed the family's new motor car, and the whole promise of his help was off.'

Lambert clenched one fist. He looked as if he might be about to smash it through the window. 'We kept on writing . . .'

'But what about the Holts?' Lara interrupted.

'They'd done enough,' Lambert said shortly. 'They'd taken me.'

'But how much could they have needed?' She thought of the lavish life they'd lived these last few weeks. 'Couldn't someone have helped them? Just a measly train fare and somewhere to stay? Couldn't any of them have managed that?' It occurred to her, really for the first time, that they were her family too.

A slow tear rolled down Lambert's face. 'The British government were asking for a sum of money to be pledged as surety against any refugee, any Jewish refugee entering the country. Ten thousand pounds. So that was twenty thousand, just for my parents, the equivalent, say of . . .' Lambert shook his head. 'Half a million pounds today.'

'Half a million pounds? What for?'

'As a precaution, if they were ever to become a . . . how did they put it, "a drain on the public purse". But the British Government didn't know my parents. They would never have asked for anything. Not for themselves.'

'So . . . what hap . . .?' she attempted, and she thought of the photograph she'd seen that morning, the bright face of Lambert's sister, his mother's fierce eyes. So what happened to them all? What happened? But she lacked the courage to ask. Instead she sat beside him, her arm against his, their legs touching, her body shielding his, until eventually he turned his face to the window and slept.

The five backpacking women were all reading now. Thick paperbacks with the pages folded back. Lara ate another biscuit, took out her copy of *The Grapes of Wrath*, cried over its unrelenting pages, and when she ran out of tissues to mop her eyes with, she looked through her history books, making notes and underlining passages on the French Revolution, wondering what would happen to Kip and his family if the masses of indignant people ever rose up again. 'Let them eat cake.' She could imagine Roland's drawl, and she closed her eyes and allowed herself an indulgent moment at the front of the crowd as she waited for his public execution. But would she be safe? If she was with Kip? She shook the thought away. Lady Lara Willoughby. She heard Ginny's teasing voice. But then again, she could save him, prove he wasn't really one of them. He's mine! she'd shout, for some reason in a bonnet and white apron. He's my brother. Stop! The guillotine would screech to a halt.

But then what if she was pregnant? She felt herself grow cold just at the thought of it. 'If we had a baby . . .' She could feel Kip's hands on her, pushing her back against their kissing tree. 'I wouldn't mind.' But he would mind when he saw it. A two-headed monster, their four blue identical eyes squinting out the truth. She'd have to push it around in a pram with a cloth draped over it so that people didn't stare.

And then she'd lose him. He'd be disgusted, and she'd have to pretend to be disgusted too. But what he didn't know was that it was the one thing that bound them together. The reason why he thought she was his type. It was the thing that gave her a chance over all those other girls. Lulu, and all the unknown Lulus, and even Allegra, just waiting to grow up. But then what if it was Roland's? It made her flinch, the thought of it, but surely a baby couldn't be made from anything so brutal? She curled over on the seat, and although she tried to block it out with thoughts and prayers for being lucky, for having one more chance, the memory engulfed her – his iron heavy leg, the stink of his aftershave, the drool on her neck as he rammed her up against the wall.

*   *   *

The refugee camp at Purawala, when they finally arrived, had been a shock. The people there, Cathy had warned Lara, were displaced – had been forced out of their own country by the Chinese. She had letters, which she read to Lara, about the hardship of starting this new life, of the bravery of these people and how much help they needed to settle and make a new home.

Cathy read these letters aloud on the long train journey from Bangalore, she read them to warn Lara, but also to make her aware of how lucky they had been. Living in their little cottage in Scotland, where the toilet, however freezing in winter, was at least in a brick shed beside the house, and not, as one letter described it, in a snake-filled pit below a single slippery plank.

But once they arrived at the camp it was Cathy and not Lara who was tested. The Tibetans had already been helped. They had smart watches and Western clothes, they had tractors and a school house, and, to Lara's disappointment, the children were no longer needed to bang pots from the roof of the one building to keep the parrots off the struggling corn. Cathy looked dejected. She and Lara had been living all these years in poverty, refusing any help from Lambert, trudging with no car, not even a bicycle, to the village's one shop.

They'd eaten dhal and brown rice, meal after meal, baked hard brown chapattis on the griddle, drunk goat's milk in their tea, and here was His Holiness, just back from a trip to America, with a paunch and a gold chain and some very flashy-looking socks under his robes.

'I want to believe in everything,' Cathy held Lara's hand tightly in her own, 'but I'm finding it so hard to understand what's real.'

His Holiness stood for a while in silence, and then he looked up at the sky. 'You see?' He pointed. 'There's a dragon's tail,' and as they watched, the three of them, a single plume of purple streamed across the clouds.

'I don't . . .' Cathy turned, tearful, but His Holiness was smiling so serenely that slowly and inexplicably Cathy felt her faith restored.

Lambert didn't speak again until the next day when the train finally stopped at Calais. He had slept fitfully, refusing all offers of food, only stirring occasionally to adjust his swollen foot, and to lie down on a stretch of seats conveniently vacated by the paperback-reading Dutch. Lara had leapt up as soon as they got off and pulled down the blinds on to the corridor so that apart from a timid young man in glasses no one else dared enter their carriage. At the border with France a guard appeared and demanded to see their passports. Lara watched Lambert show his passport, saw him slip the photograph out, hold it against the flat of his thigh and then slide it back inside again. She'd never have noticed if she hadn't known to look.

Lara had slept too, waking every few hours in the grip of an uneasy fear, and then, unable to remember what it was that was so horrible, she sat still until it flooded back. I'll have to ask him, she realised. I'll have to ask him, that's all. And just then the train came to a stop.

'Dad.' She shook him lightly. 'We've arrived,' and finding his shirt soaked through with sweat, she opened his bag and took out his dressing gown. 'Here.' She helped him into it. 'That's better.'

'Thank you.' His teeth were chattering as he stepped down from the train. 'Nearly there,' and with his dressing gown unfastened, flying out around him like a cape, he stumbled towards the boat.

* * *

Lara had once heard Lambert say – she supposed it must have been to Caroline – that he refrained from asking people questions because he so dreaded anyone asking one of him. But the nearer they got to England the calmer Lambert became. His fever subsided and his eyes cleared. They sat together in the restaurant car of the boat while Lara ordered fish, mashed potatoes and peas.

'It'll be revolting, I'm warning you,' he smiled, but it was delicious. Salty and buttery and warm.

'Did you know there was a funeral,' Lara attempted, 'for Caroline? All arranged?'

'Oh,' Lambert paused. 'Yes. But I never go to funerals. It's the living I'm concerned with. Not the dead.'

'So how come . . .'

'In my life,' he said drily. 'Not in my work.'

'But won't you be sad . . .' She couldn't help herself. 'If no one goes to *your* funeral? If no one cares?' And hearing how ridiculous this sounded she added more quietly, 'Not even for Caroline?'

'No,' Lambert said. 'Not even for Caroline.' But he looked surprised.

They fell silent and Lara toyed with her pudding, a jam sponge in custard, adrenalin washing through her, rising and dropping away, until she thought she might dissolve. I'm going to have to ask him, she thought, and the realisation cut through her like a knife.

'Dad?' she ventured as the waiter delivered coffee, and Lambert looked at her sideways.

'Yes?'

They smiled at each other and quickly, before her courage failed, Lara leant towards him. 'Dad, can I ask you something . . . It's just . . . about Kip.' She watched his face. 'It's just I had this idea. I mean I heard . . . I wanted to check. Is Andrew . . .' She hesitated. 'Andrew Willoughby. Is he . . . Kip's real father?'

Lambert stared at her as if he wasn't quite sure what he'd heard. Then he leant towards her too. 'Why do you ask?'

Lara smiled but inside she was trembling. 'No, it's just . . .' There was nothing much to lose now and anyway if necessary she could run and throw herself over the rails of the boat. 'I remembered that you used to know his mother and then I heard Andrew Willoughby say something . . .'

'Andrew Willoughby? Don't believe a word spoken by that shit. It's typical of him to go round rubbishing the one woman who was loyal to him. The one woman who would never have an affair.' He shook his head. 'Poor lovely girl.'

'Kip's mother?'

'Yes, I was terribly fond of her. Used to take her out regularly to try and cheer her up. Especially when she was pregnant with Kip – she was terrified, poor thing, that she was expecting another girl and that her marriage would be over. But in fact once Kip was born, once Willoughby had his son and heir, he pretty much ignored her. It destroyed her really – she became ill, had a sort of nervous breakdown.' Lambert said nervous breakdown as if it was a little-known medical term. 'I told her, nothing could have been worse than staying in that marriage. But being Catholic, of course, she'd never agree to a divorce.'

'So it's not you?'

'Me?' Lara had never seen him look so gentle. 'No, it's not me. But I can tell you who is mine.'

Lara stared at him. She felt a great gulf opening up inside her. 'Who?'

He put a hand out and touched hers across the table. 'You, of course.'

'Oh. Me.' And she began to laugh.

*   *   *

Lambert was almost cheerful on the train into Victoria Station and once there he commandeered a trolley and throwing their luggage on he hopped at great speed towards a kiosk where he bought one of every newspaper for sale.

'Taxi,' he shouted wildly, clutching the papers to him. 'Taxi!' And Lara saw her father reflected in the drivers' faces – a man, unshaven, half dressed, limping, foreign – as each cab accelerated past.

'Taxi,' Lara tried instead, sticking out her arm, and almost immediately there was a screech of brakes.

Lambert's flat was much as they had left it. Dark and private, even the steps of the stairs leading up to it muffled in quiet. Lara stayed and had a cup of tea, delaying the moment when the adventure would end, when she'd get the tube to Finsbury Park, walk through the tunnel of the station, hand in her ticket, step out into the real world. Occasionally her face dissolved into a smile. He likes me, she thought. Kip likes me for no reason at all. It was all she could do to control her grin. I just have to be lucky now, she told herself, and she kept her fingers crossed.

'Goodbye then.' She felt awkward when the moment came to leave. 'I hope your foot gets better.' She reached up and formally they kissed, once on each cheek. 'Thank you,' she said, 'for taking me.' She wanted to say how sorry she was about Caroline, about Isabelle, about his toe. About everything, but then through the half-open door of his bedroom she saw the giant pot of his one plant. Its familiar leaves, pale-green and heart-shaped, stretching towards the light. Lara moved instinctively towards it. 'I've always wondered, what is that plant?'

'Oh.' Lambert pushed the door wider to reveal its branches, almost spanning the width of one wall. 'It's a Zimmerlinde. My little sister sent the seed to me in a letter. It's the only thing I've ever tried to grow.'

They stood and looked at the Zimmerlinde together. 'Well, obviously, that's not the original one.' His voice was low. 'But I take cuttings, every decade or so.'

Lissia, Lara wanted to add, but she stayed quiet.

'Bye then,' she said again. 'See you soon.'

'Yes. Let's meet. Maybe for supper?'

'All right.' Laughing, she turned and gave him a hug.

'Goodbye.' Lambert stood at the top of his stairs and watched her as she ran down.

'Bye then.' Lara waved from the front door, and Lambert raised his hand to her in silence, watching after her till she was gone.

ACKNOWLEDGEMENTS

I'd like to thank my friend Georgia Shearman for sharing her memories of India with me, and her mother Sarah Shearman for an early fact-checking read. I'd also like to thank Mark and Domitilla Getty for their generous hospitality, for taking me to the Palio, and for steering me towards *La Terra in Piazza* by Alan Dundes and Alessandro Falassi, which proved to be invaluable. Also Alexander Afriat for answering my many queries and my editor Alexandra Pringle for – as well as her warmth and generosity – putting us in touch. I am very indebted to Kitty Stirling for answering my questions, and once again, thanks to Shawn Slovo for providing a quiet room in which to work. Enormous thanks too to Manuela Zainea for childcare, to my agent Georgia Garrett for continued support, and my invaluable first readers Julie Myerson, Bella Freud and David Morrissey.

A NOTE ON THE AUTHOR

Esther Freud was born in London in 1963. She trained as an actress before writing her first novel, *Hideous Kinky*, which was shortlisted for the John Llewellyn Rhys Prize and was made into a feature film starring Kate Winslet. She has since written four further novels, *Peerless Flats*, *Gaglow*, *The Wild* and, most recently, *The Sea House*. Her books have been translated into thirteen languages.

B L O O

Also available by Esther

Peerless Flats

Sixteen-year-old Lisa has high hopes for her first year in
London. But squeezed into a temporary council flat with her
bohemian mother and a little brother obsessed with foxes, she is
not off to the best start. Ambitious to be more like her
glamorous sister, Ruby, who lives life
through the city and re-
fusing to lose fantastic will
her life.

'Attending, s still, truthful voice becomes not
only a necessity' Jonathan Coe

'A highly talented writer' e Lively

ISBN: 9 7807 475 544 3/ Paperback / 7.99

Order your copy:

By phone: 01256 302 699

By email: direct@macmillan.co.uk

Delivery is usually 3-5 working days.
Postage and packaging will be charged.

Online: www.bloomsbury.com/bookshop

Free postage and packaging for orders over £15.

Visit Bloomsbury.com for more about Esther Freud